I0762873

PRAISE FOR AIMIE K. RUNYAN

"Delicious, page-turning, and ultimately relatable. Book clubs will devour this story of love, life, and lost (and found?) connections."

—SARAH JIO, *NEW YORK TIMES* BESTSELLING AUTHOR OF *INSIGNIFICANT OTHERS*

"Aimie Runyan has written the perfect book for foodie readers, romantics, and anyone who has ever dreamed of a do-over. Sabrina Sorenson has plotted a meticulous career in the restaurant industry, honing her palette in hopes of becoming a Michelin inspector—but a holiday dig from her critical mother has her wondering if she's chasing the wrong goals. When a mysterious airport ticket inspector gives her the opportunity to revisit past crossroads in her life—failed relationships, jobs not chosen, ladders unclimbed—Sabrina has the chance to discover what she truly wants. I finished *Missed Connections* with a big smile and an even bigger craving for a craft cocktail, a perfectly plated strawberry marzipan tart, and a plane ticket to Europe."

—KATE QUINN, *NEW YORK TIMES* BESTSELLING AUTHOR OF *THE ASTRAL LIBRARY*

"A feast of culinary delights, a fairy godmother, and a chance to rewrite the past? Yes, please. Textured with regret, soul-searching, and second chances, *Missed Connections* is thoughtful, heartfelt, and magical. Truly a novel you'll want to savor."

—HEATHER WEBBER, *USA TODAY* BESTSELLING AUTHOR OF *MIDNIGHT AT THE BLACKBIRD CAFÉ*

"With its razor-sharp understanding of high-end restaurant culture and its moving exploration of life's turning points, *Missed Connections* will resonate with fans of *The Bear* and readers drawn to the emotional what-ifs of *The Midnight Library*. A compelling meditation on ambition, regret, and belonging. Don't miss this excellent book!"

—BARBARA O'NEAL, BESTSELLING AUTHOR OF *THE LAST LETTER OF RACHEL ELLSWORTH*

"What if you could revisit the moments that mattered most? *Missed Connections* answers that question in a beautifully written, fast-paced novel filled with mouthwatering food, emotional depth, and just the right touch of magic. Aimie K. Runyan explores ambition, love, and second chances with heart and honesty. With a determined heroine you'll root for, this is a novel you'll savor long after the last page. It's my favorite book of Runyan's yet."

—ELIZA KNIGHT, *USA TODAY* BESTSELLING AUTHOR OF *LOST IN THE SUMMER OF '69*

"An elegant, magical journey through one chef's globe-spanning past as she seeks discernment about her future. Full of delicious food and far-flung places, I loved joining Sabrina as she revisits pivotal moments of her life."

—RACHEL LINDEN, AUTHOR OF *A SPRINKLE OF SWEET SERENDIPITY*

"Fans of *The Midnight Library* will devour this delicious story of a woman who gets a magical opportunity to re-do pivotal life choices. With the fascinating backdrop of culinary culture from New Orleans to Copenhagen to Paris, this whimsical tale is full of hard-won insights about work, love, passion, and family. I was utterly entranced by the mystical airport from which our heroine boards flights to key moments of her past—gaining wisdom, standing up for herself, and ultimately, creating a fulfilling pathway ahead. You'll be wishing for your own enchanted airplane flight . . . Enjoy the ride!"

—LAURA RESAU, AUTHOR OF *THE ALCHEMY OF FLOWERS* AND *THE RIVER MUSE*

"In *Missed Connections* Aimie K. Runyan enchants the reader from the first word, striking the perfect blend of whimsical magic with the emotional depth of a story about a woman journeying back in time to relive her life's most pivotal moments. Journeying through the culinary world of Michelin restaurants, readers will practically taste the dishes, feel the heartache, and find themselves pondering the timeless question: What if I had the chance to redo life's big moments? It was a book I wished would never end."

—GRACE HELENA WALZ, AUTHOR OF *GOOD HAIR DAYS*

"A poignant story about timing, fate, and emotional risk. Runyan captures longing with grace and restraint. Romantic without being sentimental. A quietly beautiful read."

—LAURA F., BOOKSELLER ON NETGALLEY

"What would you change about your life? This book offers you a look into what might have been. The incredible characters and chance to look at your own life in retrospect will hopefully let you see what you have now and accept or cherish it."

—THERESA HESS, BOOKSELLER AT MACDONALD BOOK SHOP IN ESTES PARK

"*The Wandering Season* is a delightful journey of self-discovery, romance, good food, and a little magic. I devoured every word and, although the ending was perfectly satisfying, I can't deny wanting just a little bit more. I eagerly looking forward to Runyan's next offering!"

—KATHERINE REAY, AUTHOR OF *THE LONDON HOUSE* AND *THE BERLIN LETTERS*

"Aimie K. Runyan has knocked me out with *The Wandering Season*, a lyrical book about a young woman's modern-day quest to find out who she really is and how to fulfill her creative dreams. Rich with exquisite descriptions of food, family, international travel, as well as fully believable instances of magical realism, this book has everything I love in a story. Brilliantly written, Veronica's journey will stay with me for a very long time."

—MADDIE DAWSON, BESTSELLING AUTHOR

"It's a rare book that feeds both your soul and your body, but that's exactly what Aimie K. Runyan's *The Wandering Season* accomplishes. For anyone who has ever looked in the mirror and wondered where they really came from, this story combines the realities of modern DNA testing with a sprinkle of magical realism to bring the past to life. *The Wandering Season* is the perfect palate cleanser and an utterly delicious tale of self-discovery."

—SARA GOODMAN CONFINO, BESTSELLING AUTHOR OF *DON'T FORGET TO WRITE* AND *BEHIND EVERY GOOD MAN*

"Some books are simply a joy to read. Aimie K. Runyan's *The Memory of Lavender and Sage* is one of them. Sensuous . . . dreamy . . . romantic . . . *The Memory of Lavender and Sage* is a mélange of tastes and smells, magic and romance. Aimie K. Runyan weaves a sumptuous tale of mystery and magic, family and friendships, reminding us that it's never too late to find the home of our heart."

—LORI NELSON SPIELMAN, *NEW YORK TIMES* BESTSELLING AUTHOR OF *THE LIFE LIST*

"In Aimie K. Runyan's signature heartfelt voice, *The Memory of Lavender and Sage* is a warm, generous, and utterly satisfying novel about the power of kindness, character, and finding purpose and love where you least expect it."

—ANN GARVIN, *USA TODAY* BESTSELLING AUTHOR OF *THERE'S NO COMING BACK FROM THIS*

"Aimie K. Runyan wows in her latest atmospheric novel . . . *The Memory of Lavender and Sage* reminds readers that every moment should be savored and that, sometimes, the simplest pleasures are the greatest gifts. Runyan has proven herself as a standout voice in women's fiction. I was captivated from the very first line."

—KRISTY WOODSON HARVEY, *NEW YORK TIMES* BESTSELLING AUTHOR OF *THE SUMMER OF SONGBIRDS*

"*The Memory of Lavender and Sage* is an enchanting novel that sweeps you away to France on a journey of self-discovery, uncovering family secrets, and learning how love lives on. Friendships are forged, romance is cultivated, and magical moments abound in the captivating small French town. For readers who love *Under the Tuscan Sun* and *Chocolat*, this is your next heartfelt, delightful read."

—JENNIFER MOORMAN, BESTSELLING AUTHOR OF *THE MAGIC ALL AROUND*

ALSO BY AIMIE K. RUNYAN

The Wandering Season

Mademoiselle Eiffel

The Memory of Lavender and Sage

A Bakery in Paris

The School for German Brides

Across the Winding River

Girls on the Line

Daughters of the Night Sky

Duty to the Crown

Promised to the Crown

WITH J'NELL CIESIELSKI AND RACHEL MCMILLAN

The Liberty Scarf

The Castle Keepers

Aimie K. Runyan

Missed Connections

Published by Harper Muse, an imprint of HarperCollins Focus LLC, 501 Nelson Place, Nashville, TN 37214, USA.

This book is a work of fiction. The characters, incidents, and dialogue are drawn from the author's imagination and are not to be construed as real. Any resemblance to actual events or persons, living or dead, is entirely coincidental.

Any internet addresses (websites, blogs, etc.) in this book are offered as a resource. They are not intended in any way to be or imply an endorsement by HarperCollins Focus LLC, nor does HarperCollins Focus LLC vouch for the content of these sites for the life of this book.

ISBN 978-1-4003-5326-2 (ePub)
ISBN 978-1-4003-5325-5 (TP)
ISBN 978-1-4003-5327-9 (downloadable audio)

HarperCollins Publishers, Macken House, 39/40 Mayor Street Upper, Dublin 1, D01 C9W8, Ireland (https://www.harpercollins.com)

Library of Congress Cataloging-in-Publication Data

CIP data is available upon request.

Art Direction: Halie Cotton
Cover Design: Grace Cavalier
Interior Design: Chloe Foster

Printed in the United States of America

26 27 28 29 30 LBC 5 4 3 2 1

For Kerry Schafer, aka Kerry Anne King,
without whom this book may have driven me insane.
You are an amazing crit partner, nurse, author genie . . .
and, above all, friend.
You have my humble thanks.

Cooking is like love. It should be entered into with abandon or not at all.

—HARRIET VAN HORNE

Of all the high-end culinary guides produced by major tire manufacturers, the Michelin Guide is easily in the top three.

—SAM DENBY, HALF AS INTERESTING

The *Brigade de Cuisine*

Developed by Auguste Escoffier in the nineteenth century, the hierarchical kitchen-brigade system was born of Escoffier's experience as an army chef in the Franco-Prussian War (for more on that conflict, see my novel *A Bakery in Paris*) and is still used in fine-dining establishments the world over, often using the original French terminology. The modern restaurant kitchen has adapted these roles to fit their needs, but the hierarchy has remained much the same for a century and a half. The following terms do not comprise an exhaustive list, but they may help some readers better appreciate certain details in *Missed Connections*.

BACK OF HOUSE:

- *Chef exécutif*: Executive chef who manages the menu and the vision for the kitchen but is not directly involved in the running of the kitchen unless also serving as head chef.
- *Chef de cuisine*: Head chef in charge of the day-to-day operations of the kitchen who makes final decisions regarding the menu in conjunction with the executive chef, if there is one, or the general manager and the sous-chef if there is not.

- *Sous-chef*: Deputy chef, second-in-command of day-to-day operations and the head chef's right hand. The sous-chef leads service in the absence of the head chef and plays a key role in the smooth running of any kitchen.
- *Chefs de partie*: Station chefs are responsible for a specialized area of the kitchen. Examples include:
    * *saucier* or sauce chef
    * *pâtissier* or pastry chef
    * *rôtisseur* or roast chef
    * *entremétier* or vegetable chef
    * *chef de tournant* or swing chef (substitutes for any station lead)
- *Commis chef*: These entry-levels chefs assist the station leads. They may specialize in one area or move from station to station as the head chef wishes.
- *Escuelerie*: The staff of dishwashers and kitchen porters who keep the kitchen clean and running efficiently.

FRONT OF HOUSE:

- Restaurateur/CEO: Responsible for the business side of the restaurant and its branding. Nowadays, usually represents investors for a larger "restaurant group."
- General manager (GM): Oversees the day-to-day running of the business end of the restaurant and is charged with making the restaurateur's vision come to life.
- *Maître d'hôtel*: Assists the GM and organizes staff schedules. Oversees seating and makes sure all is running smoothly during service.
- Sommelier: Wine steward who curates the wine list and works with the head chef for pairings. Manages bartender and cocktail servers.

- Expediter: The crucial link between front and back of house. The expediter ensures all orders for a table are served at the same time and helps pace the timing of individual courses.
- Servers: Led by the head waiter, the servers are the public face and beating heart of every restaurant.

Prologue

MAY 2000

SANTA BARBARA COAST, CALIFORNIA

Serendipity.

The word sags under the weight of the expectation it evokes. One can hardly read it without the mind racing into a dozen flights of fancy. If a person is fortunate enough to encounter the serendipitous, will it be something as momentous as discovering the cure for cancer in a lab mix-up? Or will it perhaps be something more mundane . . . like finding a ten-dollar bill in last year's winter coat? Is it presumptuous to say that serendipity is *ever* mundane?

After all, that ten-dollar bill might give a young woman an excuse to treat herself to a coffee before going into the office.

While waiting in line for her coffee, she might fall into conversation with a tall and handsome stranger.

The conversation with the tall, handsome stranger might bolster her confidence, and she'd finally be bold enough to ask for a promotion at work.

She might, in time, become a leader of that company. A company that will ensure that very same cure for cancer is readily available across the globe, free of charge, and save countless lives. Including that of the tall, handsome stranger.

A ten-dollar bill just might be all the serendipity it takes . . .

But in this case, Serendipity is a charming seafood restaurant on the coast of California, forty-five minutes from Solvang, where the lovely Sabrina Sorensen has spent her entire young life. The darling girl has no idea how apt the restaurant's name is, nor will she for quite some time.

It's Sabrina's thirteenth birthday, and she's dressed in her finest: a new A-line periwinkle-blue dress that plays up her Nordic-blue eyes. The dress is nice enough, but it pinches at Sabrina's chest. But it was the dress her mother, Robin, insisted on because it was "the most appropriate." Rather than choosing a dress that fit properly or altering the garment to accommodate her daughter's developing body, Robin preferred to purchase a too-small brassiere to flatten Sabrina's bosom. The result isn't entirely effective, but it is wholly uncomfortable.

In a similar vein, Sabrina's hair is styled in two long, blonde braids. Not stylish, but pretty and neat. Robin believes that allowing preteen girls to dress and style themselves like adults leads to smart mouths and small acts of rebellion in the beginning. But if the unruly behavior is left unchecked, it results in a late-night summons to the county jail with bail money in hand.

Sabrina hates the childish clothes and hairstyle, but if she'd put up a fuss, it might have risked her birthday dinner. So she wisely decided that dressing like a child to please her mother is a small sacrifice to pay for being treated like a young lady by her father.

Tonight, there is no older brother competing for their father's attention. No younger sister to spill milk all over the table or cry at the slightest provocation. No mother to constantly scold and correct. Just an evening for Sabrina to be with the one person she feels truly understands her. Her father is dressed in a suit, which makes Sabrina feel as if he's taking the evening just as seriously as she is.

"What looks good, Sabrina?" Her father, Jannick, an immigrant from Copenhagen, prods his daughter. His eyes dance with merriment rather than reproach. She's studying the menu with all the seriousness of Scripture and looks terrified as she peruses the list of unfamiliar dishes.

She casts her eyes downward. "I don't know."

Her mother, while well-meaning, is always so quick to make decisions for her daughter that Sabrina often finds herself cowed when faced with them. Sabrina also knows her mother doesn't exactly approve of this outing, which makes Sabrina even more hesitant.

In the past few weeks since Jannick formed his plan, Robin had mentioned several times—loudly—that when she herself had turned thirteen, she'd been more than happy with pizza and ice cream with three of her friends at the local pizzeria. It was, in Robin's view, fancy enough for a child. After all, the red-and-white checkered tablecloths had been made from actual cloth rather than plastic. Anything more is an extravagance.

Serendipity, with its blanched linens and polished crystal, is akin to a fairy castle in Sabrina's eyes. More than an extravagance, it is the stuff of dreams.

But Jannick, thankfully, had been able to win Robin over to his point of view. Sabrina is sure her father is the only person who could persuade Robin to agree to anything she wasn't already in favor of. But Jannick has always been a special case for Robin. He'd gone from being a poor carpenter's apprentice when he first arrived in Solvang to becoming one of the most respected architects in the region.

He supports his family admirably and revels in the opportunity to take his children on excursions such as these. Jannick hopes to impart his love of fine cuisine to at least one of his children. Their oldest, Brian, seems all too firmly entrenched in the meat-and-potatoes camp, much to his father's dismay. Their father-son outings generally consist of professional ball games in Los Angeles, where nothing on the menu is more complex than a hot dog. The baby, Chloe, at five years old, still thinks chicken tenders are the pinnacle of haute cuisine, though Jannick holds hope her palate will mature in time. But with Sabrina, the timing is just right.

Jannick had already prepped Sabrina in proper restaurant etiquette—beyond the basic table manners that had been instilled since she was old enough to hold a spoon. The hurdle will be getting over her fear of trying new foods, a fear that developed as a result of her mother's strict policies against food waste.

Jannick couldn't fault his wife for her fastidiousness in this area; he'd known hunger himself a few times in his life. But it did discourage the children from any spirit of adventure when ordering off a new menu.

"Take a chance. It's not the end of the world if you don't like it, *min skat*." He reaches across the starched white linen of the tablecloth. "Let's pretend we're Michelin food critics. We'll order—and eat—like the professionals."

Her keen eyes narrow. "Michelin? Like the tire company?"

Jannick smiles broadly. "The very one. They began reviewing restaurants and hotels in France to encourage road trips when automobiles were new."

She considers this a moment. "So their tires would wear out faster?"

He chuckles, the corners of his eyes crinkling in the way Sabrina loves so. "Already thinking like a businesswoman. Precisely right. But their little red guides evolved into something far bigger than they ever envisioned. They became the standard by which all fine-dining establishments are measured the world over."

Sabrina sits mesmerized by her father's words. "How is eating like a critic different from the way normal people eat?"

He meets his daughter's serious expression with equal solemnity. "First and foremost, we don't have to pretend if we don't like it."

"Like with Mom's meatloaf." As soon as she says the words, Sabrina looks as though she wants to leap out of her chair, snare the words with a butterfly net, and swallow them back inside.

Jannick doesn't bother to suppress a laugh. "Just so. Your mom's feelings would be hurt. But a professional chef doesn't have that luxury. He or she must take criticism as it comes, analyze it for whatever truth it contains, and learn from it. As nice as they are to receive, a chef can't grow from compliments alone. They need honest criticism too. A plant may love the sun, but it needs rain just as much to take root and flourish."

Sabrina nods, absorbing her father's words like gospel. Her eyes widen. "So how do we order?"

"We each get an entrée, a main dish, and a dessert, but we don't get the same ones so we can sample each other's, and we get to experience twice as many offerings. As we eat, we'll give each dish our honest appraisal." Jannick grins as his daughter's face lights up at the prospect. It was a grand meal indeed when the family shared an appetizer at a restaurant. Dessert was almost always drugstore-brand ice cream or nothing at all. A full three-course meal per person seems an unthinkable luxury.

She is about to be introduced to a world where an entrée is not a basket of mozzarella sticks served with lukewarm marinara sauce or a greasy platter of potato skins filled with cheese and bacon crumbles—a few chives thrown in to remind the clientele that the dish is, academically speaking, a vegetable. The entrées here are bite-sized morsels meant to awaken the palate and tantalize the patrons for all the delights about to reveal themselves. A true amuse-bouche in the purest sense of the term.

Jannick continues his lecture. "We order with an eye for the chef's signature dishes. Pay attention when the server mentions the specials. You can often tell from their expression if a dish is truly a chef's special creation made to take advantage of the best produce of the season, or if it's just a hodgepodge of ingredients the kitchen wants to use up before they turn. For that reason I generally avoid soups and salads when dining out."

Young Sabrina listens enraptured, brow furrowed like a young scholar hungry for the knowledge imparted by a sage elder.

He removes a small package from his jacket pocket and produces a leather-bound notebook and fine writing pen she can use to jot down her musings. He promises to make these outings a regular occurrence, and she'll have the notebook at the ready to record her assessment of their dining experiences. It's the most grown-up gift she's ever received, and she's positively tingling with the prospect of more dinners like these with her father.

The kindly waitress, an older woman with a maternal aura, bustles from table to table but can hear every word as father and daughter discuss the virtues and demerits of the various entries on the menu. When she knows they've settled on their choices, she stops by their table.

"This must be a very special occasion." She addresses Sabrina with the same respect she would an adult, because she senses in her very bones this is what the girl craves. "I trust the young lady has found something to her liking on the menu?"

"I would like the crab cakes, the macadamia nut–encrusted Alaskan halibut, and the pit-hiver for dessert."

"A good *Pithivier* is a delight," Jannick corrects mildly, not condescending to wink or even look in the waitress's direction. "I love anything with puff pastry and almond crème. Good choices, *min skat*."

"Oh, I forgot to ask about the specials." Sabrina looks as though she realizes she'd forgotten the back page of an important exam.

"Chef has a seafood cioppino on for tonight, as well as a *Canard Montmorency*, which is duck roasted with bourbon-soaked cherries." The waitress knows Jannick will be looking for her tell, so she doesn't bother trying to hide which dish is being used to clear the fridge and which one the chef spent three weeks perfecting.

"I'll have the duck." Jannick changes his choice of main dish without hesitation. "With the escargots in Chablis to start, and the Grand Marnier soufflé for dessert." Now he does glance at the waitress with a knowing look.

As they weren't ordering from the prix fixe, custom would dictate that the server would take their order for each course separately, but he could teach her this next time. And there would be many more next times.

For the next two hours the waitress delights in hearing their running commentary on the food: everything from the ingredients, the choices in plating, and her own service. Thankfully they've found the latter exemplary. Jannick has infinite patience for the girl's questions and revels in teaching his daughter all the moving parts in an establishment such as this. The kitchen hierarchy, from the *escuelerie* to the chef de cuisine himself, is explained not like a pyramid, with the head chef at the pinnacle, but more like the precise inner workings of a watch. No cog, large or small, is less essential than another. If one cannot perform, the whole apparatus fails to function. As an architect he understands that better than many seasoned chefs.

When there is just enough of a lull in the kitchen, the waitress brings Chef Nathan out to speak to them, and Sabrina reacts as though she's being introduced to the lead singer in her favorite rock band. Nathan will ride that high for weeks, bless her. Her questions are erudite beyond her years, and chef and father are both impressed with the insightfulness of her queries, which range from the technical "How are you able to get the crust on the halibut so crunchy without burning?" to the more philosophical "Do you think it's better to use local produce, even if it means limiting your menu?"

She'd noticed several of the items on the menu had been imported quite some distance and, having learned about the concept of a "carbon footprint" in school, is wisely convinced that the food industry—perhaps the most essential industry in existence—must be at the forefront of sustainability measures.

The waitress isn't meant to intervene, but she can't help but become attached from time to time. Along with the check, she brings Sabrina an enamel lapel pin in the shape of a red flower with six petals and a small pearl in the middle. The shape is not unlike the Michelin Star logo, though a bit more refined. The girl beams at the waitress and envelops her in a parting hug.

Father and daughter leave with their stomachs replete and their hearts brimming even fuller. Her dreams are born that day, and her father's mission of opening his daughter's palate—and her mind—to the world is already more complete than he realizes. Heartache is waiting for that special, sweet child. The time will come when the waitress needs to intervene and guide her back to her path . . . But for now, she can be in no hands more loving and capable than her father's.

So the waitress will bide her time, silently keeping tabs on Sabrina as she grows from gangly child to grown woman until such time as she needs her.

Chapter 1

DECEMBER 23, 2024
DENVER, COLORADO

Get it together, Sorensen.

I've been in enough job interviews that this should be old hat, but even fifteen years into the chase, I've never been to one where my hands didn't shake. From my first gig in New Orleans, fresh out of the Culinary Institute of America at twenty-two, to my last job as general manager of Maison Ortense in Paris, each one sent me into something just short of a panic. Despite this, I land the jobs I want more often than not. Sometimes competence matters more than confidence. And at this stage of my career, I'm able to fake the latter better than most.

I have been working toward becoming a Michelin Guide inspector this whole time, each job another rung climbed on that oh-so-competitive ladder. I've chosen each position with an eye toward making my application to Michelin irresistible . . . when I do finally work up the courage to send in my application.

I also keep an anonymous food blog—The Anonymous Epicure—on Substack to serve as a running portfolio of my food-writing skills that I'll use as part of my application. It has gained quite the following and has been a nice little side hustle that gives me practice reviewing on the sly. It's also a financial lifeline in this hopefully brief period of unemployment.

I am actively trying to convince myself that this job as GM of 540 Blake in Denver is the next step up on the ladder and not the setback it feels like. There is no way I am going to blow my chances and apply to Michelin after a failure. I have to wait until my career is on an upswing.

Fun fact: No one but those in the most secret of Michelin's bat caves (okay, they're probably normal offices, but I enjoy picturing them as bat caves . . . don't take that from me) knows the exact number, but it's widely understood they receive *thousands* of applicants for every opening they post. Sure, a huge number of those aren't even close to qualified, but if even 5 percent of applicants *are* qualified, it's one of the most competitive jobs in the world.

It's the job I've wanted since I was thirteen, and I've never considered doing anything else long term. I've made it a point to move on as soon as I feel too comfortable. And I've had jobs I've loved. Absolutely loved. But when that happens, I pack up for a new city and a new job before I decide to settle there forever. Though in the case of Maison Ortense in Paris, the decision was made for me. I'd been hired as GM to help debut head chef Joëlle Durand earn back the third star that was stripped from the restaurant when legendary chef Éugenie Rosier retired.

It's Michelin's custom to remove a star when the baton of a master is passed on to a protégé. The idea is that the chef needs, and deserves, the chance to prove themselves. Our investors gave us two years to reclaim the honor, and when we failed to do so, both of us were unburdened of our employment and replaced with new blood. Seeing Girard Bodin, Joëlle's cocky sous-chef, take over her place had been a blow. They wanted to throw him in right at the holidays, perhaps to prove he was up to the challenge. Or perhaps to deny Joëlle the chance to demonstrate—again—that she is a world-class chef worthy of following in Éugenie's footsteps.

It's not that I wish Girard and the new GM ill . . . I just don't put a lot of energy into wishing them well.

It didn't matter to the investors that we'd worked our asses off and had done some damn fine work. It didn't matter that a third star is never ever guaranteed. It didn't matter that the Parisian restaurant scene is one of the most insidious old boys' clubs in existence and all manner of decks were stacked against Joëlle. The dirty little secret is that once a woman like Éugenie shatters the glass ceiling, it re-forms again right beneath her feet, this time reinforced and bulletproof, like the windshield of an armored car, so other upstart women can't reach the same heights.

But as unjust as it is, there is nothing to be done. We'd been given a timeline to make it happen, and we failed to meet the benchmark. Fairness never entered the equation.

Since leaving Paris a few days ago, I have succeeded in being philosophical about this career setback. Most of the time. Perhaps we *could* have done things better. Perhaps not. It's not out of the question that Michelin was set on making Joëlle pay her dues for more than a couple of years before restoring the third star. It's possible there would have been no way to change their minds, and we were never going to succeed in the time frame we'd been given.

But we'll never know, and no good will come of speculating how it could have turned out differently. Though, I confess, in darker moments the temptation to Monday-morning quarterback the situation is too great to resist.

I force my head back in the game. This is a job interview, and I desperately need a win. I *need* this job, even if it's not in a key city like Paris, New York, or Hong Kong.

I should be grateful to have any sort of interview, especially during the busy holiday season. I'd been surprised at the invitation—and on just two days' notice—but decided it would be worth the detour on my trip back to my hometown of Solvang, California. 540 Blake wants someone to start early in the new year, so the new GM would have the January lull to formulate a plan for a profitable Valentine's Day and Denver Restaurant Week, and they were willing to carve time for interviews during one of the most hectic weeks of their year. The investors must be worried and want someone in place to right the ship's course.

I've never spent much time in Denver, apart from layovers in their infernal airport, but the city is fast becoming a player in the industry and is worth paying attention to. Each city has its own quirks, and I'll need to learn them in order to succeed. I've arrived early enough to eat a meal here before the designated interview time. Incognito—Michelin-inspector style. It will give me more to talk about in the interview, and I might decide to write the place up in my blog for the sake of content, but only if I don't land the job. Conflict of interest is never a good look.

To work at Michelin, one has to be a chameleon. Not easy for me, who at six foot two stands out no matter how hard I try to camouflage myself. In other cities I would dress for a business meeting. I generally stick to well-tailored clothes in good fabrics, usually in dark colors. Boring but convenient. It's easy to hide in a sea of pin-striped suits.

Unfortunately, Denver, as I gathered from quick research, is too casual for the smart suits and dresses I wear in other cities. I've opted for my usual preferred travel garb—dark knit wide-leg pants and top with a duster jacket. Comfortable for hours crammed in a plane seat but still put together enough for a job interview in one of the most casual cities in the US.

I step out of the car and stride into the building, moving as though I belong there. The feeling that I am somehow an impostor is ridiculous; I am just a diner like any other. The interview is an hour and a half away, and this is my chance to see what I'd be working with if this job comes to fruition.

It's time to chase the nerves away and assess the place with my Michelin hat on.

I scan the dining room from the other side of the currently vacant host stand. Patrons are wearing enough denim and performance fleece to prove the cursory research right—pinstripes here would have stood out like a red dress at a funeral. I was raised in the California casual aesthetic, sure, but could all these people possibly be coming in from or headed out for hiking or skiing? Do Denverites really go to work dressed like this? I shake my head and wait several more minutes for the host.

I take advantage of the host's absence to begin my appraisal. At first glance 540 Blake is your typical trendy hot spot for upscale food. Understated all-lowercase signage on the outside. Minimalist décor on the inside. Starched white tablecloths, substantial flatware without embellishment, sleek glassware, stark white floral arrangements with spindly branches. Lord spare me, strands of bare Edison bulbs hang from the ceiling. It's like the proprietor has taken a checklist of all the must-haves for a high-end modern eatery and followed them meticulously. Ruthlessly, even. The result is that there isn't a bit of personality in the place. I feel like I am in a desert of black and white, thirsting for any splash of color. Unfortunate but fixable.

It's eight full minutes before a scowling woman comes to the host stand.

"We're full up for lunch service." She grumbles rather than speaks. She is tired and harried. And a disheveled front of house never bodes well for calm and order in the back of house. That will take some work to fix.

I summon a smile for the beleaguered woman. "I have a reservation. Meredith Turner?" A fake name I used when making the reservation—I always use one when I'm blogging, just like Michelin inspectors do, to make it harder to trace the blog back to me. I like to imagine that, in those secret bat caves, Michelin has random name generators to produce forgettable pseudonyms. The trick is that inspectors have to remember them—and can't reuse them—so I try to keep to the same standard with my blog.

The hostess glowers down at an iPad affixed to the host stand, and she heaves a sigh when she spots my fake name. I notice not all the tables are full, but the poor hostess is acting like they have a huge backup. This tells me they don't have enough waitstaff to cover their real estate. She shows me to a two-top in the corner and thrusts a menu in my hands.

I take out my phone, open a blank sheet in the Notes app, and peck out my first impressions:

540 Blake

**Service could use improvement. Cold welcome. Kept waiting.*

From a professional standpoint I am grateful that in the digital era, taking photographs of food and scrolling on one's cell phone is accepted practice in a fine-dining establishment. It sure beats the old days described by retired inspectors of sneaking off between courses to discreetly scribble notes on a covert notepad in a restroom stall. All the while hoping an overly officious staff member wouldn't check in on them during their third such trip out of concern that something was dreadfully wrong with the food.

But for the rest of the patrons, who should be fully present for their dining experience, it's a shame so many are distracted by their phones. My father would have hated it. He introduced me to fine dining in the era just a few short years before everyone had cell phones glued to their hands. Had I been my baby sister Chloe's age, introduced to the restaurant scene five or ten years later, I liked to think he'd have held my phone hostage until the bill was paid.

He *might* have indulged me long enough to take a photo of an exceptional meal. Maybe.

I'll never forget the year he took me—just me—to a place on the coast called Serendipity. It was a standard white-tablecloth, tie-preferred sort of place, but to me it seemed like a fairy palace. It's gotten a Michelin Star in recent years, but back then it was grateful to have been mentioned in the guide, even without the distinction. I'd fallen in love not only with the food, but also with the theater of it all. From the gracious host to the especially kind waitress and the introduction to the chef, it was a spectacle.

I read the menu. It isn't laminated but is a loose sheet of paper tucked into a leather backboard designed for this purpose, suggesting the offerings are changed frequently. A good sign. It's printed with elegant but unadorned script on thick linen paper, much like a résumé. Appropriate. A menu is very much a snapshot of a head chef's CV. Not the whole of their repertoire, unless they're foolish or they're running a chain restaurant with a ten-page menu, but it should represent a wide variety of their skills and talents.

The first thing I notice on the menu is the prices. They wouldn't be out of line in New York, Singapore, or Paris, but seem, according to my cursory market research, a solid 25 percent too high for Denver. That is something crucial to bring up in the interview, as one of the five criteria Michelin takes into account is "value for the money." If they want stars, they have to play it smart.

While few Michelin contenders sell their food on the cheap and their prices invariably go up as soon as they affix the red plaque with the white star on their door, value is still a consideration. It's one thing to drop a few hundred on a good meal that will leave you talking about it for weeks. It's quite another to shell out that figure for a meal that leaves you wanting a cheeseburger afterward.

The next thing I notice is a huge number of entrées that include vanilla, sweet and savory dishes alike. It's unconventional as a signature flourish, and I hope the effect won't be too cloying. I'm fond enough of the flavor, but too much of any one note can be tedious. But if it's the chef's trademark, it would be my responsibility to select dishes that highlight it. Ingredient quality is another tenet, and I hope the chef has brought their A game with some exceptional home-brewed vanilla.

My options selected, I scan to the bottom of the menu and see the words *Executive Chef Edward Fairbanks* printed in small type.

Dammit. Dammit. Dammit.

I consider leaving then and there. I could message Nora, the director of operations for the restaurant group that recruited me. I could claim my flight was late and if I stayed for the interview, I would miss my connection back to California. That I'd risk missing my kid sister's engagement party unless I went straight to California. But if I flake on an interview, word will get around. I might not get another GM interview, and it would set my career back even further.

Edward will block me from being hired here. I'm as certain of this as I am of my next breath, but that won't reflect as badly on me as my not showing up to the interview.

I had done as deep a dive into research as I could, given that the interview was offered on short notice. Edward must be very new to the place, or else they aren't crowing too loudly about his association with the restaurant. Which, given the industry rumors about him, might be true. He had a spectacular failure in New York not long ago: a nouveau-industrial nightmare called Nava.

Out of morbid curiosity I'd taken the opportunity to eat there while on a weekend stay in the city last year, and it was as awful as the reviews said. Most newspapers and magazines either left tepid praise or omitted the place from their reviews altogether. I assume his investors had sway in publishing to bring that about. But even if they'd secured a glowing review in the *Times*—and they didn't—it wouldn't have been enough to drown out a sea of bad word of mouth among the foodie crowd.

I had referenced the place in my blog, briefly, as a place to skip if on a short trip to New York. I'd offered up one short sentence about the bad ambience and discordant flavor pairings and suggested three other "edgy" places that better managed to hit the mark. It was perhaps untoward to review an ex's restaurant, but if the chef had been a total unknown to me, I don't think I would have done anything differently.

Actually, that isn't true. I'd have done a full review and panned the place the way it deserved. But as a kind and magnanimous ex-girlfriend, I'd refrained.

It would seem he came to a less competitive environment to start over. But the investors won't plaster his name all over the place until he's earned some accolades. Accolades in the form of a red-and-white plaque one affixes to the front entryway.

Knowing Edward, this has to be eating at him. He lives for the recognition that comes with being an executive chef. To have his name kept on the down-low would be the worst sort of blow to the ego. I almost feel sorry for him. Almost.

I *am* glad to see he isn't making the same mistakes with garish ambience and discordant flavor pairings. If anything, he's erring too far in the other direction. He couldn't even come up with a name that was more exciting than the address, for crying out loud.

I decide to stay the course. Chances are, an executive chef isn't in-house on a Monday. I'd escaped seeing him at Nava, and my luck may extend far enough to avoid an encounter here. I'll do the interview and save as much face as I can.

I bury my face in the menu and pray I can stave off embarrassment.

But fate has *really* decided to mess with me these days.

"Sabrina fair, listen where thou art sitting," a familiar voice croons from above me. "Under the glassy, cool, translucent wave."

I look up from the menu and there he is. Edward. Not Teddy. Never Eddie. Always . . . Edward. His bronze hair is a little grayer around the temples, a few more lines at the corners of his eyes. Still devastatingly handsome. And quoting the Milton poem for which I was named, which is a low blow. My mother envisioned a delicate water nymph of a daughter, not a sturdy Viking maiden—a fact she reminds me of often.

I study Edward's face. Has his ego mellowed with age? Unfortunately, my experience has shown the opposite is more likely. Chefs' egos age like whiskey: They don't mellow. They become more complex and nuanced. More potent, oftentimes. But mellow? No.

I pause for the briefest of moments and consider the possibility of lying to his face and telling him that he must have mistaken me for someone else. But, unfortunately for me, I am a terrible liar. It's also unlikely that my doppelgänger is walking around Denver. Copenhagen? Maybe.

"I didn't know you were much for Milton." I like to think my words are laced with confidence and bravado, but I probably just sound like I have a cold. "It's nice to see you, Edward. Or Executive Chef Fairbanks, if you prefer. Well done, you."

His black chef's coat with *Fairbanks* emblazoned on the right side above the words *Executive Chef* is sleek and fitted. He must have gone to the expense of having it tailored rather than deigning to wear something from a garden-variety uniform supply shop. Very on-brand for him.

"What brings you to Denver?" His eyes are on me, assessing. Classic Edward. Always analyzing. Always scrutinizing.

"Oh, just a long layover on the way home for the holidays. Lots of travel lately, and I couldn't bear the thought of airport food for another meal. You know how it is. And when I heard you had a new kitchen, my curiosity got the better of me." There. Not entirely true, but believable.

"I'm flattered you'd take an interest after all these years." I think I detect a flicker of sentimentality cross his face but dismiss it just as quickly as the machinations of my own mind.

"I've always rooted for you, Edward." *Even if you didn't believe me.* The unspoken words hang heavy in the air over our heads, like a noxious plume of kitchen smoke we both want to escape.

He averts his eyes for a moment and clears his throat. "What looks good to you?" He gestures to the menu I've set aside. I'm unsure if he's taking my order or asking for an assessment of his repertoire, but the answer is the same.

I glance back at the menu. "I was drawn to the scallops for the starter, the lamb for the entrée, and the vanilla bean panna cotta with the gingerbread *espuma* looks especially intriguing for the dessert?" I voice it like a question. There is nothing in the rules against asking the staff, even the executive chef, what's good that day.

He nods. "Good choices. Add a beverage pairing: white, red, and a dessert cocktail to go with it, and you've got yourself a meal. Want to see the wine list, or do you trust me?"

I consider. "Both, actually. I'd be delighted to follow your advice, but I'd love to see what your list is like." Key information I'll need for the interview. I might as well ace it since I'm here.

"Are you doing the sommelier thing these days?" His eyes sparkle as they search mine, hunting for information.

"Not now, but I did several years back. Boston. Eight years ago? Nine?" It seems like a lifetime.

His brows rise. "Impressive. Coming right up."

He strides off to the kitchen, and the surly hostess provides the wine list a few minutes later. Her expression has softened somewhat, but she looks bone weary. She almost trips over her own feet as she hands it to me.

"So sorry." She reddens as she rights herself. "Our expo quit last week, and I've been doing two jobs. Dead on my feet."

She snaps her jaw shut as she realizes she probably shouldn't confide this in a patron. It explains a lot. The expediter is the link between the front and back of house. There isn't a role more important in the running of a restaurant. Efficient waiters and talented chefs mean little if there is no communication between the two. To ask the host to do both roles is like asking someone to juggle flaming batons while doing figure eights on roller skates. Technically feasible but incredibly difficult. And disastrous when it goes wrong—which is a near certainty. I give her a sympathetic smile, and she rushes back to the kitchen.

Get your house in order, Edward. You know better than this.

He'd do better to run expo himself and leave the cooking to his sous than to have an inexperienced host try to do two jobs at once. And he certainly shouldn't have taken the time to visit with me when they're down a key staff member. I suspect there is a fair amount of chaos in back of house, and the previous expo snapped. Probably mid-service. Edward didn't run a Zen kitchen fifteen years ago, and I doubt very much that has changed.

In the unlikely event I get the job here, it will be quite the hurdle to get Edward to change his ways. I consider searching online to see if the previous GM ran screaming into the night, but high-end places like these do their best to keep their dirty laundry off the internet. They're classy and spread gossip by word of mouth, the way nature intended.

It's a full twenty minutes before I see the scallops and another five after that before the waiter, just as harried as the host/expo, remembers to bring the white wine Edward selected to go with it. The scallops appear fresh—always a concern of mine when eating seafood so far from the coast—and the vanilla cream sauce is a bold choice to accent them, especially with the strong undercurrent of rum. The sauce is mellow enough that it doesn't overpower the delicate flavor of the scallops and draws out their flavor without giving too "fishy" a finish on the palate. Full marks for the tenets of "mastery of flavor and cooking techniques" and "the personality of the chef represented in the dining experience" in the entrée.

I consider those criteria the most important, so it's a promising start. The Alsatian Riesling, a bit on the sweet side for an aperitif wine, has a hint of citrus that cuts the sweet notes short. A strong start overall, but the Riesling is served a few degrees too cold, which masks many of the nuances in its flavor. Not an insurmountable problem, but one that Edward should address with his sommelier.

The lamb is brought out before I can finish the scallops, which is never ideal. Colorado is known for its lamb, and I'm excited to see what Edward has done with it. Vanilla again. This time it's a vanilla balsamic glaze that is, admittedly, amazing. His saucier is very good at their job, and I hope Edward knows this and does all he can to keep them happy and on his staff. The vanilla in the glaze is distinct from the one used in the cream sauce. It's earthier and contains notes of whiskey, rather than rum, interlaced with it.

The problem is that the lamb is overcooked and far too dry to serve to a customer. The last of Michelin's tenets is "consistency between visits," which I can't yet comment on, but there isn't even consistency between *entrées*, which means the kitchen needs an overhaul. There had clearly been an issue with the scallops that resulted in them holding the lamb back too long and reheating it before bringing it out. It's usually fine to "fire" a dish gone cold once right before serving, but there's been a mix-up in communication, and the poor lamb has seen the frying pan at least two times more than it should have. The two stalks of asparagus on the side are limp and pale too. It'll be weeks until asparagus is in season, and he should have chosen a different side that's in its prime. The whole point of a frequently changing menu is to serve food in season. The red wine shows up, only two minutes late this time, but is a rather forgettable local blend.

I snap a few photos that show the lamb's dryer-than-sawdust texture and push the plate to the side. Despite the excellent glaze, it's just too overdone to finish. The dessert arrives, beautifully presented on a comically oversized plate. The waiter doesn't think to clear my entrée plate, which is left moldering at the side of the table.

The vanilla bean panna cotta is more complex than I expect, with bottom notes of cinnamon and coffee that take me by surprise. The gingerbread *espuma*—a fancy word for "foam"—is clearly a nod to the festive season and leaves me salivating. It's earned an entry in my top three desserts.

Ever.

It's good enough that, for a few moments, I don't just need, I actually *want* this job. I have visions of talking Edward into an entire themed dessert menu around the *espuma*, a Dessert High Tea before the matinee of *The Nutcracker* at the Denver Center for the Performing Arts. Sumptuous dishes to make the Sugar Plum Fairy and Mother Ginger proud. It would be a sensation. Moments after I've taken my first bite, the bartender presents me with a vanilla-infused hot buttered rum, the likes of which I've never tasted.

I consider the meal through the eyes of an inspector. Were the last course the only course, I'd insist Edward ought to get two stars immediately, and to the devil with protocol. Taking the first and last courses into consideration, I'd give him a confident recommendation for a star. But with a clunker of a main dish—the remains of which still sit festering on my table—I could not offer him my recommendation. And while service isn't an official consideration, it is a dereliction of duty not to clear a plate. Given that a decent amount of the meal has been left untouched, the waitstaff really should have asked if it was to my liking.

Edward, you are better than this. I wish chefs' coats had lapels so

I could grab his and shake him by them. So much potential. So much talent. So many needless screwups.

I start to take some notes on my phone. There are a lot of things I want to discuss with Nora. I don't relish the idea of working with Edward, but I know I can help this place run better. To get his buy-in, I would have to frame it as helping to take a lot of the day-to-day mechanics of the place off his shoulders so he can focus on his vision—which is objectively incredible.

Edward emerges and his face falls when he sees the uneaten lamb on my plate, but he says nothing about it. He arches a questioning brow.

"The dessert was absolutely incredible. The cocktail too." It's the truth and he deserves to hear it.

"And the lamb?" He glances down at the barely touched plate. It speaks for itself, but he is insistent I speak the words out loud.

"Subpar, I'm afraid." It's the closest thing to a diplomatic response I can offer without disrespecting both of us with a lie.

His eyes flash cold. No hint of sentiment or nostalgia there now. His eyes land on my phone for a moment and then fix on me. "I'm sorry to hear it. By the way, good luck with your interview . . . *Ms. Turner.* Don't forget to mention your little experiment with The Anonymous Epicure. I'm sure Nora will find it fascinating."

The glow I'd felt from the warm rum cocktail and the decadent dessert dissipate instantly into frozen mist. *Play dumb, Sabrina.* "Edward, I'm sure I have no idea what you mean . . ."

He cocks his head, his expression just a degree short of lethal. "You're not the only one keeping tabs on old chums. Your little blog got too big to go unnoticed, and you made the mistake of writing up too many restaurants in the cities where you worked.

Not to mention your voice and style are obvious to anyone who knows you. It wasn't too hard to make the connection."

Shit.

"Let me make this simple. You panned Nava, but I won't let that happen again. You mention my restaurant in your little blog *at all* and I'll make sure every chef worth their coat from Bruges to Beijing knows who you are."

"Listen, Edward, if I *did* run a blog, there is no way I'd platform this"—I gesture to the uneaten food on my plate—"even to pan it. I'd hate to alert readers to the existence of this place. Unless you turn the ship around, you deserve to fail like you did in New York."

His face goes ashen, but he regains his composure. "Appearances matter more than truth in this business, Sorensen. Plenty of people are looking for the Anonymous Epicure and would be all too happy to believe that it's you. And once your name is out there, it will be hard to regain that *anonymity*."

His cards are all on the table now. He has the power to block me from getting this job. I'd resigned myself to this as soon as I saw his name on the menu. But that isn't enough for him. He is poised to take out my blog and any shot I might ever have of Michelin too. Aside from my father, Edward is the only one I ever told about my Michelin aspirations.

And it's clear he has no compunction about ruining all of it for me.

Chapter 2

DECEMBER 29, 2024
SOLVANG, CALIFORNIA

Mom, please. You have to listen."

Robin storms into the room in a cloud of Chanel perfume, Chloe trailing in her wake. Chloe's voice, usually soft and restrained, carries effortlessly over the empty restaurant without the din of patrons and waitstaff to dampen it. The pang of panic in her words is unmistakable.

I peer down from the stepladder from which I'd been hanging fairy lights in the Oak Room of the Laerke Inn, our family's preferred event space for decades, as the dutiful spinster does when her baby sister is having a pre–New Year's Eve engagement party.

Chloe had decided to hold the party on December 29, giving people something to do in the weird void between Christmas and New Year's. A lot of her childhood friends would be in town for the holidays, and having it now would save them a trip. Plus it was a Sunday night, so the venue rental was cheap. This is totally in line with Chloe's people-pleasing mindset. She probably racked her brain trying to find the least obtrusive date that would maximize the guest list. Off-peak pricing? Even better.

"You have no experience planning these things, Chloe." Our mother's dulcet tones lace the air like an arsenic cocktail. The more she speaks, the more I'm glad there isn't actual poison handy, lest I be tempted to take a swig. She has a maddening way of speaking as though she rules by fiat.

Chloe's jaw actually drops. "Mother, what are you talking about? I plan events for a living." It's the closest I've heard Chloe come to challenging Robin in ages. Good for her.

Robin looks at her youngest with an indulgent gaze that one might give an errant six-year-old. "It's not the same thing, darling. Weddings are different. We'll do the seafood buffet like the Hansens did for Astrid's wedding." She takes Chloe's hand and pats it. "You need to trust me to organize things. It's the appropriate thing to do."

Appropriate. Her favorite word. I feel my shoulders droop in exhaustion, and the party hasn't even started. At least I haven't had time to stew about my interview. How I aced it. How it will all come to nothing anyway. How Edward needs my help to get his house in order, but there is no way he'll accept it. I've started looking at other opportunities, but it's still the holiday season and hardly anyone is hiring. The overt threat to my blog and Michelin aspirations weighs even heavier over my head. There is no way I'd cover 540 Blake or any other of Edward's restaurants on my blog now . . . even to praise them. But he is just the sort of person to blow my cover just because he's mad at the world. He thinks he should have made it bigger by now, and he hasn't.

So, yes, the upshot of being in Solvang is that there's always too much drama surrounding . . . everything . . . to dwell on my own misfortunes. The downside of coming home is pretty much everything else.

Rather than meet Robin toe-to-toe, Chloe shrinks. "Chris is allergic to seafood, Mom."

I've only met Chris, a very bland investment banker sort, three times before this trip, but I already knew this about him. He isn't just itchy-hives allergic, but ambulance-ER-anaphylaxis-level allergic.

Robin chuckles as if indulging the prattling of a willful child. "So we have the caterers make him a steak. Astrid's wedding dinner was so lovely. People talked about it for months."

The red in Chloe's cheeks deepens several shades, but she doesn't speak up. Chris shouldn't even sit near a fish tank, let alone be in a room where fish is being served. If he ever were to come to a restaurant I was managing, I'd have the kitchen on high alert to keep any kind of seafood from coming within ten feet of him. Liability is a thing.

Chloe bows her head in defeat, and I want to shake her. *Stand up for yourself, woman!* But I'm just as apt to cave to our mother as she is. I just won't be as sweet about it as Chloe generally is. The problem is that Robin has already got the whole affair planned in her mind. Once this happens, she won't accept any deviations from her vision.

Robin bristles at Chloe's displeasure. In her mind, Chloe should be radiating with gratitude at Robin's magnanimity in sharing her expertise in planning an event that's *appropriate*. Appropriate for whom, I can't say. "So what do you have in mind then? Pizza and beer? This isn't a frat party." She has her trademark steel-blue glare of disdain, which makes stronger mortals than Chloe quake in fear.

So very much in character for Robin. No one knows better than her about such things, and anyone who doesn't heed her advice is a fool. No matter that Chloe's job involves planning *movies*, which is far more complicated than any wedding our family could afford. The truth is of little consequence to Robin.

I feel the heat in my own cheeks now. Chloe is closing in on *thirty* and has fabulous taste—and she's far more in step with modern preferences than Robin. But as much as I want to go in swinging in Chloe's defense, I soften my approach, hoping it'll lead to less bloodshed in the minutes before we welcome guests. I descend the ladder and wrap an arm around Chloe's delicate shoulders. She is a strawberry-blonde pixie of a thing, and I feel like a giantess in comparison. "I sense a catering emergency. My superpower has few uses, but this is one. How may I be of assistance?"

Mom glares at me as though I've just tracked mud in on her clean white tile floors. "Now's not the time, Sabrina. Aren't there more lights to hang? You're the tallest, after all." She speaks as though my height is a personal affront. Inheriting my stature from my dad's side was the first of my many offenses against her vision for me and my future. She scans me from head to foot with her assessing eyes. "Did you really *need* to wear heels, dear?"

Chloe stiffens under my arm. "Leave Sabrina alone. I don't want my maid of honor pecked to death before the wedding."

I startle slightly. Chloe has a bevy of friends, and I was certain I'd be relegated to guest book detail. "Really?"

She embraces me, careful not to rumple her pale pink dress that looks like it might be crafted out of meringue. "Of course. Who else but my big sister?"

"Chloe, dear, we still have a lot to decide before we finalize the attendants. You have so many friends who would look so nice in the bridal party photos."

For the first time in my memory, Chloe shoots Robin a *try me, woman* look. She has always been the favored daughter precisely because she never challenges Robin when she insists on something—which is often. I likely don't fit our mother's *vision* for the wedding party: petite, delicate girls all under the age of thirty who would look pretty in whatever dress Mom picks out and who wouldn't complain about her numerous demands for the day. But Mom is trying to hold her tongue since it's Chloe's engagement party.

"Tonight's about Chloe." I accept a glass of bubbly from a waiter who's loaded a tray of glasses for the imminently arriving guests. I raise the glass in Chloe's direction, hoping to deflect Robin's attention off me. "I want to hear all your plans. I'm happy to help with whatever I can."

Chloe's face lights up, and she looks ready to launch into a rapturous speech about dress fittings and centerpieces when Mom interjects.

"I don't see how you can help from Paris." Robin shakes her head as though I've suggested lending a hand from the International Space Station. I'm momentarily dazed at how resolutely every strand in her shellacked strawberry-blonde bob stays fixed in place.

"I'm not in Paris anymore." I wish I could reel the words back in as soon as I say them. This is not a can of worms I need to open tonight.

"So I suppose you'll be wanting your old room back?" Robin looks half exhausted, half delighted at the prospect. She'd love nothing better than to have me back under her roof to boss around until she's had her fill—a limit we've yet to find. More than anything, she's thrilled at the idea that as the one of us three who's been the most likely to ignore her advice, I'm apparently the biggest screwup. This smarts because, at least at the moment, it feels extremely true.

"No, I have some prospects in Denver." It's a lie, but the best cover I have.

"Denver? For heaven's sake, why?" Robin looks horrified, as though I've suggested I'll be renting a stall in a barn rather than an apartment.

"Yes, I've already begun settling in." Another lie. Everything I own is currently in my hotel room upstairs. Any furniture I acquire in a city is generally secondhand and left to benefit whoever takes over my lease after I move on or be donated to the nearest thrift. The life of a Michelin inspector is nomadic: three weeks of travel per month and 275 reviewed meals per year. I have done my best to adapt myself to life on the go so I'll have the stamina and fortitude I need when I finally get the job. Though I freely admit that the idea of a home base with decent furniture and things like decent kitchen equipment and throw pillows—unnecessary, extravagant throw pillows—sounds wonderful at times. But then again, I wonder if I get used to a decent mattress and a nice sofa, will it be harder to go back on the road?

I shove the thought away and turn to Chloe, refusing to put more gas on Robin's perpetual fire of martyrdom. "I have tons of contacts in catering. I'll hook you up."

Chloe beams at me. "I knew you would. I had kind of an off-the-wall idea for the food, actually. I was thinking street food. With cute stalls and everything. I can call in some favors and have them made custom to look like stalls from places we've visited and loved. Something different, you know?"

"Oh how fun!" I can envision the whole thing now: tacos al pastor and tamales to pay tribute to their trips to Mexico with a churro station for the kids. Arancini from Italy and banh mi from Vietnam. The stalls are a super-clever touch, and the right caterer might even be willing to buy them after the wedding for use at future events. A list of contacts starts swirling in my brain.

A picture of a stereotype fit for *Merriam-Webster*: Robin actually clutches at the rope of pearls around her neck. "Heavens, no. Why not hold the wedding at a theme park if you're going to make a joke of it?"

Chloe steams and I open my mouth to defend her. "I think—"

Robin holds up a hand to silence me. "Nice try with the diversion, but we weren't done with you yet. Tell us why you left that promising job in Paris for some pokey old cow town?"

I stand straighter, eschewing my usual tendency to slouch in my mother's presence. "It's not about the location; it's the job. It was time to move on, so I did."

I suspect Robin has loved telling all her friends about the far-flung European cities where I've worked. Occasionally I found myself on the East Coast but have avoided the US west of the Mississippi from a professional standpoint since I went away to school. Not because there is any shortage of incredible restaurants here, but, well . . . to paraphrase Elizabeth Bennet, it is possible for a woman to be settled too near her family. And me moving someplace as prosaic as Denver would give Robin a lot less to boast about.

She puts one hand on her hip and heaves a dramatic sigh. "How typical. You got bored and left. How many jobs is this now?"

I do the mental math and opt against full disclosure. "Just the right number."

"That's quite enough sass for one night, thank you." She takes a swig from a flute of champagne. "And quite enough aimless job-hopping for one lifetime. Once Brian and Annabelle and the kids head back home, you can have your room back and we'll discuss your plans."

Before I can say, "Like hell we will," she spins on her heel and shoots one last look back at Chloe. *We aren't finished here.*

"I'm so sorry, Sabrina. I'd hoped she'd be mellower tonight since it's a special occasion." Chloe puts a hand on my arm, and I can feel the sympathy radiating off her like heat off asphalt. Great. She thinks I'm a screwup too.

I turn to Chloe, refusing to succumb to the tears that threaten. "Listen, we're going to make a pact, right here and now. Neither of us is giving in to her. You're going to have the wedding you want, and there is no way in hell I'm moving in with her."

I hold up a pinkie to seal the pact, but Chloe doesn't reciprocate, her eyes downcast. "Good luck. You know how hard it is to change her mind once she's set on something. And she's in rare form today too. We told her we're covering the cost of the wedding and she's acting like we told her she isn't invited."

Suddenly I'm glad there was "simply no room" at Robin's house for me to stay this holiday season. With Chloe and Chris in from LA, along with my older brother, Brian, his wife, Annabelle, and their kids in from Portland, it *is* a pretty full house. The little ones have taken over my childhood bedroom, and Mom thought I'd be "more comfortable" in a hotel. Which I had to reserve and pay for myself. And, wow, I'd be conveniently on-site to start preparations for the party long before anyone else thought to show up.

I wrap an arm around her shoulder once more. "Oh, hon, that's simple. If she were writing the checks, she could call the shots without compunction. You took that from her and she's hacked off."

Chloe's eyes spark with her own threatening tears. "I didn't mean to hurt her feelings, but it's important to Chris that we 'stand on our own two feet' as he says."

"You have *four* feet between the two of you." I point down in the direction of her fabulous shoes, wagging a finger back and forth. "Don't let him discount yours."

As an associate producer for a midsize studio in LA (read: she plans everything for everyone and acts as the executive function center of the brain for everyone on set), Chloe isn't making a tremendous amount of money, especially when compared to Chris, but she is immensely talented and lucky enough to be making a living doing what she loves. But I worry the small paycheck means Chris and the rest of our family see her work as less valuable. I certainly won't be one to talk about paycheck size once Michelin happens, but the work still matters.

Fun fact: Michelin Guide inspectors are paid roughly on par with public school teachers and are required, by the nature of the job, to live in some of the highest cost-of-living areas in the world. My latest positions have paid well, however, and I've lived well below my means. I've socked away as much of my wages as possible for years, along with some money from Dad's estate, so I'll be able to buy a small place outright wherever Michelin sets as my home base. The hope is that I'll be able to live comfortably on my salary without the burden of rent or a mortgage.

Chloe brushes a kiss on my cheek. "Thanks for that, Rina." I smile at the use of the nickname that has fallen out of favor with everyone but her. "I'm going to need you, I think. Mom is set on having the reception *here*. It will be like every other family event for the past century, and it's not what Chris and I want. I'd hoped having the engagement party here would help appease her."

I hold up two fingers in a scout's pledge. "As maid of honor, I vow your venue and catering will be exactly what you and Chris want. Not a bit of seafood on-site." I make a mental note to discuss security measures, like passwords, with the caterers and other vendors. I wouldn't put it past Robin to go over Chloe's head and try to make changes to suit her own tastes despite the whole thing being on their dime.

She kisses my cheek and dashes off toward Robin to tend to some detail or another before the guests arrive, which should be any moment. Seeing no restaurant staff with free hands, I fold up the stepladder and haul it out of the dining room, looking for someone out in the inn's lobby to whisk it away. Of course Brian and Annabelle aren't here yet to help. She's probably doing a livestream from Robin's kitchen, making organic purées from scratch for baby Bailey or some such thing. Annabelle is happy to be the life of the party, so long as she doesn't have to break a sweat to make the party happen.

That's where I come in. The consummate spinster who's expected to make herself useful while the pretty young things like Annabelle and Chloe get their time to shine.

I stop off in the ladies' room to make sure my moonlighting as an electrician hasn't left me too rumpled. I'm wearing a cobalt-colored sheath dress. Silk, designer, and well-made, but secondhand like most of my better clothes. Understated but festive. The black patent heels were perhaps a mistake since Robin is in attendance, but I developed the habit of wearing them in Paris. I already stood out so much there, a few more inches didn't make much difference.

I return to the dining room and admire the effect of my handiwork. I not only strung the lights but also oversaw the delivery of the centerpieces, directed the staff on the best layout for the tables, consulted the chef on the menu and head count, and generally made sure the space was shown to its best advantage. The restaurant is a bit outdated, but we've hosted so many special occasions here over the years, it feels like an extension of Robin's living room. The restaurant doesn't have any stars yet, but it does merit a mention in the guide, which is great for a small place so far outside LA. On the exterior the inn conforms to the Solvang aesthetic: a quaint white building with dark timber framing designed to pay homage to the town's Danish roots. The inside is—as my father's people would call it—*hygge*. Comfortable, cozy, familiar. As an added bonus, the entire town is still decked out for Julefest, the town's month-long Christmas festival, and looks like something fresh from a Hallmark movie.

As hard as it is to come home, the Danish flair of Solvang always makes me think of Dad, and I take complicated comfort in it. I don't know if I can claim much aside from looks from my Danish side, but an appreciation for making people feel at home—*hygge*—is one Danish principle I do aspire to. I like to think it's part of the reason I've been called to the hospitality business and why I care that patrons in my restaurants feel welcome. And why serious reviewing by places like Michelin matters. They set and uphold standards that ensure everyone is treated like an honored guest.

I see Robin fussing with one of the centerpieces I've already aligned perfectly with the table.

"Please stop messing with those." I gesture to the centerpiece that is now off-kilter.

"That's rude." Mom hisses her words as her eyes flicker to the door to make sure no one is here.

I step closer and use my height to its full advantage to tower over her. "Right backatcha, lady. I've worked all day on this while you all were off getting your hair done, so leave it alone."

I move the centerpiece back to its original place, never breaking eye contact with her. I swear I can hear a low growl escape her throat, but I refuse to retreat.

"What's wrong, Robin, really?" I use even tones, hoping to engage her in a real dialogue. "This isn't about catering or my moving to Denver."

"I have no idea what you mean. This is a lovely party for a lovely couple." I've skated too close to something resembling meaningful connection, so the ice shields rise to save her from the indignity of having to be emotionally vulnerable. "And since this is probably the last one of these I will get to throw, I ought to do my best to enjoy it."

I ignore the jab at my single status. "You should enjoy it because you're celebrating Chloe and Chris. That's reason enough." I accept another flute of champagne and turn back to Robin, who is, to her credit, trying to collect herself.

"And who says I'm not?" She avoids looking at me altogether with an expression of such pained annoyance, I hope Chloe doesn't see and have her night spoiled.

"Listen, I don't want to fight. But I do want you to take it easy on Chloe with the wedding. She and Chris will do a fine job. Let them come to you for help where it's needed. Your relationship will be the better for it."

Robin purses her lips. "I'll manage my relationship with your sister without your interference, thank you."

"Wow, a serious family meeting, and you didn't think to invite me?" Brian's booming baritone sounds behind us. "I'm hurt."

Robin's demeanor changes in an instant. Golden Boy Brian is now on the scene with his Stepford wife, Annabelle. No doubt my impeccable niece and nephew, Bailey and Asher, whom I'm convinced have never been permitted near a speck of dirt in their short lives, are probably in the care of three specially trained nannies with résumés good enough to get them posts in the Secret Service. They'd want a spare in case one is taken out by sniper fire in Robin's living room or some such equally likely disaster.

Robin. Loves. Annabelle.

"Not at all, dear. Sabrina and I were just finishing up a little chat, weren't we?" She shoots me a glare that dares me to contradict her.

I lock eyes with my brother and pray silently that he can somehow defuse her. If anyone can, it's her precious baby boy. Perhaps, with Annabelle's help, he can persuade Robin that Chloe's ideas are brilliant and creative. But Annabelle is off taking footage for her feed, and Brian seems more interested in working his way over toward the bar than playing referee. Not that I blame him.

The guests begin to arrive and Robin's face brightens. "Oh, there he is. You two stay here and I'll be right back."

Brian turns to scan the room. "Did Bradley Cooper just show up? Or whoever it is Boomer moms drool over these days?"

I am mid-sip, and a chuckle reverberates in my champagne flute. "I wouldn't put it past Robin to try to get some A-list celebs here for the event. Though whom she's trying to impress, I don't know. I've been wondering that for close to twenty years now."

"Don't be so hard on her. She's just trying her best." Brian gives me a scowl as though Robin is a small child passing off a lopsided cake for dessert at some important dinner and I am the persnickety hostess who insists on perfection.

I successfully keep my tone low. "Trying her best to do what? To be supportive of Chloe and Chris? Not so much."

"It *is* possible for you not to get involved for once. Let Mom and Chloe work it out between themselves." Brian speaks as though reminding his son, Asher, to use a fork instead of his bare hands for the third time in the course of a meal.

I hate when he takes on the "man of the family" persona, as though he can dictate our behavior. I take a step closer, taking advantage of the two inches I have on him. "I wish I could, but you know full well Mom will just steamroll Chloe into whatever she wants, and Chloe will spend the whole day hovering over Chris with an EpiPen, miserable in a venue she doesn't want. Chloe deserves better than that."

Brian rolls his eyes and wanders off toward Annabelle, who is holding her phone at arm's length, yammering away to her adoring fans. As usual he will be of no help.

The sound of the arriving guests drowns out my frustrated inner monologue, and I decide to play my part and make sure the food and drink are circulated without a hitch. If people are well fed and the champagne flows freely, the better the chances people will stay civil. I'm greeted by a flurry of relations, many of whom I haven't seen in ages. I'm about to greet my ancient aunt Carlotta when Robin uncharacteristically loops her arm in mine. "Come, I've someone I want you to talk to."

The dread washes over me as she hauls me across the dining room. It's either some long-forgotten relative, one of her boring-as-beige-paint friends, or . . .

"Darling, you remember Tim, don't you?" She purrs like a cat who caught the mouse.

Tim Espersen. The literal boy next door from my childhood. Mom had pushed us together at every opportunity, but I'd resisted. He had been a foot shorter than me, pimpled, and a massive computer nerd. I wasn't popular or charming either, but I preferred hanging out with my dad and futzing around in the kitchen to forced social situations where neither party would have enjoyed themselves.

But the Tim before me looks nothing like the Tim from high school. He's tall and confident, and his skin has mercifully cleared up.

"We had four years of English and science classes together, and a few other classes too. I think I can dredge up a memory or two." I extend a hand toward Tim and wink. I actually wink. What on earth is wrong with me?

"True story. I could never keep up with Sabrina in English, but I like to think I gave her a run for her money in science. Except chemistry. You slayed in chemistry." Tim flashes a grin as he accepts my hand in his.

"True enough. Cooking is just edible chemistry. It's the science I could wrap my head around." I'd never considered that Tim considered me an academic rival, but it made sense. We both graduated in the top five of our class. I barely edged him out for salutatorian, but I'd not been all that interested in competing against him so much as against myself.

Robin chimes in with her fake titter she pulls out for social situations. "Yes, our Sabrina is quite handy in the kitchen. I'm shocked no one has swept her off her feet yet."

It takes more than a little self-control to refrain from turning for the door. I instead decide to turn the conversation in the way Robin will hate the most. "I'm six foot two. I'd hate to meet the brute capable of sweeping me anywhere."

I'm rewarded with a glower. Robin *hates* being mocked. Which is likely why I enjoy it so much.

Tim, to his credit, ignores Robin's death stare and accepts a flute of champagne from a passing waiter and tips it in my direction. "It's great to see you, Sabrina. You look the same as you did in high school."

I snort. "So you come to my family's party just to insult me? Real nice, Espersen."

Robin elbows me discreetly but not playfully. She apparently missed that Tim is laughing at my rebuke. She is also incapable of letting the conversation flow without moderating it. "Tim is working in computers in Silicon Valley. Making quite the name for himself too."

Tech means dollar signs and prestige to her. I don't look over to see her saccharine expression as she daydreams of his opulent house and posh lifestyle. As she envisions living vicariously through me if Tim and I were to become an item. I don't think my stomach can handle it, but I keep my game face on for Chloe's sake. "No surprise there. Tim was always destined for the tech life. I had no doubt we'd all be using some product on the daily with the name Espersen on it."

A slight blush rises in his cheeks. "Yeah, I developed an algorithm that a lot of apps are using . . ." He goes on to list several, three of which are currently occupying prime real estate on the front page of my phone. He hasn't just made it in the tech world; he owns it. Best of all, he's the smart sort that manages to keep from becoming a household name, because who wants that?

"Wow," is all I can muster.

Robin nudges me a step closer to Tim. "Sabrina has been working in Paris until recently. We're all very proud."

I look back at her to check for signs she's been abducted by aliens. Remarkably, there are none.

"I knew you'd be a sensation, whatever you did." Tim looks genuinely happy. "So if you're not in Paris anymore, where are you?"

I decide to keep my lies consistent. "Denver. It's great there. Good skiing, fabulous hiking." I have never skied and only rarely hiked, but at least I've read both are true.

Robin clears her throat. "Yes, well, Sabrina's career has led her all over the world. Who's to say it won't lead her back to California?"

I don't give her the satisfaction of looking at her with disdain but lock eyes with Tim instead. "My plan is to stay in Denver awhile."

"Plans change, dear. Especially yours, it would seem." Robin fairly purrs the insult.

God how I wish Dad were alive to rein her in. He was the only one who could make her see how unreasonable she was.

I force myself to breathe once again. Just being in Robin's presence makes me forget how. Just as she is trying to railroad Chloe into her vision for the perfect wedding, she's pushing me to settle here so I can be open to the mere *possibility* of dating Tim. She's publicly implying that I am so desperate and my career so unimportant, I can drop everything for the mere prospect of a relationship. And embarrassing me spectacularly in the process.

I beam a Hollywood-worthy smile. "Tim, it was so great seeing you. If you're ever in Denver, give me a shout, okay?" I shake his hand and turn back to the crowd to mingle. Of course I *won't* be in Denver, most likely. And I didn't give him my card. But it was at least a pretense of politeness.

Robin follows hard on my heels. "What are you doing? He is *such* a nice boy."

I, through sheer force of will, love for my sister, and fear of the American prison system, narrowly avoid throttling Robin right there in the Oak Room. "I'm sure he is, but you don't have to ram him in my face. He's just making small talk, and you act like he's on the verge of a marriage proposal. You were embarrassing me."

"Embarrassing *you*?" Her expression goes cold. "Maybe it's just as well. He's a family friend and it would be awkward. Even if it worked out for a while, you'd find an excuse to end things. It's the same with men as it is with jobs for you: You never stick with anything long enough to really give it a chance. It's sad, really."

I scan the room and see that Chloe is enmeshed in her crowd of admirers, enjoying her moment in the sun. She won't notice if I leave. I set my champagne flute down on the nearest table. I don't spare a glance backward at Robin as I exit the dining room. Out of the corner of my eye, I see Tim working the room with a confidence I never would have expected of him.

I have worked so hard to get where I am. Sacrificed relationships—even friendships—to get closer to Michelin. It has meant upheaval and change, yes, but Robin should be proud of me and my accomplishments, even if she's not fully aware of my end goal. That's a mother's job, isn't it?

But between Robin's spiteful words, the awful encounter with Edward, and the unrelenting feeling I let down Joëlle and Maison Ortense, I am beginning to feel the weight of it all. Is going after the Michelin job at the expense of almost everything else in my life really worth it?

I've had some amazing experiences these past fifteen years, but it doesn't change the fact that I feel alone in the world, even in a ballroom filled with my "nearest and dearest." And I have felt that way for some time . . . and I'm not sure *any* job can fill that void.

Chapter 3

DECEMBER 30, 2024
BURBANK AIRPORT

I have to get out of Solvang. It's not the most rational decision, but I trundled myself out of the hotel at 4:00 a.m. and drove to Burbank Airport in my rental car. It's not as close as Santa Barbara Airport, nor does it have the volume of (comparably) cheap, direct flights to almost anywhere in the world like LAX. So it's both inconvenient and expensive, which absolutely feels on par with my life right now. But I want to get farther than Santa Barbara as soon as I can, and I simply can't face the bustle of LAX right now, and it's one of the few airports I actually *love*.

The exterior in particular feels like the airport depicted in every sappy 1960s romance movie—and it has been used as such plenty of times. One can practically see a tearful farewell between Doris Day and Rock Hudson unfolding as you step onto the sidewalk in front of the gracefully curved terminal building. Sometimes a bit of old Hollywood charm is exactly what the soul needs. Along with a tankard of cold-brew coffee strong enough to wake my ancestors. But that will have to wait.

I sidle up to the ticket counter line, already seven people deep despite the early hour, laden down with two suitcases that contain all my worldly possessions and a large designer backpack—secondhand and made of supple deep green leather—that I use for carry-on items too valuable or precious to check.

Of course there are prosaic items inside, like my laptop and earbuds, which I can't afford to replace at the moment. But more important are the sentimental items that even my stern pragmatism, born of fifteen years of constant moving, hasn't managed to pry from my grasp. In hard moments such as these, I often clutch the bag and hold it to my chest, letting the comfort of the items inside seep through the porous leather and envelop me like the perfumed steam of a sauna.

Among my small trove of treasures is a small case with my meager collection of jewelry, including an amethyst necklace from my parents when I graduated high school and amber earrings that had belonged to my paternal grandmother that Dad passed on to me when I turned sixteen. I wear both frequently and consider them my good luck charms. Not especially valuable, but irreplaceable. But prized above all else is my dad's forty-two-year-old Michelin Guide to Paris that is dog-eared and marked up with his bold script that is still, eighteen years after his passing, achingly familiar. It's highlighted with all the places he'd been in his youth and annotated with his impressions of them.

I spent a good deal of my scarce free time in Paris tracking down his old haunts. Some of the establishments had faded into the dust, while others were generations-old icons that had weathered more economic downturns and setbacks—like global pandemics—than most of us would see in our lifetimes. Monoliths of the Parisian gastronomic skyline much in the vein of the Eiffel Tower.

Every time I ate at one of the restaurants from Dad's guide, I yearned to see his face across from mine at the table. So much so, I kept notes on every meal and compared them with his once I was back in my apartment. I could hear his voice on the restless breezes of autumn as they rushed by my window. I could imagine too vividly the animated conversation we might have about the heavenly roasted duckling at La Tour d'Argent. I imagined taking him to compare the decadent savory and sweet soufflés from the classic restaurant Le Soufflé, which he'd loved, with those at the newer Le Récamier, which hadn't yet opened when he was in the city. I dreamed of chatting about it all over a cup of proper French hot cocoa at Café de Flore the following morning. I wished we could wander the streets and stumble upon the new, as-yet-undiscovered gems that might be the icons foodies flocked to three generations from now.

Dad's guide had been in the discard pile once Robin had gathered the strength to sort through his things—a task that was infinitely harder than the funeral for all of us. I'd squirreled away the guide when she wasn't looking. She probably would have objected to me resurrecting it from the rubbish with a pretense of not wanting me to develop hoarding tendencies or some foolish thing. Which would be ironic, given that she has a four-bedroom house full of belongings while I insist on being able to carry everything I own in two standard-sized TSA-approved suitcases, my beloved backpack, and a sturdy yet classic cross-body purse. I need to be able to manage trains and subways, airports and taxis, without assistance. Too often, there is none to be had.

Really, Robin just didn't—doesn't—want her judgment questioned. And ironically, I completely understand why she would have pitched it. A natty, out-of-date guidebook would appear to any other person to be a prime candidate for the trash bin when they were faced with the task of sorting through a lifetime of belongings. It just wasn't trash to me.

I clutch my backpack tighter to my chest as I approach the front of the ticket line. I have my choice of about twenty-eight cities if I'm flying direct . . . and virtually anywhere in the world connecting via the major hubs they service. In all my life I have never been in an airport without a ticket and a plan and any number of contingencies at the ready should my original plan fail. "Be present in the moment" might be a credo of mine, but "Go with the flow" is not in my vernacular.

When Michelin is the goal, whether you're a chef, a hotelier, or a wannabe inspector, there is no plan B. Because if there *is* a plan B, at some point down this long and grueling slog of a desert road, that cozy little tree-lined detour will lure any sane person away from the path they've been on for so long. And once you take that detour, diverting back to the desert road is nearly impossible.

The family in front of me accepts boarding passes and scoots off to the side, and I am beckoned forward by a young, vivacious ticket agent whose brass name tag reads *Olivia*. She is far too bright and smiling for this ungodly hour, and I fight the urge to take a step backward. I am capable of many things, but facing this sort of unbridled energy without the assistance of near-lethal doses of caffeine is almost too much to ask of myself.

But just before I close the distance from the two poles at the front of the line to the check-in desk, an older woman with soft gray curls taps Olivia on the shoulder. Olivia's face goes blank for a moment, and she scurries off as though to an urgent appointment.

The old woman waves me toward her, but her warm smile is

tempered with the grace earned from a few more decades of experience, so my feet find their way forward. "Where to, dearie?" She has a lilting Irish accent I hadn't expected. She seems oddly familiar, likely because she reminds me of every doting grandmother in a generic sort of way.

I open my mouth, hoping a destination will pop out. I'll just go with whatever city comes to mind and find a job there that will get me a step closer to Michelin. *Come on, brain.*

San Francisco? Too close and way too expensive without a *very* good job lined up.

Phoenix? Not a Michelin city, but it has loads of potential.

And Tucson, a UNESCO City of Gastronomy, is just an hour away. Blistering hot place to live for much of the year, but amazing work is being done with Sonoran Mexican food there.

Or I could try Chicago, which I've always felt is underrated.

Do I want to go back to the big leagues and try New York? Maybe New Orleans again, or somewhere in the Southeast where Michelin will finally be expanding in the coming months?

Stay domestic or go abroad? Expand my horizons and go somewhere in Asia for the first time? Practicalities swirl in my brain. Expenses, language barriers, and job possibilities all compete for what little bandwidth I am working with.

"I—I don't know."

I don't. And it terrifies me.

I always know my next move on the chessboard of life. Usually several ahead. But Maison Ortense was meant to be my last stepping stone before I applied to Michelin. For the first time in my entire life, I don't *have* a next move queued up. From nowhere, tears spill over the rims of my eyes, and I worry I am going to collapse into a blonde puddle on the floor of Burbank Airport.

This is not who I am. This is not how Sabrina F. Sorensen (yes, my middle name is Fair—ugh) conducts herself. I want nothing more than to have a mentor and a friend to lean on right now. And while I have left an impressive string of jobs in my wake, I don't feel like I have much to show for them. What have I been doing with my life but chasing a dream? Which is great if you catch it. But for the mortals down here on the ground who don't make the cut, what's left?

It's not that I don't have choices. I could excel in any number of dining and hospitality jobs. Enjoy them, even. But when so much of my life has been devoted to making myself worthy of this job, how can I face the world if I fail? How can I live with *myself* if I never get the chance to try?

I let the tears fall and stare into the woman's gentle blue eyes and shake my head. "I just don't know."

"Oh, this won't do at all, will it? Come with me, dearie." The ticket agent, whose brass name tag reads only *Ticket Agent*, rather than her given name, vacates her post and meets me on the other side of the counter. It's like the relic of a bygone era when people in service only needed to divulge the job they performed and were still afforded the privilege of anonymity. While I am not one to romanticize the past, I do wonder if that was a perk we've lost.

Olivia emerges from somewhere and resumes her place at the counter as though nothing has happened. She motions the next person forward, her bright smile affixed like she's advertising whitening toothpaste.

I follow the Ticket Agent down a hallway toward what I assume is a series of airport offices the general public doesn't have access to unless something is seriously amiss. Because of my breakdown, is she taking me to some sort of airport infirmary to have me evaluated by a physician before they let me near an aircraft?

Instead of a sterile doctor's office, I'm shown to what looks like the most elegant VIP lounge I've ever seen. It looks like it's out of an opulent 1950s or '60s movie set with plush oversized chairs, wooden tables shined to a mirror finish, and a gleaming bar area with abundant food and drink.

"This is so beautiful." I step into the room and struggle to take a full breath. I've been in my share of airport lounges, some of them objectively swankier, but this one is unique somehow. The atmosphere is otherworldly in a way I can't articulate. Welcoming, soothing, but with an underlying vibe of uncanny valley I can't shake. It doesn't feel quite *real*.

First of all, I've traveled in and out of Burbank Airport enough times to know this lounge does not exist on any airport map available to the masses. It's possible this is a private lounge they don't advertise to the public, or even garden-variety frequent flyers. But this seems unlikely given the lost potential for profits to be made from such a place.

Second, it's completely empty of other travelers. It's still very early in the day, but it's one of the busiest travel weeks of the year. Even if it's super exclusive, the place should have at least a few bleary-eyed celebs and hedge fund jerks looking for their complimentary coffees. Or mimosas, depending on how challenging their holiday celebrations have been.

Third, and most important, my gut tells me something is off, and that is a feeling I've learned to ignore at my peril.

What I don't feel is fear. Things may seem strange or "wrong" somehow, but I am not in danger. I'll let this be enough for now.

"You look white as a sheet, dearie." The Ticket Agent pats my arm like she might her niece's. "Let me get you a fresh coffee. It'll set you to rights."

She glides off toward the polished mahogany bar and emerges a few moments later with a brimming stoneware mug rather than a flimsy paper cup. In the other hand, she has a plate with a sesame seed bagel filled with bacon, egg, and cheese. My default American breakfast with healing powers far beyond Michelin stars. How she knows that this simple breakfast is my ultimate comfort food, I don't know. She gestures to one of the open tables and I join her. She places the mug and plate in front of me.

"I added just a dollop of caramel to the coffee. You look like you could use the extra boost."

I accept the cup gratefully. I'm usually a strong black coffee sort of person, but I have been known to add a square of chocolate to sweeten it when the mood strikes. Something more complex than table sugar that will play off the rich coffee notes instead of masking them. I take a sip of the coffee and try not to groan from pleasure. It is, without reservation, the best cup of coffee I've ever had in my life. This is no garden-variety grocery store coffee.

"Where did this come from?" I sniff the cup, trying to parse its origins for myself. I'm usually able to nail down a coffee's origin with reasonable accuracy—a sort of coffee sommelier—but this one is hard to place. It seems to have the complexity of beans from Ethiopia and the bright, clean flavor I associate with Costa Rican varieties.

She sits with me, having fetched a mug for herself. "It's a blend of my own, dearie. I keep a bit here for caffeine-related emergencies. And, not to boast, but I make my own caramel too."

"Boast away. You're in the wrong business." I clutch the coffee mug possessively to my chest. "You should be running a coffee empire. I could introduce you to some people." I take a bite of the bagel sandwich and don't even try to conceal a groan of pleasure this time. Ambrosia fit to accompany the caramel-laced nectar.

She chuckles. "I've had a great number of careers in my lifetime, and this is where I belong right now. But thank you for the compliment. Now tell me what on this green earth has a lovely young lady such as yourself crying at my ticket counter before dawn."

Despite my usually reserved nature, something about this woman has caused my inhibitions to lower, which should, all by itself, cause me to raise my shields. But it all comes tumbling out of my mouth in a tear-laden confession. My mother's insistence that my life is somehow inferior or broken because I haven't yet attached myself to a man hits particularly hard, especially because I *have* felt lonely lately.

Miraculously, this grandmotherly woman doesn't seem fazed by my trauma dumping. It's a nice change. Whenever I've tried to confide in Robin, she never lasts more than about two minutes, after which she tries to one-up me with a tale of her own misery or tells me to buck up and work on my online dating profile. Which I don't have.

I even confess my Michelin desires, which I never do. And in doing so, I realize that the job I've dreamed of for so long now feels less like my fifteen-year plan and more like a childish whim of an eight-year-old who dreams of being an astronaut. What harm is there in telling her when those goals and aspirations seem as far away as a moon landing is to that starry-eyed third grader?

The Ticket Agent clucks her tongue sympathetically. "Oh, dearie, that's a lot to be getting on with. No wonder you didn't know where to go."

The caffeine and protein have begun to enter my bloodstream, and I am beginning to feel more human. And more aware that not ten minutes earlier, I had a very public meltdown. In front of this very nice woman who probably isn't paid nearly enough to put up with such nonsense. "I am so sorry I panicked on you. How idiotic of me."

"*How* inappropriate *of you*"—Robin's voice echoes in my brain.

That woman really is incapable of leaving me alone. She's managed to imprint herself in my inner voice . . . which is something I'll eventually need to unpack with a therapist when I get around to hiring one.

"Dearest Sabrina, you never need to apologize to me." She reaches across the table and pats my hand the way a mother would do. The way I've wished countless times that Robin would do. A tingling warmth washes over me. Is this how most people feel around their mothers or other maternal loved ones?

"Thanks." I usually am one to shrink away from being touched by a stranger, but I don't move my hand. I also don't remember telling her my name or showing her my ID. We hadn't gotten to that point at the ticket counter. She seems so familiar, but I can't place her at all. "Do we know each other?"

"That doesn't really matter, dearie." Her insightful eyes search mine. "You're at a crossroads in your life, and you need a friend to help you find your path."

A friend. Do I have any of those? A few pals from high school or culinary school? Perhaps. But we don't really keep in touch. Other than that? It's mostly colleagues. And while I might be able to call in some favors to help me land another job, it feels like I need more than my next job at the moment. "I suppose I do, but I'm not sure how you could possibly help."

"I'll wager I can help more than you think." An unmistakable glint of mischief twinkles in her eyes.

Have I found myself in the clutches of some mischievous fairy? "But why would you want to? What's in it for you?"

"Helping people is my job, and I get the satisfaction of knowing I've done it well. That's reward enough for me, dearie. Now tell me if I've got it right: You're out of work, and on top of it, you've been working toward a goal your whole adult life, and now you're questioning if you really want it. Or if, indeed, you've sacrificed too much for something that may not ever happen despite all your years of hard work."

Statistically? Very unlikely to happen, actually. But I don't say that out loud. I simply shrug my agreement.

"Well, that *is* an uncomfortable place to be."

"Have you ever felt this way?" The question is an impertinent one, but perhaps this stranger and I are beyond those sorts of boundaries. At the very least I'm not likely to see this woman again, so I don't have to wear the embarrassment too heavily.

"I'll say this: I don't think a being lives as long as I have without some measure of regret. Regrets just take on different shapes and colors from person to person. The things we do, the things we wish we'd done. More common than anything else, the countless things we wish we'd done just a *bit* differently. We all have them and they're all a cross to bear. The trick is keeping those regrets small and learning how to haul them around with as much grace as we can manage."

"Wise. I'm not sure how good at grace I am, though. Tall and awkward is more my thing." I cross my arms over my chest like a Kevlar vest, realizing I left my own comfort zone behind about a half hour ago.

She stares into her mug a long moment before meeting my eyes. "I think you're graceful enough in the ways that matter.

There isn't a single person in this world who doesn't find themselves in a situation like yours at some point. If not, it's because life has been far too easy for them and the right decisions have been handed to them at every turn. Or else far too hard, and life has denied them the privilege of choice. You're fortunate enough to be in the middle, Sabrina."

I'd not thought of it that way. Here I sit in a comfortable airport lounge faced with any number of choices, each one ready for me to select it from the proverbial hat. Some are probably good. Maybe even great. Others might be disastrous. But they are all mine to make. But what if I make yet another mess of things?

"You're right. I just need to pick a city and make the most of it." I set the mug down on the table with a resolute thud. "I can do this."

"Hold on now. That isn't quite what I meant. We're coming in on a new year, and I think it wise for you to look back on your life before making the leap to a new city and a new job. You may learn something that will be useful."

I snort and gesture to the lavish lounge. "Do you have a crystal ball or a scrying bowl somewhere in here so I can watch my life like reruns of an incredibly boring TV show?"

And for a moment, it doesn't seem the most ridiculous thing to find in this place, and I worry I've insulted her.

She waves a hand. "Oh, I don't put much stock in such things. Far too unreliable. And I find actually being in the moment is far more impactful than watching it passively, don't you?"

I shrug. "I suppose?"

She presses further. "If you could go back and relive a moment from your past, undo a mistake, take a chance, or just do something differently, what would it be?"

I don't hesitate. "I'd go back and hold the ladder for my dad."

I was at the Culinary Institute of America in New York, three thousand miles away, when he took his fall. I can't say the number of times I've wished I'd been there. How much would be different if just a few things had gone differently.

The Ticket Agent shakes her head. "I'm sorry, dear, but there are certain paths in our past that are written for us as they must be. It was your father's time, unfair as it was."

I stand from my place. "Who are you and how do you know this?" Things are getting too eerie for me, and it's time to seek the normalcy of postholiday travelers celebrating the final hours of the season by being positively beastly to one another.

"Like I told you, I'm a friend, dear. I've just known you a bit longer than you've known me." She smiles and makes no move to stand. She's completely relaxed and doesn't seem anxious to stop me from running for the door.

So, inexplicably, I don't.

Because the fact remains that I have nowhere to go and no one waiting for me. I'm certain if I turn my phone on, it will have a zillion missed messages from Robin and Brian telling me off for leaving early. Possibly a message from Chloe telling me she's sorry she didn't have the chance to say good night. Social butterfly that she is, it probably didn't even register with her that I headed out just as the party was getting started. But no one would be saying they missed me or urging me to hurry home because they genuinely like my company.

I flop back in the chair and stare at the retro—or possibly vintage—light sconce on the wall as though it might contain the answers to all my woes.

"What else, dearie?" The Ticket Agent speaks as if I didn't just nearly storm out of this surreal lounge. Perhaps she knows I'd never find my way back to the real airport if I left. I'm tempted to go test the doors to see if I'm locked in here against my will, but it hardly seems worth the effort. If the Ticket Agent wants me here, I don't think I have much choice but to stay.

I let my mind wander a bit, and it settles on the disastrous encounter with Edward. The interview with Nora went fine. Great actually. We made a good impression on each other, though none of it mattered. They wouldn't risk alienating the talent to bring in a general manager he didn't endorse. But what if I'd never met him? What if he were just a talented chef like any other who needed some guidance from a business-minded GM like me?

"I wish I'd never met Edward Fairbanks. I wish I'd ignored him at the bar all those years ago and met him for the first time at my interview."

The Ticket Agent shakes her head. "No, dearie. He may be quite the pill, but you were always meant to meet him when you did. My advice would be to think a little smaller than saving a life or cutting someone out of yours entirely. You'd be surprised at the difference a small decision can make."

I ponder further. We'd parted with a rather public shouting match back in New Orleans—not my proudest moment—and not spoken again until our fateful encounter in Denver, despite being in the same field. And reconciliation doesn't seem to be in the cards.

If I'd kept my temper under control, I just might have left on good enough terms with Edward to have a shot at the Denver job. And if I could succeed in doing for him what I wasn't able to do for Joëlle, I just might be able to revive the dreams of Michelin that seem to be smoldering amid the embers of my career.

"I would go back to end things with Edward on better terms."

The Ticket Agent gives a small smile. "Not bad. Why don't we give it a go?"

She hoists my backpack over her shoulder and gestures toward the Jetway door I didn't notice before. I remain stock-still.

She looks back in my direction. "Do you trust me?"

I obviously should say no. I don't know this woman or anything about her. She doesn't fit the profile for a serial killer, but those are always the best ones, aren't they? But the strange truth is that I *do* trust her. Despite all reason and logic, I nod.

"Come with me, then. No need for your luggage just now. Your pack will suffice." She pats my green bag and gestures toward the door. She opens the door to a private Jetway, and I'm now certain this is some sort of secret celebrity hideout to which the plebeians usually don't get access. I have never been on a flight from Burbank that didn't board outside.

The Jetway looks nothing like the modern ones at other airports but, like the lounge, feels straight out of the golden age of air travel. She escorts me into the plane, a private jet that appears to be from the same vintage but is as pristine as a plane straight from the factory line. If there is such a thing as a new airplane smell, this one has it. Leather upholstery, polished wooden tables that smell of lemon Pledge, and carpets that look freshly vacuumed.

The Ticket Agent senses my anxiety as I take in this veritable time capsule of an aircraft. She smiles her warm smile, and my shoulders lower an inch. "Choose your seat and get settled." The seats are more like sofas. There's easily room for three passengers at one, each with an oversized table, perfect for use as an in-flight desk or dining table.

She spends a few moments fussing about and hoists my backpack in the overhead bin.

"Anything you'll need will be in your pack. And if things go badly or you find yourself displeased with your destination, all you need to do is head back to the airport."

"Am I the only one on the flight?" I look around and don't even see evidence of a pilot onboard.

She places a hand on the edge of the massive seat. "No one can take this journey with you or for you, dearie. And I can only offer you one more bit of advice for now."

I look at her expectantly.

"You may be going to New Orleans with an objective in mind, but be open to new paths and options. What you think is important may be far less crucial than you believe. And remember, you're always free to come back here whenever you wish."

The Ticket Agent leaves back up the Jetway, the door of the aircraft closing behind her. A mechanical voice tells me to fasten my seat belt, and the jet engines roar to life.

Chapter 4

NEW ORLEANS

The aircraft seems to do little more than taxi and take off before landing again. An animated female voice comes over the plane's intercom system.

"Welcome to New Orleans. Outside, it's a balmy seventy-two degrees, perfect weather for a Cajun Christmas. We hope you enjoy your stay, and as always, thank you for flying with us! We hope to see you again soon."

The seat belt lights switch off and the doors open. I grab my backpack from the overhead bin and walk toward the aircraft door that has opened onto another Jetway, just as old-fashioned as the last. On a table in the Jetway there's a newspaper. I scan the headlines about the winter weather putting a damper on holiday travel in the north and lots of excitement about the local NFL team hitting the playoffs. But then my eyes fix on the date:

December 22, 2009.

The night of the Christmas party where Edward and I had our very heated, very public breakup. I am known for having a very long fuse, but Edward was foolish enough to find out what happens when the flame finally meets the tinder. He'd said some cruel words. Maybe, just maybe, I can smooth things over so that even if I don't get the job at 540 Blake (I doubt I can smooth things over *that* much), he might reconsider destroying every other aspect of my career.

I pause to breathe and try to recall more details of my life in 2009. I am all of twenty-three years old and working in my first-ever adult job. I look down at my body. I do feel and look fifteen years younger.

Nice.

Whatever weird hallucination this is has its perks. I consider . . . Maybe I've fallen off the ladder at Chloe's party, and this is all a concussion dream? Logical, reasonable.

But it all feels far too vivid to be a manifestation of my subconscious.

As I walk down the Jetway toward the outside world, I continue to take stock of myself. My clothes have changed, and I am now wearing my signature black chef's pants and one of a million white tees I owned in this era of my life that would disappear under my chef's coat at work. Robin had sent me a boxful of quality white tees when I mentioned my work uniform. She insisted quality cotton was worth the investment. They were a luxury in this time of austerity in my post–culinary school years, and I thought of her every time I slipped one on.

That was one of the last of those sorts of gestures she made. Over the years I struggled to figure out what I'd done to bring about their end, but I always came up at a loss.

But now isn't the time for Robin. I realize, as a bead of sweat forms on my brow, that I shouldn't have agreed to come on this weird little trip. Not without asking *a lot* more questions. Chief of which would now be, "Is time travel involved?"

I've seen enough movies and read enough novels to know how

dangerous time travel can be in the fictional realm, and I know better than to test my luck when my own future is at risk. I don't know if anything I do here will impact my real life or if this is some sort of weird simulation. This could be the worst sort of butterfly effect disaster, and I don't want to travel back to my own time to find that I've mangled everything. I shudder at visions of myself managing a failing Waffle House in rural Alabama. Not that there's anything wrong with honest work like that, but it's not what I've spent fifteen years bleeding for.

Or worse, I don't want to find out that my actions have somehow caused someone else's life to implode, even inadvertently. The enormity of that possibility is just too much to contemplate.

I can't do this.

I turn and jog back down the Jetway, determined to reboard the aircraft. I'm not doing this without more knowledge in hand. I reach the plane only to find the door is shut. I pound against the smooth white metal of the cockpit, but it stays resolutely closed. No magical flight attendant comes to rescue me.

And I don't expect them to.

I have no facts to work with, only my gut intuition. And it's telling me that it's too soon to go back. I have to believe the Ticket Agent was honest when she said I am free to come home whenever I want, but I'm beginning to think I am obligated to give this . . . experiment, for lack of a better word, a shot. I don't know if that means a few minutes, a few hours, or even days or weeks. What I do know with certainty is that the plane door is definitively shut, and I have no alternative but to continue to the terminal.

I curse my own impetuousness for agreeing to get on that plane so easily, for not having a better sense of self-preservation. But there is nothing for it now; I have to figure out how to make the best of the situation I've gotten myself into.

December 22. I try to remember what I did that day before the ill-fated Christmas party. It doesn't take long to recall I was on the lunch shift at La Fontaine Mirabeau and hopping busy because of the holiday season.

My wrist is devoid of a watch; I never wore one when I worked back of house. I dig around in my backpack, hoping the Ticket Agent's promise about it containing everything I would need is accurate. Inside are the contents of the workbag I usually carried in those days, including my first-ever smartphone. This one was a graduation gift from Brian who, by this time, was already doing well up in Portland in his swanky software job.

I'd first scoffed at the idea of being held captive by the device but found it indispensable for keeping my ever-changing schedule straight, being available to my supervising chef, and snapping photos of an especially good plating. I've not been without one since.

The time on the front of the phone reads 9:47 a.m., and there is a glaring red reminder that, yes, I have to work that day. I remember clearly that I was expected to report by 10:00 for lunch service, and I always made a habit of showing up at least twenty minutes early to prep my station.

I'm already late.

But do I have to work? Can I just go explore my life and skip out on service? Tempting, but every neuron in my body is telling me I need to go where I would have been and let my life unfold.

I slip on the backpack and rush down the Jetway. At the other end I find myself in Louis Armstrong International Airport, as I expected I would. Unfortunately, it's a solid thirty minutes from my restaurant in the French Quarter. A crowd of holiday travelers, all looking merry and bright as the cliché goes, meander about.

I think back to what was going on at the time. The economy was slowly improving after the recession, and the general mood of the country was brightening. I remember culinary school being a tense place to be in the middle of an economic downturn. Restaurant dining, especially of the middling to upscale sort, was one of the first things people cut from their budgets. But by the time I graduated, things were looking up, even if they weren't totally better.

I start to dash to ground transportation, hoping there will be an obliging taxi at the ready, but it dawns on me that in 2009, I was not the sort of person who could afford a half-hour cab ride. I presume my old wallet is in the bag somewhere, and it probably has a lovely colony of moths making their home in it, Looney Tunes–style. I'll have to pray the bus schedule is in my favor.

The airport buses only run every ninety minutes, so if I haven't hit it just right, I'll be disastrously late. And this is a gig I don't want to ruin for past me . . . if indeed that's a risk. It's probably better to assume my actions here have consequences for my future, so I'll act accordingly.

"Princess, you running late?" A familiar baritone sounds behind me.

I swivel my head to see Jean-Rémy, the sous-chef from La Fontaine Mirabeau, jogging to catch up with me. He's in his sixties but is robust for his age, so it doesn't take long for him to catch up with me. Tears well up in my eyes as I take in his lanky frame, warm features, and salt-and-pepper hair, cropped close to his head. I throw my arms around my old friend, having wished for just this chance more times than I can count.

Jean-Rémy was my first mentor and guide. He saw my skill and wasn't about to let me waste my time as an *escuelerie* (the fancy restaurant term for dishwasher) and insisted our boss, Antoine, promote me to *commis chef*—the lowest rank in the kitchen who is actually trusted near food. And despite having no outward signs of poor health, Jean-Rémy will die of a massive heart attack in about five years. Despite lots of emails and texts, I won't see him in person again after I leave La Fontaine Mirabeau about six months from now.

I think back to my breakdown at Burbank Airport and the feeling of friendlessness. Had Jean-Rémy survived, he'd have been the first person I called when everything went wrong. He might not have had all the answers to fix my future, but he sure as hell would have tried to help me find them.

It's no exaggeration to say that I wouldn't be where I am without Jean-Rémy. Rather than letting the *chefs de partie*—the station chefs—order me around haphazardly, he had organized a proper apprenticeship for me where I could learn each rotation in detail. I dig around in my mind and remember I was likely working with the *poissonnier*—seafood chef—that month. I bet that if I raise my hands to my face, I'll still have the scent of briny oysters clinging to my fingers despite countless washings. He made sure I left his kitchen knowing how every cog in the back-of-house machine works.

"Girl, are you okay?" Jean-Rémy chuckles into my hair.

My behavior is definitely strange for 2009 Sabrina, even if 2024 Sabrina feels totally justified in acting like a sentimental fool.

"Yeah, fine," I lie. I discreetly wipe away the tears that had threatened to spill over. "I, uh, was worried I was gonna be late. Antoine's always a bear about it this time of year, ya know. I just cut the timing too close."

"Don't you worry, sweetheart. I got you." He wraps an arm around my shoulder, warm and avuncular, as he used to do.

I remember now, he'd been traveling to New York to see his

daughter Melisse, who is roughly my age, perform *The Nutcracker* with the New York City Ballet. She was one of the ensemble dancers, but it was her first role as a professional, and he wasn't about to miss it. He'd had to threaten to quit to get Antoine to let him take the time off in the middle of the holiday rush. Even Antoine and his massive ego knew he couldn't run the kitchen without his sous.

The sous-chef really is the backbone of the kitchen in most restaurants. Executive and head chefs are essential for providing vision, sure. The head designs the dishes and creates the menu, but the sous-chef has the impossible task of taking sometimes-whimsical dreams and making them a reality. Or they have the even harder task of telling their boss that their vision simply isn't workable in a mortal kitchen bound by the constraints of time, finances, and physics.

We find Jean-Rémy's car in the garage, and he maneuvers onto the streets of New Orleans with practiced grace. "Something isn't right, Princess. You'd better tell old JR about it."

I smile despite everything I'm trying to process. The only one he allowed to use the nickname JR was himself. His family had been in the city for literal centuries, rising up and down the social ladder as the fortunes of the Black elite waxed and waned. Many of his forebears had ties to the NOLA food scene as well. With such lineage, he embodied the soul of Créole culture—and its food—more than anyone I'd ever met. His daughter Melisse was one of the first to move away, and he was immensely proud of her career. And for good reason. She's a rising phenom in the dance world and has brilliant prospects.

"It's just been a very weird day after a very long week." I hope it sounds believable. It *is* true, just not in the way he thinks it is.

"Don't I know that. You're in hospitality in the holidays. No weirder days or longer weeks to be had, Princess. I don't think that's everything, though. But you'll tell me when you're ready."

"Thank you." He had always been like this. Never pushing, always open. I remember wishing Robin, with her incessant prying, would take a few lessons from him. "It's a little complicated. Nothing serious, though."

"Is that Edward fella treating you okay?" Jean-Rémy's hands tighten on the steering wheel.

I wish I could open up to him about the mess of an encounter Edward and I had in Denver, but that would be impossible to do without sounding insane.

"Um, things are fine." It sounds stupid, even to my ears. How can I explain to Jean-Rémy that fifteen years down the road, Edward will pose a threat to me holding on to the job I fought to get for so long? There's no way to make it sound like I'm not crazy.

"He taking you to the big to-do at the Esmeralda tonight?" Jean-Rémy takes his eyes from the road to glance over at me.

"That's the plan." Edward is the newest sous-chef at Hotel Esmeralda and fought hard to get the job. Their holiday party is a huge deal on the New Orleans food scene, and as a key employee, he's expected to be there and be charming. And as his girlfriend, I am lucky enough to score a place as his plus-one at this top-tier event.

"Well, that's good. He needs to take you out and show you off. Don't let him treat you like anything less than the princess you are. Got it? I'll be keeping an eye on the pair of you tonight to make sure he does." With one of the best reputations in the industry, Jean-Rémy is a perennial fixture on the guest list. I didn't see him there the last time, but I'm glad to know he'll be there if I need him this go-round.

Past me had been elated to rub elbows with the who's who

of the NOLA restaurant scene, but present-day me knows how the party ends. I overheard him making a derogatory comment about my work at La Fontaine Mirabeau and called him out on the spot.

I didn't say anything he didn't deserve, and I'll defend that even after years of replaying this night when sleep wouldn't claim me. What I do regret is doing it publicly. It's not that he didn't deserve to be embarrassed either. His behavior merited a good dose of humiliation, but making a scene is beneath me. Perhaps fifteen years of maturity has made me see it, but the public shaming was a lot like junk food. Enjoyable in the moment, a little cathartic, but leaves more regret than satisfaction in its wake. Maybe if I'd done things differently, my career wouldn't be in peril.

But the party is still hours away, and I have to survive the lunch shift before I can figure all that out. I'll have to let the question percolate in my brain as I work. I find myself both intrigued and terrified at the prospect of a "redo" on this lowlight of my life.

We finally arrive at the staff parking near La Fontaine Mirabeau, and Jean-Rémy glides his wheels smoothly into his assigned spot. I lean over and kiss his cheek. "Thanks for saving my rear."

He chuckles. "Anytime, Princess."

Antoine gives me the evil eye as I arrive ten minutes past staff call and a full thirty past when I usually arrive. But Jean-Rémy shoots back a look of his own. "She came to get me at the airport. Saved me at least an hour."

Antoine nods, expression softened. Losing ten minutes of my time is nothing compared to an hour of Jean-Rémy's. It's a lie, of course. And it occurs to me that Jean-Rémy never questioned *why* I was at the airport. Bless him for that. There is no excuse I could have concocted that he would have believed anyway. There's no time off for a grunt like me this week. If I'd postured turning in my notice like Jean-Rémy had done, I'd be currently unemployed. I am utterly dispensable.

But over the years, I've been working as hard as I know how to make that less true.

Jean-Rémy deposits me at the fish station, where Marc, our lead *poissonnier*, points wordlessly to a heap of oysters that need shucking. I glance at the menu posted and see we'll need them not only for the gumbo and the charbroiled oyster platter, but for the lunch special of southern-fried oysters as well.

As I pick up my knife, I can already feel my fingers ache from the effort of shucking the eleventy billion oysters for service.

And I can't wait to get started.

Chapter 5

Lunch service is a blur, but I feel invigorated by the adrenaline. It's been ages since I've been part of a kitchen staff, and something is magical about the kinship found there. Comrades in arms, all baptized in the fire of our first dinner rush. Even the newest kid washing dishes understands the hustle. Respects it.

I should be beat, but as I leave the restaurant with a parting kiss on Jean-Rémy's cheek, the bounce in my step is undeniable. Even though I dread the party I have to show up for in two hours, I am high on kitchen magic. Despite it being ages since I was in New Orleans, I find my old studio apartment with no trouble. The keys are securely zipped in my backpack's inside pocket, and it seems the Ticket Agent wasn't kidding about it having all I need.

I take a long, luxurious shower, hoping in vain that the smell of oysters hasn't permeated my skin so deeply that it's become part of my personality. I sacrifice liberal amounts of body wash and shampoo in the endeavor and will chase them with a spritz of my favorite perfume. It has notes of coffee and spices, with a floral undertone to soften it just enough that it doesn't take away all the hard edges. It's subtly foodish without being an overly sweet "gourmand" scent I never felt was right for me. I love the idea of some confection with notes of praline and chocolate, but they come across as too juvenile for someone built like a Viking warrior woman.

No, the earthy spices and hint of lilting jasmine are better suited to someone like me. Robin gave me a bottle for Christmas when I was in college—the year before Dad died—and I'd been addicted ever since. She has a knack for picking out the perfect perfumes and colognes for people, I have to admit. Even as broke as I was back in this era, I permitted myself a bottle of the stuff every year, hunting desperately for sales or at least a decent "gift with purchase" promotion that would help me cut back on my makeup expenses for the year.

I'd made a special thrift run to find the perfect dress for this event and discover the spoils of that hunt in my closet. I run my fingers along the silhouette of the dress I'd been too timid to wear ever since that night. It's long and red and makes no effort to conceal my height or other attributes I've been conditioned to conceal. I'd purchased it in a moment of confidence and wondered whatever happened to it in the years since.

I rarely got rid of clothes, preferring to maintain a small wardrobe of high-end pieces purchased on consignment or at thrift that would last, but this must have been one of the rare pieces I'd sacrificed back to the gods of Goodwill. Returning some underused pieces back into the wild is the ethical thing to do, after all.

The holiday party at Hotel Esmeralda is legendary. While we at La Fontaine Mirabeau close for a family dinner prepared and served specially by Antoine and Jean-Rémy, Hotel Esmeralda sets aside their ballroom for a lavish spectacle of a party for their employees as well as VIP patrons and the who's who of the hospitality industry in the city. The passed hors d'oeuvres are always next level, and the specialty cocktails flow like water. I didn't have much time to sample either on my first iteration of this timeline.

Dressed, coiffed, and made up, I admire myself in the mirror, pleased with the effect. It's jarring to see my face with fewer lines and the bright skin of youth, but this young face lacks some of the character of my thirty-seven-year-old one. The lines had been etched there with fifteen years of well-earned laughter and tears, triumphs and tribulations. I'm glad to know I won't feel a sense of loss when the time comes—and I assume it will—for me to leave my dewy skin behind and go back to the present day.

All the while I worry about how I will react when I see Edward again. Every part of me is compelled to act as though nothing is wrong. To allow events to unfold naturally and see where things lead. But do I have the fortitude to do that? How tempting will it be to head off Edward's hateful comments before they happen? To defuse whatever anger is bubbling under the surface before it comes spilling over? Or to simply choose not to be in the room when the words are spoken? I don't know how long his little tirade might have lasted if I'd not interrupted it the first time, but I can probably gauge things well enough from my memory to avoid the scene if I want to.

But that doesn't feel right either.

Edward needs to see me and my reaction to his words. So at the sound of the car horn that has just blared on the street below, I go downstairs and meet Edward and deal with the night's events as they come to me.

Even from his profile, which I admire as I slide into the passenger seat of his beat-up coupe, he is as alluring as ever. Most people, and I must say men in particular, develop a swagger when they reach a certain level of competence in their chosen field. Edward radiates it. The swagger isn't off-putting, though, because he's earned it. He's climbed the ranks to sauté chef in short order, due to nothing but his own talent. He and the saucier are the lead station chefs, and it's quite an accomplishment for someone so young.

The electricity between us is there, as though no time has passed for me at all. His gorgeous bronze hair begs to be tousled. The proud line of his nose longs to be kissed. Slowly. By me. I had often looked back on my time with Edward and wondered if the chemistry I remembered was just the product of nostalgia, but now it seems like my memories have done a disservice to what we shared. I can't find it in me to care that future Edward might destroy me. *This* Edward is young, ambitious, and full of hope. And he is, by every indication, very into me.

He leans over and pulls me into a deep kiss. The kind that says, "I have nowhere else to be and no one else I want to be with," that leaves me gasping. All the dreams of being a culinary power couple come rushing back, and I hate myself for enjoying the familiar tingle of longing a bit too much. This is the man who is hours away from disparaging me in front of his friends.

I remember every word I overheard him say as though they were etched on my heart. Moreover, this is the man who, a decade and a half later, is threatening to ruin my career with precious little cause.

But I find I can't hate him. This Edward hasn't done these things . . . yet. Maybe he'll surprise me and this time it will be different. But in any case, I have to play along for now.

"Hey." He rests his forehead against mine. He's tired from his shift, glad to see me, and both excited about and dreading the party all at once. I used to be able to read him like a book. Not unlike how I had been able to read my dad's moods . . . And I missed having someone I felt that connected to.

"Hey." I try to react to him as I would have done, so I rub his knee, remembering the joy of such familiar contact with him. With anyone, really. I don't want to calculate how long it has been since I felt free enough to touch someone this way. Or how long it has been since someone touched me.

Another kiss or three and we reluctantly decide to proceed to the party. The engine in his ancient Mazda stalls once before roaring back to life. "Sorry," he mutters to the universe in general rather than directing it specifically to me.

Driving a crap car isn't generally a sore point for younger chefs; rather, it's a badge of honor that you're still in the time-honored trenches of paying your dues. Not so for Edward. I know in his heart of hearts, he has his eyes on the Emeril-Lagasse-Gordon-Ramsay-esque levels of fame that come with fancy cars. Or at least cars that don't make noises that cause people to duck out of fear of a nearby robbery.

"How was work?" I try to keep my tone light and brace myself. Just as powerfully as the mutual chemistry has resurfaced, the memory of having to walk on eggshells around him after a shift tags along. This I don't miss at all, and I remember the lightness I felt once I got over the initial pain of the breakup.

His workplace back then was volatile, and the answer to the question could go in a number of extreme directions. One day he could extoll his triumph for an hour when the head chef complimented his efficiency. The next day the same head chef would be a talentless buffoon with no vision because he didn't like a new dish he'd auditioned for inclusion on the menu.

"Well, given the event we're headed to, I think it's safe to assume I spent a whole lot of time making canapés and mini quiches. Not exactly riveting." His tone is indifferent, meaning the day wasn't stellar, but it wasn't awful either.

I pat his knee. "I expect a less-than-riveting day in the kitchen is a nice change of pace this time of year." I have to speak as though it's my first Christmas in a professional kitchen, so I don't offer anything more insightful.

He looks world-weary as his eyes scan the traffic. "It was just a time suck."

"I'm sure Jerome is grateful you delivered for him." I don't add that I've learned in years since that volunteering for these less-than-exciting tasks, rather than being "volun-told" to do them, frequently *is* a deciding factor in promotions in the restaurant world. Often, reliability is more sought after than raw talent. It doesn't matter if you're this generation's Jacques Pépin if you don't show up and seek opportunities to show off your skills. Opportunities like these.

"Sure. Kitchen karma, I guess." His hands are tight on the steering wheel, and I know he is just trying to assuage me. He feels like he's spent the day as a kitchen grunt, and there is no making him feel better about it.

I see his point, to an extent. It's important not to make yourself so available that you're taken advantage of, but showing a willingness to be a team player is essential. Even more so is proving that you don't have such an ego that you see certain tasks as "beneath you." I've seen head chefs wash dishes when the situation called for it. But things are far more convivial at La Fontaine Mirabeau than they are at Hotel Esmeralda. My coworkers want to see me succeed, and most of Edward's are either indifferent to his attempts to ascend the culinary ladder or downright hostile toward it.

I wonder if reminding Edward of this lesson is why I've been sent here, but as Edward pulls into the employee parking near Hotel Esmeralda, I decide it might be worth nudging him toward this truth. It's the best guess I have, and all I can do is hope that I can guide him toward a kinder version of himself.

Chapter 6

I enter Hotel Esmeralda on Edward's arm, enjoying the warmth of his flank against mine despite the muggy air of the ballroom that's already overwarm from the heat of too many bodies. The ballroom really is one of the most sumptuous spaces in New Orleans, and I'm glad for the chance to see it again.

In years past, the appetizers passed by tuxedo-clad waiters have been first rate: smoked salmon, caviar, savory-filled pastries—some classic, some experimental. Last time I was in this timeline, Edward hadn't cooked for the party. Perhaps something small has changed for him as well, like making all the lights in traffic instead of being held up. Maybe this time he arrived on time and was roped into the job . . . A shiver trickles down my spine like a frigid bead of sweat as I consider how many other things may have changed *just* enough to make a world of difference.

I try not to think too much about it, or it will paralyze me from doing anything. I focus on how this shift may be presenting Edward with a golden opportunity, and I hope he's brought his A game to these appetizers. Aside from my unfortunate lunch at 540 Blake, it has been a long time since I've sampled his cooking, and I'm dying to try Edward's interpretation of these dishes for myself.

I'm several years newer to the business than Edward, so I know fewer people here, but I don't feel as daunted by the sensation now as I did back then. Now I am used to being in rooms of people I don't recognize, it being a rather critical function of my work. Young Sabrina was worried about being a wallflower and feeling left out and awkward. Present-day me (I refuse to call myself *old me*) considers this an opportunity to observe and learn.

"Hell, Cecil Granby made it. He hasn't bothered to come in four years. I wonder what dragged him out?" Edward discreetly gestures toward a man who is actually wearing a smoking jacket unironically. He is quite possibly the only person I've ever met who can pull off the look without coming across as an absolute loon.

The Rolodex—and given the year, it feels like a Rolodex—in my brain whirs to the card for Cecil Granby, the owner of Le Métropolitaine. It's one of the most exclusive eateries in town, on par with Hotel Esmeralda. Perhaps even more posh. It also has a long and storied past, invaluable in history-steeped New Orleans, that Hotel Esmeralda lacks. Edward's boss, Jerome, and Cecil are longtime friendly rivals. I have the advantage of knowing Cecil's pet-project restaurant in New York will earn its first Michelin Star in 2012. Jerome, despite efforts to break into Michelin markets, hasn't yet been successful. From the scuttlebutt in the industry, their little feud turned from friendly to hostile shortly after Cecil's triumph.

But one point on which Jerome and Cecil, and most of the culinary establishment, can agree is that New Orleans not being a Michelin city is a crime against gastronomy. I don't dispute this. Only just now in my own timeline is Michelin expanding to New Orleans and across the Southeast, an honor far past due to this culinary gem of a city.

We'd not been courageous enough to introduce ourselves to Granby before, and I have a strong feeling that this is exactly what needs to change. Moving from Jerome's kitchen to Cecil's would be a coup for Edward. If he plays his cards right, it might accelerate his career. I am convinced now that my role here is to make sure the two men make a good impression on each other. I can't think of anything better for Edward than getting him out of his toxic work environment.

"Let's go talk to him." I gently tug his arm in Cecil's direction.

He looks at me as though I've just suggested we serve Cheez Whiz on saltines to the guests. "He has no idea who I am."

I playfully tug on his arm again. "And how will that change if you don't introduce yourself? This is a party in 2009 New Orleans, not a Mayfair ballroom in 1805. You don't have to wait for a mutual acquaintance to introduce you."

He looks dubious but plants a kiss on my temple as he gathers a long breath. "I guess we can give it a whirl?"

I return his kiss and meet his gaze with determination. "You have nothing to lose."

I wish someone had told me the same thing at this age and a few other times in my life, but there's no time to mull over that moldy regret now.

We approach Cecil, who doesn't appear to be dismayed by our approaching him unbidden. Edward smiles, exuding confidence, and introduces himself. Edward mentions his employer and slides in a compliment about the last dishes he tried at Le Métropolitaine. Very smooth. The pair seem sufficiently impressed with each other before Edward takes a long enough pause to introduce me.

I extend my hand. "A pleasure to meet you in person rather than by reputation alone, Chef Granby."

Edward discreetly shoots me an astonished look. The version

of Sabrina he knows is much shyer and would meet the introduction with some stuttered pleasantries and blushed cheeks.

"Enchanted, I'm sure. I was hoping to be introduced to the loveliest lady here this evening, and it seems that objective has been met in the first half hour. How splendid." Utter malarkey but well delivered. He places a kiss on the back of my hand like a proper southern gentleman. He's a diminutive man, so he peers up at me without releasing my hand. I don't let the sensation of towering over him make me feel awkward. It's better to own the air in my own stratosphere. "Are you in the business as well, my dear?"

"Rather new to it. I'm working as a *commis chef* at La Fontaine Mirabeau. Just out of culinary school."

He chuckles, his accent of the Louisiana gentry thicker than swamp water. "Brava. No doubt my old friend Antoine is putting you through your paces."

I can't help but reciprocate a chuckle. "He is. But Jean-Rémy has been an amazing mentor and something of a firewall between Antoine's temper and the rest of us."

His posture straightens and recognition gleams in his eyes. "Oh, Ms. *Sorensen*, yes indeed. I've heard talk of you. If Jean-Rémy Landry has taken an interest in you, young lady, you must be a prodigious talent."

Edward's jaw twitches ever so slightly. I'm charming one of the most preeminent executive chefs in New Orleans, and I don't think he's all too pleased about it. This should be his moment, not mine, but it does seem Cecil is more interested in poaching me from Antoine's kitchen than Edward from Jerome's.

This is not at all what I want. "Oh, I'm as eager to learn as any new chef worth their bleached coat." I try to deflect the attention from myself, which contradicts every instinct I've honed to use every contact I can to advance. "Edward helped with the hors d'oeuvres tonight. Aren't they amazing?"

Cecil locks eyes with Edward, his interest piqued. "Did you make the pastry for the savory palmiers? That *was* exceptional."

Edward blanches a few shades. "No, sir. That would be our pâtissière, Lana. I made all the fillings, but the pastry is hers."

Cecil looks vaguely disappointed. "Well, they were a good effort, son. Keep plugging away." Cecil pats Edward's shoulder and moves to mingle in the crowd, but not before shooting me a meaningful look. *"You call me if you need a spot in a kitchen"* is written all over his face.

"I need a drink," Edward mutters as soon as Cecil is out of earshot.

I gesture to the champagne flute in his hand. He empties it in one gulp. "Something stronger," he mumbles before he's even lowered the glass, his words reverberating into the crystal and bouncing back in his face. He sets the flute down on an obliging tray with a clink and strides off to the bar.

Rather than chase after Edward, I maneuver toward one of the waiters with a tray of Edward's appetizers. I snag samples from two different trays to see what had made Cecil grow tepid. The palmiers, a savory take on the sweet French cookie, filled with bacon, Gruyère, and caramelized onion, look fit for the cover of *Bon Appétit* magazine. The pastry is on point, firm but flaky and bursting with butter flavor, but the fillings are dry and underseasoned. A crime punishable by flogging in New Orleans, the home of Cajun spices, I'm sure of it.

The canapé is standard: a thin slice of toasted baguette, cream cheese, smoked salmon, and a bit of dill. Like the palmier, the baguette is the best part of the canapé and is Lana's work, not

Edward's. The cream cheese is unremarkable, the smoked salmon is bland, and the dill is wilted. Rather than seeing this opportunity as an audition, or even just a chance to show off to his friends, Edward phoned in the whole thing and made tired, uninspired choices.

No one would complain about the fare tonight, but they wouldn't be talking about it tomorrow, much less next week, except to praise Lana's pastry work. *She* earned the accolades, not Edward. Worse, he was given Lana's excellent handiwork to form the foundation of something exceptional, and he let her down. Remarkably, this makes me madder than the words I know he is about to speak against me. There is little worse in my book than letting down colleagues, and that's precisely what Edward has done.

And, not for the first or last time, he has sabotaged himself.

There is nothing I can do for this Edward. I've only been here half a day but know, deep within myself, that this relationship was always fated to end when it did.

I scan the crowd for Edward and feel my stomach drop as I see him in the corner surrounded by his small group of friends from the restaurant that he trusts aren't out to stab him in the back on the way up the ladder. I remember this moment from fifteen years ago, though I approached him blissfully unaware last time. Now, I am at least armed with the knowledge of what's coming so I can brace myself for it.

I take three steadying breaths and walk toward Edward and his entourage.

"Honestly, she's a glorified dishwasher and she acts like she's actually got some talent just because Jean-Rémy said a few nice words. She's delusional."

It is verbatim what he said the first time, though we'd not been bold enough to approach Granby before. Something else inspired his diatribe all those years ago, but it's of little import what it was. The meaning is clear: Despite my efforts to sing his praises and to say the right things in the rooms that matter, every word of these insults has been living in his head, bubbling below the surface just yearning to escape. Even with fifteen years of growth and maturity, I find the barbs sting as badly now as they did then.

The difference is that now, as the old maxim goes, I know it really *is* him, not me. I'm sure I did and said the wrong things from time to time, but this outburst has nothing to do with me and *everything* to do with his own insecurities.

Last time I gave him hell right then and there in front of God, Cecil Granby, and all manner of lesser mortals. I won't let him slide this time, but I will respect myself enough not to air my grievances in public.

I clear my throat, and he turns slowly toward me.

"I—uh—wasn't talking about you?" He stammers his words, and they sound pathetic to everyone in earshot. Especially me. His friends scatter to other parts of the ballroom like so many rats. Apt, really.

"I never said you were. Sounds like you have a guilty conscience, Edward." I endeavor to remain the glacial Scandinavian ice queen. Unflappable. He isn't worth the indignity of rage and tears.

"Why don't we go talk outside?" Edward suggests, as the color drains from his face. At least he has the good manners to appear ashamed.

I spin on the ball of my foot. He can follow me or not. The cool air on the street outside is a relief after the ballroom's oppressive mugginess. It's not even nine yet, so the French Quarter is just coming to life. People are finishing their dinners and finding their way to the bars and jazz clubs. It's decadent and seedy, and not my scene at all. I enjoyed it well enough back in my twenties, but I feel utterly out of my element now.

I turn to Edward and only hope he'll make his excuses brief. I'm already longing to find my way home.

"Listen, I—" He runs his fingers through his hair, unable to complete his sentence.

"Let me help. You bad-mouthed me in front of your friends who work in the same industry as I do because you feel insecure about your own career." The words aren't laced with rancor but are as cold and as matter-of-fact as I feel.

"I'm not insecure." His response is knee-jerk. And also a damned lie.

"Then what on earth was that? A demonstration of your confidence? Sure didn't look like it from my angle." I cross my arms over my chest, silently daring him to contradict me.

He shrugs and fails to meet my eyes. He rubs the toe of his shoe absentmindedly against the rough asphalt of the curb.

"The question is why, Edward? I've done nothing but be supportive. To speak your name to the right people whenever I can. Like that one—" I gesture back to the ballroom with my thumb. "I could have talked myself up to Cecil but chose to shift the attention back to you."

His eyes finally reach mine, flashing with rage. "Fat lot of good that did. He all but said he hated my food."

The old me would have told him placating lies, but I don't have the same investment here that past me did. "He didn't. He let you know it isn't up to par. And you know what, Edward? It isn't. You phoned it in because . . . I don't know . . . making appetizers is demeaning or something? That's all on you."

"So you have it all figured out after working in a kitchen for six months and the ink still wet on your diploma?" This is the side of Edward I saw at 540 Blake. Cold, bitter. And it makes me sad that he's letting his ego choke out his talent.

I don't flinch at the ice in his gaze. "Of course I don't, but I don't need ten years in a Michelin kitchen to know you blew it today. And it's not like you to fumble. And it sure as hell isn't like you to talk about me the way you did back there. Tell me what's wrong, Edward, or I'll go back in there, find your boss, and ask him myself."

His mouth drops at my pronouncement. "What has gotten into you? You're never like this. You usually try to calm me down and smooth things over."

I toss my hands in the air. "Well, that wasn't working, was it? I'm trying a bit of tough love for a change. Your ego can handle it."

His eyes drop again, but he wills them back to mine. "I got moved to lead the brunch shift."

The breath catches in my throat. I didn't give him the chance to disclose this last time. No chef likes brunch. It's an amalgamation of bland, heavy food and some of the nastiest customers we're bound to see in a week. But I latch onto the key bit of information: lead. These changes happen when someone is getting auditioned for a promotion. If he shows some initiative, he could earn a spot as sous-chef under Jerome himself.

"Brunch sucks, but that's a *promotion*, Edward."

"It's brunch. No one cares who leads brunch." He shoves his hands in his pockets. "Hotel Esmeralda is a dead end for me."

I soften. "Maybe it is. If so, move on. But maybe it's not. Maybe you can do something innovative and make Jerome take notice. If you're lead, brunch doesn't have to be the endless sad parade of soggy waffles and curdled hollandaise if you don't want it to be. You could turn Esmeralda back into the hot spot it was twenty years ago if you're creative enough."

"Like I said, no one pays attention to brunch." His eyes stare down the street, like he's longing for an escape.

I feel every bit of my thirty-seven years as I touch his shoulder. He looks at me hopefully, wanting me to comfort him like old times. Like I always do.

Did.

But I can't do it anymore. My eyes lock with his. "Grow up, Ed. At the end of the day, restaurateurs pay attention to exactly one thing: receipts. You lead a brunch that outgrosses dinner on the regular, and he *can't* ignore you. And you could absolutely do that. But you can't just go half measures like you did tonight. You have to step it up."

He stays silent a long moment. "Listen, I'm sorry about what I said back there. I was an ass."

"Yeah, you were." I've not been sugarcoating my words up to this point, and it seems too late to start now. "I'm not sure what I did to deserve to be the butt of your jokes."

He shrugs. "You didn't have to mention that Jean-Rémy has taken you under his wing to Cecil. You know that connection would help me more than you right now."

"So I'm supposed to pretend like what you said is true? That I'm nothing more than a glorified dishwasher? I graduated from the Culinary Institute of America with top marks. I'm not some fast-food fry cook. And even if I were, I'd deserve better than that. I've never treated you with anything less than respect, and a good boyfriend would never treat me with anything less than the same."

God, saying that feels good. It's shuffling off a leaden mantle I've been wearing far too long around my shoulders. It's not the emotional diatribe I hurled at him before, but closer to an accurate assessment of his character flaws. An assessment he needs to hear.

He stays silent.

I manage to keep my anger in check, but only just. "First of all, no task in the kitchen is beneath you, not even washing dishes. The sooner you realize that, the better off you'll be. Second, you shouldn't want me to make myself smaller to make yourself look bigger."

I fix Edward with a hard gaze. Nothing. No rebuttal, no apology.

"A real man wants more than arm candy. A *secure* man would lead with the fact that I'm doing well at my job. But that isn't you. Not yet anyway. I hope it will be someday."

He takes another long pause. "So this is it, then?"

I nod. I take a few moments to gather myself to end things the way I should have fifteen years ago. "Edward, you are talented and ambitious. I admire those traits. I hope you realize they aren't enough. You have to believe in yourself before your confidence comes out in your food. What I tasted back there? It was timid. And you're better than that. Or you could be if you tried. You need to get out of your own way or you'll just keep tripping over your own feet."

He scoffs—actually scoffs—at me. "I don't need a lecture from some fresh-out-of-culinary-school kid about how to run my career."

"So glad you figured it out in the whopping five years since you've been out." I turn and leave him on the hotel steps without a second glance.

After just half a day here, it's beginning to feel like I've overstayed my welcome in this enchanting, maddening city. This tumultuous period in my life. I don't linger or make pleasantries on my way out. I take the long walk home to change and fetch my backpack and say a quick prayer that I can make the last bus to the airport and whatever awaits me there.

Chapter 7

DECEMBER 30, 2024

I experience only a flutter of panic at the New Orleans airport. The Ticket Agent didn't exactly give explicit instructions on how to return to my own time. But when I cross the threshold of the airport, finding my way back to the private lounge is as instinctual as the walk from my bedroom to the kitchen in the morning, even without the lure of the aroma emanating from my timed coffee maker.

I find the tickets and ID I need in my backpack, and it isn't long before I board the same vintage aircraft from before. A glass of champagne is sitting next to my seat, though no flight attendant is anywhere to be seen. I can't help but long for the bygone days when normal, everyday air travel was this . . . serene. And I suppose it still is for certain members of society with unlimited funds and a complete disregard for their carbon footprint.

I replay the events with Edward over and over on the almost-instantaneous flight—or whatever it is—back to Burbank.

I'm glad I had more time with dear Jean-Rémy, though I realize with a slight sinking feeling that I missed my chance at saying a proper goodbye. But perhaps it is just as well.

I'd have been too distracted by Edward to properly appreciate the moment.

I'd carried Edward's words with me for far too long. *"Just a glorified dishwasher."*

The worst of it is that I know, deep within, he never meant it. We'd cooked together far too much and had openly admired each other's skills. He was lashing out because he was profoundly unhappy at work and I was a convenient target because I was lower on the culinary ladder but climbing at a decent clip. Which was never my fault. And if he had been a better partner, he would have praised me for my accomplishments rather than speak ill of me to colleagues. I'm glad to know for certain that leaving Edward was the right choice.

Do I think he's irredeemable as a person or a partner? Probably not. He's a fundamentally decent human, but he just wasn't ready to be a great boyfriend fifteen years ago. I hope that will change for him and that he'll be able to find both professional and personal happiness.

But I wasn't the partner for him. Not then and, I'm guessing, based on his recent threats, even less so now.

His vision for his career was so big that it sucked all the air out of the room for everyone else. Back then, he needed someone who was willing to make his dreams their own. Maybe once he gained more footing in the industry, he'd have space for someone who had ambitions of their own.

Back in Burbank, the Ticket Agent greets me with a smile. "How was your trip, dearie?"

"Educational," is the best reply I can summon.

"Well, travel is the best teacher, is it not?" She pats my arm and shows me to a table. "I hope the lesson was worthwhile."

"I got a lot off my chest."

She pushes a cup of her incredible coffee in front of me, and I accept, though I have no idea what time it is or how much I'll regret the caffeine intake. The earthy, almost smoky aroma of the dark roast with the barest hint of caramel and sea salt is too much for any mere mortal to resist. "But in the end, I'm not sure it changed anything."

"Do you feel like it went better this time around?" She leaned back in her chair, her eyes assessing me.

"I was more discreet, which is good. And I think more eloquent too. Which can't hurt. I didn't let him off the hook, but I did better than just lashing out." I didn't feel as mortified as I'd felt fifteen years before. I hope that counts for something.

The Ticket Agent looks serious as she nods. "Lashing out rarely yields the results we want. Well done, you."

I brood over my coffee for a few moments, collecting my thoughts. I get ready to launch into a litany of questions about this weird experiment in time travel, wanting to know whether I'm undoing a life's work of progress by tampering with my past, when I get a buzz on my phone—my actual phone from this timeline—that I'd left on the table. The time is only a couple of minutes later than when I boarded the flight. The only time passing is when I am actually in this terminal, which is somehow a relief. I didn't lose hours out of my life reliving my time with Edward.

"Why don't you see to that, dearie. It may be important."

I know the Ticket Agent knows who is texting me and why without a glance at my screen, but I've been unsettled for so long now, I've become inured to the sensation. Tentatively, I slide it to the unlocked position to see messages from Nora.

NORA: Thank you so much for meeting with me last week. I know it must have been a bear to fit us in right before the holidays. I hope you don't mind me communicating informally?

A "but" looms heavy in the air, and I consider preemptively thanking her for her time to save myself the embarrassment of having her reject me, but I restrain myself.

ME: Of course not. And the pleasure was mine. 540 Blake has a lot of potential.

I do stop short of saying "and I'd love to help you realize that potential."

NORA: I wish I were writing with better news, but we've decided to go another direction with the GM position. You know how these things are. It's so subjective and there are a lot of stakeholders who have input in such a big position.

Read: Edward said no. Not a surprise.

ME: All too well. Personalities have to mesh for it to work. It's no simple thing.

I know this from my time at Maison Ortense. Joëlle was impeccable, but the rest of the staff didn't work as a cohesive unit. There was no sense in wishing for the job if Edward was set on making it impossible.

NORA: I knew you'd understand. The reason I'm texting is because I'd like to keep your résumé on file for our other restaurants, if you're interested. We have quite a few under our umbrella and are always expanding.

I sit a little straighter. This is a *little* brighter than the "we'll keep you in mind for future opportunities" schtick a lot of recruiters bring out.

ME: Of course. I'd be delighted to be considered.

It's something. Edward doesn't want to work with me, which is fair. But either he has chosen not to blackball me, or he doesn't have that kind of sway with the investors. I could see it going either way, but the latter seems more likely.

I show the Ticket Agent the exchange. "Do you think my trip to New Orleans did this?"

She shrugs, but her lips are curled in a smile. "It's difficult to say, but it's certainly possible. Would you like to work for them?"

"Maybe. They're definitely a growing company and might have some interesting options. Hopefully outside of Denver." *And far from Edward*. I don't voice that, but I'm sure it's etched on my face.

The Ticket Agent looks pensive. "That seems nice, dearie, but I don't sense any real enthusiasm."

I make a noncommittal hawing noise. "It seems like a step sideways, professionally speaking, but better than a step backward." I'm not sure how true that is, though. There was something to Robin's gibe about Denver being a demotion from Paris, especially in the Michelin world, but a step back doesn't necessarily mean a *setback*. I have to think of it like a long jumper bracing themselves on their back foot before making the leap.

If Nora is able to find me a job at one of her restaurants, I may be better poised to make some waves. A smaller market may be precisely what I need . . . and I just might find the courage to apply to Michelin if those waves are impressive enough.

The Ticket Agent brings me back to the here and now by placing a hand on mine. "Would you like to take another hop, dearie? It might be enlightening."

I lean back, both exhausted and exhilarated by the prospect of another visit to my past. "I get to go again?"

Her hand still on mine, she gives an affectionate squeeze. "Of course. It often takes a few trips to figure things out. Never once have I had someone decide on their perfect course after a single flight."

I take a few moments to consider. The possibilities seem too vast to fully wrap my head around. I know for sure that this next jump shouldn't have anything to do with Edward. That path feels like a dead end, and I don't feel compelled to expel any more energy on him.

The Ticket Agent's hand is still on mine. "Think about a time when you were truly happy. Maybe going back then will reveal something you need to recapture in the here and now."

I exhale as the answer washes over me in a painful wave.

Rian.

The gorgeous Irish surgeon I was madly in love with. The one I'd come *this* close to marrying. The one whose mother had driven me so batty I'd had to run screaming. My issues with Robin had made it impossible to show Orla and her interfering ways much grace. It was the last time I gave a relationship a real shot, and the breakup that hurt the most.

I've wondered so many times whether, if I'd been more empathetic with Orla, if I'd made space for her and helped her adapt to a life where she had to share Rian's attentions with me, things might have gone better for us. Maybe time and a decade of lived experiences will make it easier to manage her overbearing ways. Time hasn't helped me deal with Robin all that more effectively, but Rian isn't in the mix to make it worthwhile in that case.

"Dublin, circa 2013. I want to see if I can make things work with Rian."

The Ticket Agent grins broadly. "Oh, the one that got away. And my homeland too. Lovely choice, dearie. Grab that pack of yours and let's go."

I'd instantly placed her accent as Irish, but it's hard to envision her as being *from Ireland*. Indeed, she doesn't feel as if she belongs on our plane of existence at all. But if she is of our world, no better place than the land of leprechauns and fairies exists for her to call home.

"Okay . . ." I stand, slinging the backpack over my shoulder, and join her as she ventures back down the Jetway. I try to sound more self-assured than I feel, but the prospect of seeing Rian—and Orla—again has me just shy of shaking.

The Ticket Agent gestures to the open door of the aircraft, a trademark flight attendant smile on her lips. "Wishing you the luck of my people, dearie. Enjoy yourself."

Chapter 8

DUBLIN

The plane lands, and the dual sensations of dread and anticipation wash over me, like being splashed with a bucket each of scalding and frigid water all at once. I *really* dislike the sensation of feeling unprepared. But if I want to continue this strange little escapade, I have no choice in the matter. And I find I do want it even more than I want to feel in control of the situation.

Which is quite a lot.

I fumble for my phone as I emerge onto the sidewalk in front of Dublin's labyrinthine airport, trying to orient myself in time. The calendar app reads April 8, 2013. It's a Monday night and I am, blessedly, off work. In 2013 I was working at Baile Phadraig on Kildare Street as a saucier—the sauce master. One of the best jobs I've ever had in my whole career. The one with the most scope for creativity and imagination. I loved the job almost as much as I loved Rian. I loved Dublin too. It had the same grandeur and vibrancy of Paris and London with less affectation.

It's midafternoon now and tonight is, according to my trusty app, one of the rare nights we both have off. Rian is an upwardly mobile physician, specializing in internal medicine. He was always supportive of my career, though scheduling date nights was usually as complex as lawyers and judges scheduling trials. He boasted to his friends about my work, which was refreshing after Edward's bad-mouthing.

While I'd confided everything about my ambitions to Edward, I'd learned to be more circumspect in the four years since. I told Rian I dreamed of becoming a food critic and travel writer, though I decided to wait until we began to seriously plan our future together before getting into the details about Michelin. I thought setting up the expectations for a demanding job with a lot of travel was enough before we set a date. Brand names and specifics were just details. I didn't even tell him about my blog, which I started in this phase of my life.

Though my wallet isn't as thin as during my tenure in New Orleans, I take the bus rather than a cab into town and stop at a market I'd favored not too far from my small downtown flat. I gawk at the sprawling streets like a tourist, reacquainting myself with the city I haven't seen in over a decade.

Shortly after Rian and I called it quits, I took a job in London and never came back. Which was a shame. I'd had little chance to travel outside of Dublin and knew there were untold wonders to discover outside the city. It was one of several regrets I had from my tenure in Ireland.

But I have the chance to erase some of those regrets now.

Irish cuisine may not be spoken about in the same breath as French or Italian, but Dublin has an amazing food scene, and Kinsale is the sort of hidden gem true foodies dream about. I take my time walking the aisles of the small market, filling the little trolley with whatever looks promising. In this era of my life, I know my spice drawer contains an embarrassment of riches—the sort that would have been enough to buy my way into the nobility half a millennium ago—so my wanderings down that aisle are mostly academic. Checking to see what new and interesting blends they might have or what exotic choices might hold fun possibilities for experimentation.

I linger over a jar of Maharajah curry powder. It's an earthy blend and generally made from the highest-quality spices, including a good dash of saffron. It's pricey, but it packs a flavor punch worth every cent. I add it to the cart. The niggling little idea I had at Baile Phadraig for merging a sauce Créole with curry needs to go from concept to reality in this do-over. Aside from wishing I'd been able to make things work with Rian, I often wished I'd been less timid about auditioning dishes when I was in this job.

I won't make that mistake a second time.

I linger in the seafood section and find some catfish that looks amazing, especially since it's been imported from such a distance. I plan to make Rian a dish fit for a king and benefit from some practice before hitting the saucier station again. I carry my haul back to my flat a few blocks away. The space is dated, sure. I'm pretty sure the linoleum on the kitchen floor dates back to the Inquisition. But the kitchen itself is large in relation to the rest of the space, and the stove is one of the best home models I've worked with to date. Important, given that I spent a great deal of time perfecting my sauces at home back in this epoch of my life, and I needed the space and equipment to do it.

I begin with the sauce so it will have plenty of time to simmer before Rian's shift is over. I omit the Worcestershire sauce, which is a classic staple of the sauce Créole, to make room for the curry. A principle I've always had with sauces is to make sure there aren't too many notes competing for attention, even in something as bold and complex as this. Like the culinary equivalent of Coco Chanel's maxim about removing one accessory before leaving the house—if you're going to add a new flavor, take away an existing flavor to make room for it. The trick is not to take so much away from the sauce Créole that you wind up with an unconventional curry.

I treat the dicing of the celery, green peppers, and onion like a ritual to be observed with reverence. I slow down to take in their aroma as they simmer in the olive oil at the bottom of the enameled cast-iron pot. In go the garlic, tomatoes, chicken stock, all manner of spices, and a dash of Louisiana hot sauce that had been Jean-Rémy's favorite brand. All that remains is the curry. I add it slowly, tasting as I go to make sure the rich, earthy curry flavor comes through but doesn't overpower everything else. I take note of the precise amount I settle on in my leather-bound recipe book on the counter, just where I kept it all those years ago.

The aroma is heavenly. The adjustment of the recipe, swapping one ingredient for another, has made something better than the sum of its parts, and I remember why it is I love this work. When people come to a restaurant, they generally don't comment to their friends the next day at work that the beef was well aged or the chicken was particularly tender. They extol the sauces and spices. The elements that bring the dishes to life.

I turn to the catfish and decide that the traditional Créole method of blackening the fish would compete too much with the sauce, so I opt to pan-fry it with a light coating of breadcrumbs and a few mild herbs. It will serve as a canvas for the sauce, not its competition. The timing is perfect, as I expect Rian to arrive at any moment. In the original timeline I remember I picked up takeout. I was usually so tired on my days off, the last thing I wanted to do was cook. But now, with the chance to do it all over again, I feel energized.

Just as the sauce is reaching perfection, I feel my phone buzz in my back pocket and pull it out.

It's Orla. Of course.

I steady my breath and focus on being kind and empathetic. I refrain from cursing my own stupidity for giving the woman my phone number. Mostly.

ORLA: When are you free? I'd like to meet for lunch.

I vaguely remember any number of these so-terse-they're-almost-rude invitations from her. I probably thought not responding was a clever tactic to get her to ask more politely. Spoiler: It didn't work.

I flip to my calendar app and see I have tomorrow off at the restaurant as well. They like to try to give us a proper "weekend" when they can, even if it doesn't fall on Saturday and Sunday. Which means I don't have a good reason to put her off. And as much as I loathe it, trying harder with her is one of my prime objectives here, so stalling would defeat the purpose.

ME: How nice of you. Does tomorrow work? I have it off.

ORLA: Off today and tomorrow? Fortunate that your work schedule isn't too taxing.

Heat rises in my cheeks, the way it often did when Orla was involved. I want to remind her that a large segment of the working public does indeed get two days off in a row every single week, but I resist the temptation. *Do not engage. Do. Not. Engage.* I'm also confused as to how she knows my schedule, but I don't want to open that perilous can of worms either.

ME: Where would you like to meet?

ORLA: McHenry's. Eleven thirty if that suits you.

Fine. An early lunch will give me plenty of time in the afternoon to fiddle with another batch of the sauce in case I want to make tweaks.

ME: See you then. Looking forward.

No response.

I plate the fish moments before it gets too brown and drizzle it with the sauce just as I hear the workings of my locks. I'd loved the sound of Rian letting himself in and find that it evokes the same thrill in my chest now as it did more than a decade earlier.

He wraps his arms around me from behind and rests his chin on my shoulder, his head nestled against the curve of my neck. And I melt. As good as the electricity was between Edward and me, what I feel for Rian is fathoms deeper. There is something more meaningful here than the allure of a first serious romance. The hope of a future.

"This smells amazing, *mo chroí*." *My heart*. Lord, how I've missed him calling me that. His arms remain taut around me, though I can hear the rumblings of his empty stomach. "Any special occasion?"

I turn around in his arms and take in his beautiful face. His riot of black curls, the deep green of his eyes, his cheeks that dimple boyishly when he smiles. I plant small kisses on both his dimples before giving in to the temptation of his lips. At some cost I finally pull myself away. "I thought we both needed better than a carton of takeout noodles tonight, so I decided to cook."

"You'll spoil me, Ms. Sorensen, and I won't know how to act." He steals a few kisses of his own before he releases me to put the two plates on the table, side by side.

"So tell me what we have here." His eyes are fixed on the serving platter, not with apprehension but with genuine interest.

Rian wasn't on Dad's level, but he knows his way around Dublin's finer eateries. I describe the dish as a sort of Cajun-Indian fusion, which intrigues rather than puts him off. I am glad he has a curious palate, given that he was definitely raised by the gray-pot-roast-and-soggy-potatoes sort. His only caveat used to be that he had to be careful not to develop such refined taste that hospital cafeteria food would become unpalatable to him. To ward off this terrible fate, he had a practice of indulging in fish and chips fortnightly, and generally from the dingiest chip shop he could find. Only he could render the practice endearing.

He finally samples the dish and his eyes light up. "This is a marvel, Sabrina. Truly. Promise me you'll audition it with Padraig and Fiona."

Making a sample batch for Padraig—obviously the restaurant's namesake and our head chef—and our sous-chef, Fiona, was the requisite first step in getting a new dish included on the menu. I'd made sample dishes for Rian before, but I always concocted reasons never to share them with Fiona and Padraig, even if Rian praised my cooking to the skies. I was terrified of a no.

In retrospect, it was silly. They might have rejected a dish due to practicalities that I, as saucier, would not be privy to. In this job I don't have connections to vendors or a working knowledge of the operating budget. A no due to those reasons wouldn't necessarily reflect poorly on me unless my submission was so outlandishly expensive to produce or so discordant with the rest of the menu that I was displaying a lack of judgment.

I had been timid. But I am coming back to this time in my life armed with a lot more industry knowledge and a dash more confidence. I know now that a saucier is not an annoyance by auditioning a dish, so long as they are genuinely putting forth their best efforts. A good head chef depends on the whole staff, especially station leads, to share their ideas. It's not a privilege reserved just for the sous-chef or perhaps a specialist like a pastry chef. But I didn't believe that included *me* back in 2013.

I sample my own handiwork, and not to boast, but it's better than more than a few dishes I've sampled from Michelin-starred kitchens. It deserves a shot. "I promise. Day after tomorrow at lunch service."

Rian is taken aback by my confident tone. "You sound self-assured . . . I like it."

I realize the version of me he knows is constantly second-guessing herself. Unable to believe that she has the chops to really impress her superiors with anything more than her unflagging work ethic. She's the sort who dismisses her successes as the product of luck rather than talent. I can't say I've completely cleared the hurdle of self-doubt, but thirty-seven-year-old Sabrina believes in her abilities far more than twenty-six-year-old Sabrina did. I'm curious to see how that confidence will change the course of events here, and this time I'm not afraid of meddling in my own past. It's hard to imagine that I was well served by my own reticence.

"I'm going to do better. I won't audition every idea that pops into my head, but I want to start putting myself out there more."

He sets his fork down and places an arm around me. "I am so glad to hear that, love. Don't think of it as taking a notion. Be brave."

Taking a notion, Irish slang for "putting on airs" or having an inflated sense of ego. I always described the vibe in Ireland as being "ruthlessly humble" during my time here, so "taking a notion" is a habit most Irish absolutely can't stand.

I clear my throat. "Speaking of brave, I'm having lunch with your mother tomorrow."

He chuckles, but his face pales by several shades. "She didn't mention it when she texted me earlier. I assume it wasn't you who asked?"

I shake my head. "No, but I didn't ignore her texts either."

He pats my thigh. "I appreciate that. It would mean a lot to me if you two got on."

"I'll do better." I echo my previous sentiment about auditioning more dishes. "At the end of the day, she and I have something very important in common. We both love you."

It's the first time I've spoken these words to him in over a decade, though it won't seem that way to him. But the truth of it rings loud in my ears. I never stopped loving him. Can one ever really stop those feelings entirely? But I *did* stop fighting Orla for him, which amounted to the same result.

We finish the meal, chatting companionably about his day at the hospital—the gorier details redacted—and finish with some lemon sorbet that cuts the heat of the spices. We move to the sofa where we start, and fail, to watch a movie. And as I lose myself in his arms, I know I was wrong to give up on this man so easily.

Chapter 9

I will be civil to Orla.

I say this on repeat, like a prayer for serenity. Or a mantra from a twelve-step program.

Both feel appropriate.

I am dreading this lunch, but it's a necessary step in forging a better relationship with Orla. She insists on insinuating herself into every possible aspect of Rian's life, and it feels far too much like Robin's judgment and meddling for me to swallow it without complaint. But with some ingenuity, maybe I won't have to accept her busybody ways. The best thing to do, like with any wayward toddler, is to redirect her energy.

Her help was absolutely necessary in the earliest days of Rian's career, when residency had him pulling incredibly long shifts. Things like grocery shopping and dry-cleaning runs were legitimately out of his bandwidth in those days. Though he left residency behind years before, she continues to act like a concierge, maid, and secretary, despite his being perfectly able and entirely willing to do these things for himself. It baffled me at the time, but I understand now, in a way I wasn't able to then, that all the errand running and caretaking had given her a purpose. Every task he took off her plate left a void in her life, and he was loath to hurt her.

I can see now that I didn't deal with her interference all that well. Though in my defense, Orla had enmeshed herself so thoroughly into our lives, I began to feel there was no room for me in the relationship. I ended things with Rian when he refused to take my side in a heated argument with Orla. But maybe it was unfair of me to put him in that position. Ultimately, his relationship with Orla was his responsibility, but I could manage my own rapport with her on my own terms.

I would usually dress for a day off in yoga pants and a hoodie, but I have to do better for a lunch date with Orla. I rummage through my closet and select what passes for a spring dress here: a lavender floral piece, but long sleeved and made from thick cotton, paired with a matching cardigan. The ensemble would have been warm enough for winter attire back in Solvang, but the damp Irish weather has a way of seeping into the bones. I add some ballet flats to complete the look and transfer my wallet and keys to a smaller handbag that had been a gift from Orla, who's not fond of my habit of schlepping my beloved green backpack in lieu of a purse.

I acquired the bag right around this time from one of the better secondhand shops. I don't think she appreciated my referring to it as my work "diaper bag." I vow to be a little more circumspect with my humor in front of her.

This version of me looks a little older and wiser than me from 2009 but still youthful. I slap on some lip gloss—nothing too flashy for Orla's sake—and run down to the street. This time I do indulge in a cab so I won't look rumpled when I arrive at the restaurant. McHenry's is a cozy little place, not far from the hospital where Rian works. I'd begun my blog about this time, but I had never given this favorite haunt of ours a write-up. I'll rectify that later this afternoon.

Orla is already waiting for me at a table, her reddish-blonde hair perfectly coiffed. She's dressed in a pink pantsuit as though she'll be off to a meeting at some fancy ladies' society afterward. Maybe that is *precisely* what she needs. A group of women, perhaps a little too proud of themselves, with some sort of charity mission to keep them busy and to give them a sense of purpose.

Her initial assessment of my appearance is apparently favorable, and she coos, "How lovely you look, dear," as she kisses the air above my cheeks and I return the gesture. I was right to dress up. Orla puts a lot of stock in appearances, and I'd been stupid not to put forth more of an effort before. She eyes my dress more closely. "Is that Laura Ashley?"

I glance down at my outfit, trying to imply I'd even forgotten what I'd worn, and shrug. I know the brand but hadn't thought to look at the label. "A lucky thrift find."

Her lips purse and I wish I could pull the words back into my mouth. She intensely dislikes my thrifting habit. I consider buying well-made secondhand clothing to be the best practice, both economically and environmentally, but she sees it as lowbrow and borderline offensive. Perhaps even unethical because I *can* afford new clothes, and my thrifting deprives those genuinely in need from access to the garments I buy. She sees me as one small step above those who scour the thrift for discarded brand-name items and resell them for a giant profit. That I couldn't afford the same quality of clothing if I were buying new doesn't seem to matter to Orla. In her mind I should be happy to go into debt to look the part of a doctor's girlfriend.

Time to deflect. "Your pantsuit is so chic. You look ready to run for public office." I don't add that the office is probably the treasurer of the neighborhood garden club, given the color. The key is planting the seed of ambition in her mind outside of Rian's life.

She sniffs, much the way Robin does when she's displeased. "Oh, I consider meeting my son's . . . special friend . . . for lunch is an occasion worth dressing for. I would hope anyone who feels they're worthy of my son would feel that way about themselves."

I restrain a snort. If I disagree with her, I'm diminishing my own worth. If I agree and imply that I am worth the trouble, she'll tell Rian and anyone who will listen that I'm a terrible snob and incredibly self-important. "Taking a notion" as Rian said. There is no winning here. "How kind. Of course, the same is true for meeting with you," is the only response that feels somewhat safe. Or at least confusing enough she doesn't respond.

She clears her throat. "I'm glad you were able to get away from the restaurant today. You work such erratic hours. I've been wanting to talk to you alone." She reaches over to pat my hand. I fight the urge to recoil from the gesture that comes across as insincere.

"Oh? I'm all ears." I hope my face comes across as enthusiastic rather than reluctant.

She takes in a pained breath as she gathers her words. "I just worry that a demanding and constantly changing schedule isn't going to mesh well with a serious relationship. I know many young men these days are taking on more responsibility in the home, and I am all for that, but Rian's work simply won't permit him to participate equally at home. And there's also the matter of you two not having time off together as often as you should."

I force a smile. Just yesterday she implied that two days off in a row was an unthinkable indulgence and clearly I sit at home watching soaps and eating bonbons all day. Now I work *too many* hours. She can't have it both ways.

I take a steadying breath. "Rian came into this knowing we're both busy people. We try not to put too much pressure on each other's schedules and are committed to being fully present when we do get time together. It's forced us to communicate our expectations, and I think it's worked very well so far."

She pauses to consider this a moment. "That may be true, but Rian won't have me around forever. He'll need someone willing to keep the home fires burning. You have loads of ambition, my dear. And I admire that. Truly. I'm sure it's part of what attracted Rian to you in the first place, but professional ambition won't keep a home running smoothly."

I feel the heat emanating from my pores, surprised she can't see the steam billowing from me so violently that the chef in the kitchen could prepare the broccoli if he held it up to one of my ears. I'm grateful for a brief reprieve as the waiter comes to take our order. Orla orders a side salad for her entrée, and I follow her lead, ordering a small soup despite being hungry enough for a proper meal. I'll see to that later. This, as it turns out, is a business lunch, and in the grand tradition of business lunches, food is an afterthought. It's anathema to me, wasting the opportunity to sample something new, but I will play along. So much for the blog entry.

Once the waiter is well out of earshot, I take a moment to collect my thoughts. "Orla, I know you have Rian's best interests in mind. You and I both love him and want the best for him. We're on the same team. But he and I aren't engaged or living together. I think you're looking farther down the road than we need to be."

She leans back, her brow knitted as she considers my words.

I continue. "I don't think it would be all that . . . seemly . . ." I dislike the word, but it's one Orla is fond of. It's a bit too close to Robin's affection for the word *appropriate* for my comfort. ". . . to presume that a future together is a fixed thing. I hope Rian and I will settle down someday. Perhaps soon. But it wouldn't be right or . . . prudent . . . for me to alter my life before promises are made." *Prudent*, another word she loves.

Rian, at least in my original timeline, popped the question not long from now, despite Orla's misgivings. But Orla doesn't know this, and I hope my line of reasoning makes me seem levelheaded and forthright.

"You know, you're quite right. Very sensible, dear." She takes a sip of her tepid tap water, her eyes scanning the room before settling back on me. "I do worry so about him. Those long hours and the demanding work."

"So do I." And I do. None of her concerns are baseless. And as loath as she is to cede any part of Rian's life over to me, she likely worries about who would pick up the slack for him when she isn't able to do things for him anymore.

Rian and I have, at this point in our relationship, discussed at length how we'll carefully organize our schedules and fairly distribute household labor in the event we decide to combine households. He also has the means to hire occasional help with cleaning and the like. Past me had sworn to myself that if Michelin panned out, I'd be meticulous about keeping a freezer stocked with homemade ready-to-heat meals so Rian wouldn't have to rely on health-damaging fast foods on the many nights he came home exhausted and I was out of town. I want to ensure he's not left to fend for himself just as much as Orla does. It will take a lot of juggling, but we'll be fine. But telling Orla that these serious discussions have already taken place—without her—would just set her on edge.

I want to be open with Orla, but she isn't entitled to full disclosure either. She is not a part of this couple, as much as she might wish to entangle herself in our business.

Her expression is serious as she presses on. "I just hope you'll consider the effect a commitment will have on your career and the sacrifices that will have to be made. You and Rian will need to be honest with each other about your expectations for the future. Life does have its seasons, and we must decide how to ready for them."

An entry. "Yes, we must, Orla. Since you've been kind enough to speak so directly to me, I'd also like to raise a concern with you. From a place of love and respect."

"Oh?" A brow flies comically upward at my choice of words.

"I just worry that you've invested so much time in Rian since your husband passed that maybe you haven't taken enough time for yourself. Time to cultivate friendships and interests outside of caring for Rian. Now that he's more settled—and I'm around to help where I can—I do think you should take some time to rediscover what your passions are."

Her eyes flicker for a moment, but her face turns somber. "You know, I think that's the problem with the world today. Everyone is far too focused on their own interests and 'passions.'" She throws air quotes around the word. "In my time, we didn't think of such things."

I fold my hands in my lap. "Perhaps back then *wasn't* the right time. But, to use your own metaphor, your life has come to a new season. I'm not saying you should cast away all your cares and lead a life of empty pleasures. But you can work for causes you care about. You can learn new skills. Go back to the interests you had to abandon when Rian was born. He says you used to paint?"

She nods almost imperceptibly.

"He's seen your work. He said you were good. You're freer now than you have been in years, Orla. It might seem scary now, but it's a gift. You could stop off at the art supply store the moment we're done here and get yourself an easel, canvases, and all the paints you could ever want. You could take classes. Whatever it is that would make you happy."

She chuckles softly, as though my suggestion were a mildly amusing joke. "Please, I'm not going to become the next Cézanne at my age."

"Why not? Cézanne wasn't much younger than you when he got his first solo show." I am grateful for this bit of trivia from my limited knowledge of art history. "And not everything needs to be a quest for fame and fortune. Even if you only paint for yourself or for your closest friends and family, it would be worth it if you enjoy it."

She makes a noncommittal waggle of her head.

I decide to appeal to her high-minded side. "You could teach art to underprivileged children if it makes it seem more worthwhile to you. My only point is that you deserve to do something for yourself. Something you care about. It's a good and healthy thing."

The metaphor about the pot and the kettle looms large in my head as I wonder when the last time was that I invested much time in something that wasn't in pursuit of my Michelin career. But as Orla herself said, life has its seasons, and I am at the height of my summer. Career is first, last, and almost everything right now. And it's the same for Rian, though I know Orla doesn't consider my work to be anywhere near as *worthy* as her son's almost holy calling to medicine.

"Rian is working today, isn't he?" Orla asks after a long pause. Her crestfallen expression is thinly veiled. She used to know his schedule backward and forward. She had planned her life around it. Now, she isn't the first to know, and it stings.

I pull out my phone and open the calendar app. I have his schedule in green—my little nod to his Irish heritage—my own schedule divided into long chunks of red for work with little blips of blue for personal appointments like this lunch. There is a significant swath of green for today, and I show Orla the screen. "Yes, he doesn't get off until eleven tonight. I should bring him something from the takeaway menu."

She flags down a server for the takeout menu before I can say more. She examines the offerings with studious intensity as soon as the paper is placed before her. "I know he likes the fish here."

I force a smile. "He does like it, but he doesn't eat fish at work. It's their unwritten policy. The smell of fish in the break room isn't for everyone, and some of the staff have allergies. I thought to bring him the chicken cacciatore. He likes that very much." I don't mention I made fish for him last night. She'd see it as a challenge to provide him with the fish he *actually likes*.

She passes the menu away from herself. "Well, it seems you have it all figured out and don't need my input."

I never asked you for it.

I keep the words from escaping my lips, but only just. This is one of the things I like least about Orla. In her view, her darling son is the center of the universe, so he should be able to eat what he wants when he wants, and the rest of the staff could hang. No one works as hard as her Rian, and anyone who points out the dozens of other doctors in the same hospital who put in the same hours is simply blind to her son's greatness.

"We should bring him here for fish on his next night off." I pause another moment. "And if you'd like to bring him the chicken yourself, I'm sure he'd appreciate seeing you."

She looks slightly mollified as we settle the bill and place the takeaway order for Rian. I walk with her to the hospital, partly to keep her company and partly to ensure she doesn't double back and switch the chicken for fish, which is the sort of trick she's pulled in the past. She once went so far as to tell the waiter he'd misheard the order and abused him for his stupidity. But she's in better spirits today and I let her go in alone. As much as I want to see Rian, I know she deserves her time with him too.

Chapter 10

The following day I stand at the massive industrial stove assigned for my use and take a reverential moment of silence in the empty kitchen before setting to work. This is the closest I will ever come to performing alchemy, and the process deserves respect. I have a dozen large stockpots at my station, each to be filled with the magic potions that will elevate the flavors of the meat, seafood, and pasta we serve.

We don't open until eleven thirty for lunch service at Baile Phadraig, but I report before 8:00 a.m. to make sure the sauces have time to simmer and mature. Closer to service, either Padraig or Fiona will come by to taste them and prescribe any needed adjustments. Their word is final, and if a sauce doesn't pass muster, it can mean removing a dish—sometimes several—from the menu for that service. Many of the sauces can take hours to prepare, and there simply isn't time to start over.

Saucier is a huge promotion from *commis chef*. As the job title suggests, a saucier prepares all the sauces for every item on the menu and is considered the backbone of a classical kitchen. In a kitchen that leans French? The saucier is a deity. Every sauce is derived from one of the five "mother sauces" as laid out by the great Escoffier. All cream- and cheese-based sauces are descended from the béchamel.

The silky velouté sauce is the starting point for any sauce with a white stock like chicken or fish. Espagnole, or Spanish sauce, is the darker version of the velouté, often made with beef stock and red wine as its base ingredients. Hollandaise, egg-based and smooth, is tricky but rich and buttery when done right. And the *sauce tomat*, whether a smooth marinara or a rustic Bolognaise, is the bold flavor-filled crowd-pleaser and the basis for my curried Créole sauce.

When this job came up, I had to fly to Dublin to audition. I'd spent weeks mastering the mother sauces. I was convinced hollandaise would be the death of me, but with some help from more experienced colleagues, I got the knack of it. Once I got a handle on those, I began to experiment. I turned the espagnole into a killer bourguignonne sauce. I made a Roquefort Alfredo to drizzle on steak that made one of my colleagues propose marriage, much to the laughing chagrin of his wife, who demanded the recipe. My sauce Provençal, a derivative of the *sauce tomat*, is a particular source of pride. The recipes and techniques all come back to me with the familiarity of old friends. The best kind you can pick up after years apart like nothing has changed.

I love the first hour in the kitchen, before the rest of the staff arrives. I live for the rhythm of chopping and dicing, simmering and stirring. Adding spices and coaxing out flavors, muttering my little incantations like a witch over her cauldron—or a dozen cauldrons, in my case. Later the kitchen will be loud and chaotic when the rest of the staff arrive and set to task. When the patrons are seated, it will all reach a fever pitch, and I'll feel like an octopus longing for four more tentacles to manage everything.

And I love every moment of it. Feel inspired in ways I haven't for years. Once I have all the necessary sauces simmering away, I snag a smaller stockpot from the storage room and work on a small batch of my Créole sauce to audition.

I am so deeply in the zone that when Fiona taps me on the shoulder, I shriek and drop a spoon in the béarnaise.

"Sorry 'bout that, Sorensen. You okay?"

I fish the mixing spoon out with a ladle and move to the sink to wash the whole mess off. "Now that I've put my skin back on after jumping out of it, fine. Though I may need a day or two to recover from the heart attack."

Her expression grows awkward. "Funny enough, it's your schedule I want to talk to you about. I don't know how to say this delicately, but Rian's mum rang up the restaurant last night—mid dinner rush, mind—demanding to talk to Padraig about your schedule. Asking for fewer and more consistent hours so you have more time for Rian."

I drop the spoon, this time on the floor. I pick it up and fling it in the sink. "She. Did. Not. Tell me no one put her through."

Fiona crosses her arms over her chest and casts her eyes downward. "We eventually put her through. She wouldn't stop ringing the place, and we couldn't have the reservation line tied up."

Of course caller ID is a thing in this era, but they're still using a landline for reservations. They don't have the capacity to easily block her number like we do nowadays. And knowing Orla, she'd just start calling from other phones until she got what she wanted.

"Oh my god." I grip the edge of the stainless-steel sink for support. And I know immediately this is all because of the lunch yesterday. Because I offered her my empathy and expressed my willingness to help manage things for Rian when she isn't able, so she's butting in again to ensure I make good on my promise. She never tried this in my original timeline because I'd never made such overtures of solidarity.

"Needless to say, Padraig isn't pleased. Thankfully his own mother-in-law is the overbearing sort as well, so he has some compassion for you and your situation. But his patience isn't infinite." She doesn't look reproachful but rather pitying, which feels significantly worse.

I fight the urge to fling an entire pot of velouté sauce across the room, but I have neither the desire to clean it up nor the time to make another batch. "Heard, Chef. I'll talk to her. I'll let her know she's never to call the place for any reason. Even if it's for a reservation, it'll come through me."

Fiona pats my shoulder like a comrade in arms, which we are on many levels. "As a friend, I highly recommend making sure Rian is involved in this conversation. Preferably leading it. I've been married ten years, and my mother-in-law is generally a lamb, but when a boundary needs to be set, it's on Liam to pull out the map and pencil to draw it out for her, so to speak. Let Rian be the bad guy. She'll still blame you, but she'll know Rian's on your side and her hands will be tied."

How I wish that were true. But Rian is so devoted to Orla that he would never make good on threats to break or even lessen contact over a violation of boundaries, and she bloody well knows it. This is going to be a headache, no matter how much more compassion I bring to the table this time.

"Listen, I know it's grand altogether, but mothers pull this codswallop a lot when their boys get serious with a girl. She's testing the waters to see what she can get away with. Just stand firm and it'll pass. Unless you guys have a baby, in which case all bets are off."

I groan at the idea of how insufferable she'll be if Rian and I decide to have kids. That has never been high on my list of priorities, and she makes the prospect entirely unappealing. I can't imagine how little patience I'll have for her micromanaging while trying to balance childcare, work, and the demands of marriage.

"Thanks." I'm utterly deflated, knowing I'll have to confront this situation head-on as soon as Rian and I are alone in the same room together.

"I appreciate you dealing with this. But on the bright side, Padraig thinks the world of you. I tolerate you better than I do most people. We see great things for your future here. Now let's see how everything is coming along today."

I stand aside as she takes a dozen tasting spoons and tries a bit of each, cleansing her palate with a bite of water cracker between samples. The grimrod—a saffron hollandaise with a bright lemony finish—has earned her praise. I'd spent weeks perfecting it in this timeline, and I am beyond pleased to learn I haven't lost my touch.

"What's this one?" She indicates a smaller pot, less than a quarter of the size of the others, with a bubbling red sauce with a tomato base. A frisson of anticipation burbles in my stomach. This sensation—anxiety tinged with adrenaline—has never lessened.

"I've been experimenting with a sauce Créole. Adding a dash of curry with the traditional Créole spices to try an East-meets-West sort of thing. I'd love your thoughts, Chef." My nerves force a lapse into formality, but hopefully she'll consider it a sign that I'm taking the audition seriously.

She finds another clean spoon, and this time she spoons a small amount of the sauce on a thin slice of baguette.

Her expression shifts from thoughtfulness to something like . . . delight. "Sorensen, if Padraig doesn't use this on *something*, I will personally tell him he's an eejit to his face."

I laugh. "No, you won't. You're nothing like that reckless. But I appreciate you even joking about it."

She takes another spoonful for another slice of baguette. "Well, he'd deserve it at any rate."

I can't contain a smile. "Thanks for the vote of confidence. I've been toying with this one for a while." A decade longer than she realizes or than I can ever let on.

She takes a third helping. "It's damned fine work. I'll send Padraig over to try it when he's in."

A lilting tenor voice cuts the air. "Next time you use one of your three wishes for a man to appear, I'd pick someone a helluva lot better looking than me."

Fiona, as his next in command, is permitted a snort of derision at his self-deprecating humor. "Sorensen's got a winner here, Chef."

"I'll be the judge of that." He accepts a sample of the Créole sauce on a baguette from Fiona. I try not to hold my breath in anticipation, but I fail miserably at the task.

Padraig doesn't spare me a glance but locks eyes with Fiona. "You're right. I'd be an idiot not to put this on the menu."

Fiona's eyes float heavenward as if she's offering up a prayer for patience. "I swear you have the hearing of a bloody bat."

Mischief glints in his hazel-green eyes. "Not a thing is said in this place that I don't hear."

She shakes her head. "Like I said, you're part bat."

He places the sample plate in the sink and leans against the stainless-steel tub with the ease that comes with literally owning the joint. "Sonar would be a cool nickname, but I don't suggest you try it out."

"Chef Sonar would be a mouthful," I reason.

"Cheeky, Sorensen. I like you, but don't get cocky." But I'm rewarded with a wink and a playful punch on the shoulder.

Fiona pulls us back to the matter at hand. "What do you say we try Sorensen's Curry Créole with a sautéed cod as the special and see how it plays?"

I speak up. "A pan-fried catfish would be better. Or shrimp. With rice would be best." This is a breach of etiquette, to be sure, and thirty-seven-year-old me needs to remember where twenty-six-year-old me is on the food chain.

I cast my eyes downward a beat and allow heat to rise in my cheeks, though I really don't feel embarrassed to make suggestions like I used to be. I just need to be more deferential in my delivery. "I mean, if you wanted to go for the classic choices that pair with the Créole. Obviously it's up to your vision and what we have to work with."

He locks eyes with Fiona again. "Scare up what she wants. Both options, if you can. Put them on the specials board as soon as you confirm the order. And talk to her about the other thing. Before service."

He walks off and I am proud of my success in keeping my mouth from hitting the floor. He loves the Créole sauce I'd been too reluctant to share before. I wonder now if I hadn't been cowed by Edward's failures in that area at Hotel Esmeralda. I'd not thought of it before, but it really may have been a case of a secondhand toxic work environment.

My expression turns from shock to questioning as I turn my gaze from Padraig's retreating form back to Fiona. She clears her throat. "So, we've been talking about promoting you to sous."

I gasp audibly. Saucier is a reach position for me at this stage of my career. Sous is a massive leap. "Are you serious? Sous?"

There is no trace of mirth on her face. "You're young, but you've got more talent than the last ten *chefs de partie* we've hired. We think it's the logical step for you, and we find more and more we have the receipts to justify a second sous. And it's not without some self-interest on my part. If you can share the duties of the sous with me, I might actually be able to get a vacation more than once every six years."

I pull her in for a hug, American style. "That would be so amazing."

Fiona accepts the embrace with a chuckle, like a dog lover might accept the exuberance of an over-affectionate Labrador. "I'll take that as a yes. But bear in mind, this will mean longer hours, and Rian's mam is already in high dudgeon over your schedule. You'll have to get everyone on board. Or at least on board enough to stop calling our reservation line."

It's a very good thing Orla's not in the room, as I am once more sorely tempted to throttle her for such outrageous behavior. "You've got it. I'm ready to start anytime."

"Oh, my lamb, in case you didn't realize, your training has already started. Sauces and both specials are on you today. Good luck, darling."

Sous-chef. In less than five years. It's a huge accomplishment in such a short time, but I feel ready. And if the response to my lunch special is an indicator, I *am* ready. I didn't take these risks the first time around, and to see how different things could have been if I'd taken more chances on myself is immeasurably satisfying. Being just bold enough to let the chef taste one sauce has been enough to launch my career ahead by years.

I now know how I would answer the viral internet meme, "If you could give your eighteen-year-old self one piece of advice, what would it be?"

After the afternoon I spent, it would be, "Believe in your skills and take more chances. Don't be afraid to fail. Don't be afraid to ask for help when you need it. People want you to succeed more than you realize."

Fiona had given me a massive hug of her own after the service, and I'd received more than a few accolades from the rest of the staff who'd quickly gotten wind of the potential promotion.

I float on a cloud of adrenaline all the way home, and then promptly crash on the sofa as the high subsides. It's a few hours before I stir, awakened by the rustling as Rian enters my flat, laden down with takeout from our favorite Chinese place. My stomach rumbles at the smell that emanates from the containers.

"You are a knight in shining armor. Nay, a prince among men." I sit up to admire the grand assortment of food he procured for us and pull him into an embrace.

He brings with him a sense of peace that I remember craving for months after the breakup. It's the same calming warmth that makes him an exceptional doctor. That makes Orla feel needed. That makes me feel at home, despite the thousands of miles between me and my place of birth.

He plops down on the couch next to me and plants a kiss on my cheek. "Now, you'll kindly remember I'm an Irishman," he chides in an exaggerated brogue. "I don't put much stock in titles and royalty."

I wrap my arms around his neck. "Oh, very well, you're simply my hero."

"Well now, that's an honor I can accept." He kisses me, deeply now, and I love lingering in the scent of him. He doesn't wear anything with fragrance because of his work, so he just smells . . . like Rian, without chemical-laden products to mask his natural perfume. As he pulls me into his arms after eleven years apart, I can imagine how comfortable it would be to make a life with him. And I am grateful the opportunity isn't lost forever.

"How did your day go?" I ask once I can bear to break away from his kisses long enough to take air. He worked a punishing shift yesterday and we both worked long hours today, so we haven't had time for more than the most cursory of check-ins via text.

"Mmm." He nuzzles my neck by way of response. "Not too bad. Mam brought me chicken two days in a row. Was nice of her. Saved me from a long shift fueled by cafeteria food. And she remembered the fish thing."

I don't mention that I reminded her about the fish ban. I'll let her take that win. Old me probably wouldn't have, but I'm wise enough now to know that it doesn't have to be a competition. As someone who loves and wants to look out for Rian, the more people I have in my corner in the matter, the better.

He stiffens slightly in my arms. "I forgot to ask; did lunch go well enough? No bloodshed?"

"Perfectly fine." I plant another kiss on the side of his face. "I think we have a better understanding." It's an exaggeration, but it *is* one of the best interactions Orla and I have ever had, so I'll give her high marks on a sliding scale.

He stares at me, his jaw slack for a moment. "Heavens above, did you lace her drink with zolpidem? Not that I'd blame you, but probably not the safest thing to do as the girlfriend of a doctor. It could get traced back to me, and the paperwork is a real hassle when you're up to ninety with work and all."

I thwack him playfully with the pillow I'd been using during my nap. "Ha ha, very funny. I don't even know what that is or how to spell it."

"You Yanks call it Ambien. And good. I won't have to worry about keeping my script pad under lock and key. Seriously, though. Glad you two got on. I had nightmares about it going arseways." He begins to pull the cartons from the bag and I fetch plates and decent chopsticks from the kitchen. He's always been reluctant to say anything, but I know the tension between Orla and me eats away at him. I hope, even more for his sake now, that I'm able to improve our rapport.

"I've been going about things the wrong way. I'm going to navigate my relationship with her differently moving forward." I could launch into my realizations about my complicated relationship with my own mother coloring my view of Orla's involvement in Rian's life, but I don't want to sour the mood. I consider telling him how my promotion is conditioned on Orla not pestering the restaurant while I'm working, but it's better if I have that chat with her myself. We made headway at lunch the other day, and I'd like to keep up the relationship building on my own terms. If I have to rope in Rian later, I will.

Despite the dark circles of fatigue under his eyes, his face brightens and he looks revivified . . . and not just from the prospect of the sesame chicken and lo mein he's heaping onto his plate. "That sounds grand. Nothing in the world would make me happier than you two making friends. Truly."

"Then that will be my objective. You deserve all the things that will make you happy." I take a serving for myself and settle next to him on the sofa. He sets his plate down after a few bites.

"You really are a dream, you know that?" He wraps an arm around me again, food forgotten. "I'm not sure what else could make me happier in this very moment."

I set my plate on the coffee table next to his. "Well, I can try. I got some amazing news at work. They're training me for a promotion to sous-chef. Apparently, they've been discussing it for a while, but they were impressed with a dish I auditioned, and it tipped the scales."

He squeezes me harder. "Sous? Really? I thought saucier was a huge promotion for you."

I lean my head on his shoulder. "It was. But they think I'm ready. And I do too. I nailed it today."

"It's nothing more than you deserve, Sabrina. That sauce was out of this world." Our mouths meet again, and I let myself revel in the joy of his caresses. The sweetness of his kisses. Dinner will have to survive a round in the microwave.

We pull apart sometime later, and I curse our feeble bodies' need for such prosaic things as oxygen. His kisses felt far more sustaining, his arms far more nourishing than anything I could concoct in a mortal kitchen. He cradles my head against his chest, and I despise myself for letting Orla tarnish what Rian and I shared.

But the beauty of this gift from the Ticket Agent is that it gives me the opportunity to correct that past wrong. I can create boundaries and enforce them like an adult, but I can also show her far more empathy and grace than I did before.

"Sabrina?" My name rumbles in my ear from the depths of his chest where my head is resting.

"Mmm?" I hesitate to break the mood by opening my mouth. Everything I want to communicate with him is expressed clearly enough without words.

His voice grows husky. "Sabrina, *mo chroí*, I love you. I want to make a life with you. Say you'll marry me?"

I raise my head from his chest to meet his beautiful green eyes. I say nothing, sure I have somehow imagined the words. Looking back over the footage of our relationship from the past, I realize this was not the night he proposed. We'd had a pleasant enough evening in the previous version of our life together, but like so many of the nights when we both worked, it had been filled mostly with takeaway, shop talk, an episode of some inane show or another, and him heading back to his flat when one of us started to nod off, or else him passing out on my lumpy sofa until morning.

In the previous iteration he'd proposed a few weeks down the line at our favorite upscale restaurant that we frequented for special occasions. He'd worn a smart suit and slipped the ring in a glass of champagne, claiming it was so cliché it was charming. It had been perfectly choreographed, right out of the how-to-propose playbook. It was unimaginative, but I had said yes because I wasn't hung up on a storybook proposal. Not that a proposal on my secondhand sofa after long shifts at work is the stuff of legend, but it feels more heartfelt this time. Genuine and true.

"Yes." The word squeaks on my lips. I swallow and find my voice. "Yes, I'll marry you."

He envelops me so tightly his words are muffled, but I make out, "We'll make a grand life together, the pair of us."

And I believe him. Of all the men I dated before Rian and since, none of them have communicated as well as he does. Even more important, I like the version of myself that I am with him. Despite my short temper where Orla was concerned, I was a more considerate person when I was with Rian. I thought about his needs and concerns more than I ever had about another partner. Not to the point of being totally self-effacing, but far more selfless than I'd been at other points in my life.

Maybe this was the trip I needed, armed with an extra decade of experience and a little more kindness directed Orla-ward. Maybe this is where I should stay.

"We will." My words are confident as I lose myself in his kisses.

I think I've found my way back home.

Chapter 11

There is nothing quite like the joy of producing a simmering pot of perfectly smooth béchamel or taking in the enrapturing scent of a lemon-forward hollandaise. Despite my added responsibilities at work, I take the time to breathe and let myself feel the magic of what I am creating.

I've spent a full week in this timeline, and I am in full training for my position as sous-chef. I've auditioned two dishes so far and both were selected for inclusion as that day's special. My lamb chops in peanut sauce were accepted with minimal adjustments, and my cedar-plank salmon with a lemon beurre blanc was declared perfect as it was. It was a spectacular week.

To top it off, Orla has taken the news of our engagement with more grace than she did the first time, and I'm now in possession of a lovely emerald ring—a family heirloom passed down from Orla's grandmother. Not only had she been willing to bequeath the ring to Rian to give me, but she'd also included a thick chain from her own jewelry collection so I can wear it safely around my neck when I'm in the kitchen. The ring is exquisite but far too cumbersome to wear in a kitchen. And emeralds, being significantly softer than diamonds, run the risk of getting cracked in the bustle of a dinner service. I was touched she'd thought of this.

The Orla I'd known never would have made such a kind gesture, and though my memory is hazy, the ring I returned to Rian all those years ago was something far more understated from a jeweler. Orla hadn't trusted me with an heirloom, and I might not have wanted one anyway. Now I see it as truly being welcomed into the family fold and appreciate the gesture for that reason.

"Let's see what you've done with the quail." I can hear Fiona's voice before I see her. She's been giving me an ingredient every morning to see what I can come up with as part of my training, all while preparing as many as a dozen sauces for the rest of the menu. It's a tremendous amount to keep straight without going completely mad.

I present her with a roasted quail sliced into thin strips and drizzled with a ginger-lime glaze. The sauce packs a punch without masking the delicate flavor of the quail, which is absolutely top notch all by itself.

Fiona takes a moment to consider the flavors as she samples three bites from different strips. She's checking for the consistency of the sear and how the sauce lingers on the palate. "I honestly hate how talented you are, Sorensen. It's indecent. I'll put it on the specials board."

That makes three dishes for three in one week. I don't bother to conceal my glee. "Brilliant."

She pats my shoulder. "You're delivering on your promise, Sabrina. Padraig is happy with your work."

Butterflies begin to jiggle in my gut at the compliment, but I hesitate. "Why do I sense a 'but' in there?"

She exhales slowly. "Orla called again."

There it is. The butterfly wings are now coated in sharpened steel, and dozens of the finest filleting knives are slicing me from the inside. "Oh god, I'm sorry. I'll talk with her. I thought we'd smoothed things over, but I'll make sure she understands . . ."

Fiona shakes her head. "No, no. She was lovely for the most part. I spoke with her. I understand congratulations are in order?"

I count to ten in my head slowly. We told Orla we didn't want to make the news public just yet, especially at work. I haven't even told Robin yet, knowing she'll book a venue in Solvang and start texting me pictures of centerpieces within forty-five minutes of her getting the news. But Orla has let the proverbial cat out of the bag, so there's no sense in denying it. I pull the ring on its chain out from under my chef's coat and show it to her. "Yep. Rian proposed last week. I didn't want to make a big deal out of it."

She admires the ring and lets it fall back on my chest with a thunk. "We're all happy for you, Sabrina. We love Rian and think he's great for you. Not that our opinion matters."

"It does matter," I interject. "A kitchen is a family and it's never a good sign if the family doesn't approve of the beau, right?" I realize I am actually far more concerned with what Fiona and Padraig think of my marriage to Rian than what Robin or my siblings think. I don't know if that says more about me and my ever-distancing relationship with them or how unapproachable they can be, but I set that aside for now. "So what was Orla calling about, pray tell?"

"She wants to host an engagement party here for you two. We found an open date three weeks from now, and obviously we can make sure you have the time off and we'll give her the family rate. But she had very specific requests for the menu, and we thought you ought to have some say in it before we greenlight it all officially." She hands me a paper with notes hastily written in her loopy script. Orla is the sort to speak quickly when she's in her stride, and it's clear Fiona was struggling to keep up with her.

Beef Wellington, creamed potatoes, Brussels sprouts, vanilla wedding cake.

No no no.

Beef Wellington—a classic but stodgy. It'll please her friends, but most of the people in Rian's and my age group will find it heavy and staid. Especially as we enter the warmer months.

Creamed potatoes—fine, if a bit prosaic. A very heavy side to serve with a heavy main.

Brussels sprouts—a winter vegetable. There are so many better options for spring and early summer.

A vanilla wedding cake—outside of the scope of our kitchen and will take away from the impact of the actual wedding, for which we don't have an actual date. The menu is all wrong in so many ways. I hand the paper back and rub my eyes. Rian and I aren't even ready to formally announce our engagement, and she's signing contracts to host a party. I count to ten again. *She's trying to help, she's trying to help.* I repeat the mantra in my head. At least I think it's in my head until Fiona starts laughing at me.

"Yes, she is. She didn't sound interested in hearing the options we generally offer to the public, assuming we'd do what she wants because you work for us. Which is mostly true. But I don't have to tell you what's wrong with all this. It'd be a fine classic menu for December, but . . ."

"It's a hot mess for summer." And the task falls to me to convince her that fresh produce and lighter fare would be better for the event. It could be lovely with something like quail, some greens, and a bright, lemony dessert.

Fiona puts a comforting hand on my shoulder. "Listen, let us be the bad guy here. We don't want events to flop, so we stick to the set menus for the most part. You know how far we can go off book, so I'm going to trust you to work this out with her."

I shake my head. "Thanks."

"I know you can reason with her. It's going to be lovely." Fiona takes another look at my array of simmering stockpots and breathes in like she's in a florist's shop. "Really, truly revolting how talented you are. Carry on."

I sigh and give the pots that need it a good stir to exorcise the butterflies-turned-angry-knife-wielding-demons wreaking havoc in my gut. I understand Orla's impulse to plan a party for us, but she could have worked *with* us to pull it all together.

Generally, I keep my phone in my work bag in the staff room, but I neglected to do so today. I give in to temptation and pull my phone from my back pocket.

ME: Did you know your mom is planning an engagement party? In three weeks?

RIAN: She mentioned it. I said it would be fine. I figured you wouldn't mind. It might sate her need to plan enough that she won't try to commandeer all the wedding plans.

I count to ten . . . yet again. Fat chance. This is going to be the signal to Orla that all the wedding plans are now under her purview.

ME: A heads-up might have been nice. I hadn't told anyone at work, and she called my boss to arrange to have it **here.** Did she tell you that?

RIAN: Shite, no, she didn't tell me where she was

planning to have it. Just grand. I'm sorry she did that. I'll talk to her.

Well, that's something. Rian hasn't blindsided me; it's all Orla. Which, I hate to say, is on-brand for her.

ME: Listen, the menu she wants is basically off the table. She has to work with our catering menu. She may think it's just a party with a few friends, but if the guests have a bad experience because she insists on off-season produce or something, it affects the restaurant's image.

RIAN: Okay, I have to go. But remember she's just excited and wants to do us a good turn.

ME: I'm glad she's excited, but when she roped in my place of work, she roped me in too. My boss came to me and told me to handle it, and we *have to* get her in line.

I don't mention that my promotion hangs in the balance—but I know it does. Perhaps my very job if she's too big of a pill.

RIAN: Understood. I'm sorry this happened, mo chroí.

Invoking his endearment. A low blow.

ME: Thank you for that. Let her know that I appreciate the gesture.

I slip my phone back in my pocket and try to turn my attention back to my sauces and prep for the specials. Thankfully nothing has scorched or curdled thanks to Orla's imposition on my day, and the muscles in my shoulders slowly start to uncoil as I find my rhythm again. Twenty minutes later, I feel the familiar buzz of my phone in my pocket, and I pull it out to look.

> ORLA: I'm not sure why you bothered Rian at work about the party. He was well aware of the plan.

Yes. She probably ambushed him with a call right after his shift when he was ready to fall on his face with exhaustion. She likely prattled on, and he acquiesced to get her to hang up the phone. I've seen it happen.

> ME: But I wasn't. And this is *my* work, Orla.

I breathe. I need to soften this.

> ME: I think it's incredibly sweet of you to host a party for us and I'm glad you're excited. I'd just appreciate taking over communication with the restaurant moving forward. It will make things easier for me here. I hope you don't mind, but it's important.
>
> ORLA: I don't see how planning a party will work if I can't talk to the restaurant myself. That sounds dreadfully inconvenient.

One. Two. Three . . .

> ME: I promise it will be lovely. I have to get back to work now, but we'll get together and talk it over soon.

I put my phone back in my pocket, hopeful that I've been successful in at least stalling Orla's one-woman crusade to bring back classics from the 1960s. I try to lose myself in the cadence of my work, but I'm off my game. And knowing it irritates me further. But this isn't like an office job where you can log off your computer for twenty minutes and go for a walk around the block to clear your head. The best you might manage is a good primordial scream in the walk-in if you time it just right.

Just like the old saying: If you're going through hell, just keep going. If you don't soldier on, sauces split. Sauces curdle. Sauces scorch. Some are fussy enough you need to add herbs or spices at the right moment in the process, or they simply taste *off*. There is no room for anything but my best efforts.

When Fiona comes to do her final tasting before service, my heart is fairly wedged in my esophagus. I peer over her shoulder, unable to play it cool. Nothing seems to have gone disastrously wrong, for which I am grateful. But at this stage in my career, it's expected that I can do better than just avoiding catastrophe. Fiona and Padraig expect excellence, and frankly so do I.

"Not bad." Fiona's praise, while never glowing, seems especially restrained. Sauces are a special sort of magic. Edible alchemy. They require focus and devotion, like any other self-respecting magic brew. I've tried to give my all to today's crop, but they know I'm not at my peak. And Fiona can taste it. She won't begrudge me one service that's below my usual standard, but she won't tolerate a pattern.

Not bad, but not *great* either. Fiona just had the grace not to voice that last part out loud.

I am going to have to convince Orla, for the sake of my work, to give the restaurant a wide berth while I'm working. And me with it.

The reasons for leaving Rian come bubbling back to the surface. As I begin plating for the service, laser focused on getting the specials just right, I exhale and hope I can steer my relationship with Orla back on course for the sake of the relationship I have with Rian.

A relationship I desperately want to save.

Chapter 12

I don't see why this is such a big deal. Can't the restaurant accommodate her? It's beef Wellington she's asking for, not sautéed moon rocks." Rian is stretched out on the sofa in his posh flat, an arm slung over his eyes.

Rather than seated next to him, I'm in the plush blue armchair Orla chose to complement the sofa's sleek cordovan leather. The carryout—shrimp in my Créole sauce—that I brought home from my shift at Baile Phadraig is moldering on his coffee table, but not because we're absorbed in each other. Orla has, despite not even being present, managed to sour our evening.

I try, without complete success, to keep my tone measured. "Rian, we have catering menus for a reason. The rules apply to me too. Padraig didn't go off book for his *own daughter's* wedding dinner last year."

Rian rolls his eyes. "I really don't want to be in the middle of this."

A low growl dies in my throat. "I don't either. You should have warned me this was coming, and you could have very easily headed all this off at the pass by suggesting she hold the damn thing elsewhere."

He removes his arm from over his eyes and angles his head to give me a wary glare. "So this is my fault?"

"Partly." Past me would have put the blame squarely on Orla's shoulders, but that wouldn't be entirely fair. Part of Rian's job is to protect my toes from getting trodden on by Orla and her interference. "How would you react if my mother barged into your hospital demanding you do a nose job for her?"

His annoyed glare could blister paint. "You know I don't do that. I'm an internist, not a plastic surgeon."

I lean closer to him, my voice low. "If pressed, could you do it?"

He sits up and shrugs, taking a bite of the shrimp. "Maybe? It wouldn't be ideal. She'd get a better result with a specialist."

I lean back, thread my fingers, and cradle the back of my head. "Wow. It's almost like you have a set . . . what's the word . . . a *menu* of services you're trained to provide and refer patients to a different doctor if their needs fall out of your bailiwick. Fascinating."

He gives me an icy stare. "I hardly think it's the same thing."

I don't break my gaze. "The stakes may not be as high, I grant you, but it really is the same. Your reputation is crucial to your job, isn't it?"

He nods.

"Same for us. If you start performing the odd nose job with mixed results, people might talk. Same for us with off-book catering. If we go beyond our expertise, we can't guarantee a good result, and our reputation can't afford it. Can we be somewhat flexible? Sure. But Orla has to follow the rules the same as anyone else."

He slouches against the sofa cushions, looking deflated in both senses of the word. "I guess I see your point, yeah."

"I hope you *do* see it." I could let things go here, but I decide to press one more issue. "Now last question: If my mother barged into your hospital demanding a nose job, would you want to deal with her on your own, or would you want me to help manage her?"

He tries to play it off. "Well, I've never met your mother . . ."

It's clear he wants me to drop it, but I refuse. "Answer the question, Rian."

He sighs. "Yes. I suppose I'd want your backup."

Not good enough. I dig my heels in further. "Be honest. You'd want me to handle her so you wouldn't have to be the bad guy with your mother-in-law."

"Fair play. I suppose that's true." He's lying limp on the couch, as though all of this has sapped his last bit of energy. I recognize now that this is a ploy he's been using to engender my sympathy. I don't know if it's deliberate or if it's a response that's been conditioned by his interactions with Orla, but I won't fall for it.

"Right. Because it's easier to take heat from a bio parent than an in-law. And you *know* you'll have an easier time getting through to her than I will. I'm asking you to do this for me, not just for the sake of my job and my professional reputation, but to set the tone for our marriage." I remember Fiona's metaphor. "This won't work if you aren't the one drawing the boundary lines. Orla won't bother even looking at the map if I'm the one holding it."

"Grand. I'll do my best to reason with her." His sigh is one of such dramatic intensity, I worry that, brilliant doctor though he is, he missed his true calling on the stage.

"Rian, trying isn't good enough. Your assignment is a simple one: Tell her she has to either follow Padraig's catering menu or find somewhere else to host the party. Either choice is perfectly fine by me. I'll personally help her tweak our menu to her liking—within limits—or research the right alternate venue if we can't make our menu work for her. But you need to present her with those two options and not make me look like the bad guy."

He sits forward again and takes a few more bites of food before responding. It isn't just theater—he's genuinely tired from a draining day at work, and I wish I didn't have to rope him in on this, but she's left me little choice.

"I suppose I must." His words sound like defeat.

"I'm glad you see reason." Finally. And he needs the full truth. "My promotion depends on her not intruding at the restaurant. They've made that clear."

His eyes widen. "Really?"

I let out a shaky breath. I probably wouldn't have been bold enough to tackle this head-on eleven years ago, but I am now. "Explicitly. She calls the restaurant. She tried to ask Padraig himself to reduce my hours so I can spend more time, I don't know, taking care of you? I appreciate all she's done for you, but I can't allow her to interfere with my career. Or our marriage, for that matter."

He rubs his face with his hands. "She thrives on helping people, Sabrina. And that's exactly what she thinks she's doing."

"I get it, Rian. I do. Her heart is in the right place, but she needs interests and hobbies outside of micromanaging your life. And mine. She'd never interfere with your work as she's tried to do with mine."

He opens his mouth to object but stops. His decision to censor his comment is a wise one. "Of course. I'll have a chat with her as soon as I can. Is morning okay? I don't have to go in until late, and I'll make more headway with her if I'm not knackered after a shift."

I start to say, "Sure, that's great," but the sound of a key in the lock, followed by footsteps in the hallway, stops me short.

Of course Orla has a key to Rian's place, even though I don't yet, and she doesn't bother to knock. She enters the living room carrying a garment bag and feigns surprise at the sight of me. She knew full well I'd be here.

"Oh, Sabrina, how lovely. I didn't know you'd be over tonight." She eyes the takeaway containers with suspicion. Even though I made the food myself, she probably doesn't consider it a "home-cooked meal."

"We both have the evening off," I point out. "We spend those evenings together as a general rule."

"Oh, yes yes yes. Well . . ." She looks at Rian, then at me. "Just as well you're here. I think I finally managed to talk some sense into that Fiona woman. The menu is all set. And I have a surprise for you."

She unzips the garment bag to reveal a long lace gown in a warm shade of candle-glow white. The vintage must be 1940s or '50s.

"What's this?" It can't possibly be what I think it is. She wouldn't possibly presume to buy a wedding gown for me without me in attendance. Asking to go with me to find my own gown would have been impertinent, but she can't possibly be so far removed from reality that she thinks this is appropriate. Is this how our wedding planning would have gone if I hadn't called things off last time?

"Your wedding gown, silly goose. Now I know how much you like thrifted things, so I've been scouring all of Dublin's second-hand shops to find just the right gown. It's an old Irish design house, Ordaithe. They just don't make gowns like this anymore."

I resolve to be diplomatic, though I feel my grip on my filter slipping with each tick of the second hand on Rian's mantel clock.

Orla approaches me with the gown so I can see it closer. It is a lovely thing—handcrafted lace over rich duchesse satin. Impeccable French seams the likes of which no one sees anymore. But it's not me. I always envisioned a plain sheath gown, something modern and without fuss. I'd dreamed of a reception in a modern art gallery, not something traditional in a drafty old stone church hall, which I know in my bones is exactly what she wants.

The dress is also made for a woman a foot shorter with the frame of a hummingbird.

"Orla, it's very nice, but there is no way this gown will fit me."

She waves a dismissive hand. "Oh, seamstresses can work wonders these days."

"Um, I don't think it works that way." It's the most measured response I can summon. This isn't like medical technology that has made huge advances in lifesaving treatments. Seamstresses might have a few new tricks up their sleeves, but to my knowledge, none of them involve magic fabric that expands to fit the wearer. Letting out a quarter inch at the seams might be possible, but that's nowhere near enough to accommodate my frame. I doubt even panels would be adequate—even if matching lace could be found.

It is, objectively, a gorgeous gown, but it's not for me.

Rian shoots me a pleading look. *Please indulge her. Please make this work*.

But I can't.

I shake my head. "Orla, I really appreciate the gesture, but seamstresses are bound by the laws of physics. It won't work. Maybe we can find something together."

The last words turn to ash in my mouth. I do *not* want to go wedding dress shopping with this woman, even to make Rian happy. Given my druthers, I wouldn't take Robin either. Maybe Chloe, but most likely I'd prefer to do a round or two on my own before bringing in a small brain trust to break any ties.

"But you have this one, dear. Let's not be wasteful." She turns to Rian. "I've saved the date at the church and the hall for October. We'll have Sabrina's little restaurant do the catering, of course." She glances back to me with a saccharine smile.

One . . . two . . . three . . . "We don't cater off-site events—"

"Oh, I'm sure they will for you, dear. If they like you as well as you claim." The barb in her words isn't even concealed.

I shoot Rian a death glare, but he remains conspicuously silent.

"Orla, the restaurant doesn't have the *licensing* to do off-site catering. Nor the equipment. It's not possible. Rian and I can handle the planning on our own. We appreciate your help, but we can handle this."

Orla shoots me a withering look of her own. "There are several months left for them to get all that in order. I'm sure they will. Now, I'll leave you two to your evening. So much left to plan, you know."

"Orla—"

But she's on her way out with a click of the door before I can voice my displeasure.

Rian has the sense not to meet my gaze directly. I point to the door she just exited. "She. Is. Insane. We don't even have a date . . ."

He flops on the couch once more. "She's just excited, Sabrina. Cut her some slack."

I hear my brother Brian's voice echoing in my ears with those words. *"Cut Mom some slack. She's been through a lot."* Well, so have I. I lost Dad too. We all did.

And Orla may be excited about the wedding, but it's *not hers*.

I am the *bride*, for heaven's sake. I should have a say in the planning of it.

A say in my own damned dress.

But that isn't even the worst of it.

"Rian, that loon is going to get me fired. You *have* to stop her."

He throws his hands up in despair. "You see how she gets, Sabrina. I'm not sure how I can get through to her. And it's not like you'll be working at Baile Phadraig forever."

"Well, no, but I can't afford to get a bad rap because of her. I'll need Padraig as a reference when I move up."

"You don't think you'll want to slow down a bit once we're married? Once the kids come along?"

I feel the wind deflate from my lungs. "Slow down? Kids?" We always talked about kids—or most likely *a* child as a distant possibility. Ten years down the road . . . if ever. Rian has never seemed exceptionally keen on starting a family. If anything, he rather seems on the cool side of indifferent to children in general.

"Orla isn't getting any younger. If we want her to help, it may be wise to get a jump on things. And it's not like you *need* to work once we're married."

I stand there slack-jawed, staring at him. "This isn't the life we discussed at all."

He closes the lid of the takeout container and crosses to put it in the fridge, his appetite vanished, same as mine. "You think everything will stay exactly as it is? That getting married is just moving in together and sharing bills and deciding what's for dinner?"

"Mainly, *yes*." I stand rooted to the ground where I was standing when Orla left. "I don't see why it requires me to change my thoughts about having children or to deprioritize my career. That isn't what I signed up for and you know it."

"I thought you'd change your mind when reality hits." He shuts the door of the fridge and leans his head against the freezer.

"But you're right. None of those changes need to happen overnight. I'll talk to her about the catering. Your work makes you happy and you should stay with it as long as it does."

"How generous of you," I seethe.

He looks at me with tired eyes. "Don't be that way, Sabrina. I am serious about wanting to make a beautiful life with you."

I know he speaks the truth, but for the first time since I hopped backward, I wonder if his version of a happy future and mine look the same.

"I think I need some space, Rian. I'm going home."

His face falls, but he doesn't press. "I understand." He picks up the garment bag Orla left behind and hands it to me. "Take this with you, yeah? It would mean a lot to her if you tried to make it work."

"Why? It's not an heirloom or of any special significance. She found it in a thrift shop. Without me."

He sighs. "It's just a dress, Sabrina."

"It's *my wedding dress*, Rian." I'm pretty sure I've gone from Nordic ice queen to full Viking warrior princess now. He simply heaves another sigh and thrusts the bag into my hands.

Despite wanting to shove it down his throat, I take the bag and escape down into the cool evening air on the street below before I say words that no cosmic redo can ever erase.

Chapter 13

I can't bring myself to hang the dress in my closet. Hanging it there feels like accepting that I will somehow make this dress work for my wedding. Though how I could possibly bend the laws of the natural universe to make that happen, I don't know. I have never been the sort to dream of my wedding, but dress shopping is the one exception. I would never be one of the brides who drops the equivalent of a year of my salary on a dress, but I would love the experience of finding the perfect gown for myself.

So for several days the dress stays in its white plastic garment bag on the crusty coatrack the previous tenants left behind. The gown somehow glares at me with judgment and disapproval on Orla's behalf, without the benefit of having eyes. I am stretched out on my sofa after a long shift. Usually, I'd be filled with the urge to text Rian by now, but I find myself dreading it. Despite all his oh-so-sincere claims to the contrary, when the chips are down, he always sides with Orla.

And that is just how things will be with him until she's gone.

And given that she is a vibrant woman in her very early sixties, she's got a lot of years left in front of her.

A lot of years left for me to juggle pleasing the pair of them and always dropping the most crucial balls. A lot of time left where I am forced to cope with her judgmental attitude and his pleas to keep the peace with her.

The prospect is exhausting.

And I have almost made up my mind to go back to my regular timeline. Almost.

But I love my job here. It is, without question, the best job I've had to date in terms of scope for creativity. If I had to choose one job for the rest of my career that wasn't the coveted Michelin gig, it would be this one.

And despite everything with Orla, I love Rian. I've spent more time missing him than I ever realized, and the idea of leaving him again hurts more than I can fully process. That's why I've tried to reason with her. That's why it hurts so much that it isn't working.

I've been home an hour when I hear the vibration of my phone on the coffee table.

RIAN: Everything okay? You've been quiet. Busy at work?

I consider downplaying my conflicted emotions, but I don't see how that will help the situation improve.

ME: Just been thinking about things. And yes, busy at work.

And that is true. I can feel the pressure in the kitchen weighing heavier on me as the days go on and the expectation to outperform the previous day's efforts becomes more apparent. From Fiona. From Padraig. From the whole of the kitchen staff who are also silently casting their votes as to whether I'm ready to ascend the ranks to sous. No position in the kitchen impacts their day-to-day in the kitchen quite so much as the sous, and they are all forming their opinions. And Padraig, because he is a good head chef and a helluva leader, will listen to them.

RIAN: Thinking good thoughts, I hope. About me.

I smile at how transparently he casts his line to fish for a compliment.

ME: Very often.

I say it because that is true as well. Even as I'm fuming about something Orla has said or done, I still find my heart fluttering when I think about Rian. But it isn't the whole truth. And if I love him, he deserves nothing less than that.

ME: Some not so great thoughts too, if I'm being truthful.
RIAN: What about, exactly?

I swallow a sigh. I can see him hoping and praying I'm about to vent about some persnickety colleague instead of his mother.

ME: I really don't want your mom to commandeer our wedding. Or the rest of our lives, for that matter. And I absolutely don't want to plan a family around her wants and needs instead of our own.

I exhale slowly. It was a lot to get out, but it feels good to express it.

Rian is conspicuously silent for several minutes.

RIAN: You knew coming into this how important my mother is to me.

ME: As she should be. But I'm important too. It's our wedding, not hers.

RIAN: Listen, she's traditional. Her mam planned her wedding. She thinks it's her duty to plan mine.

ME: If she were really a traditionalist, she'd know it's my mother who'd be calling the shots. And we'd be getting married in Solvang.

He takes another long pause.

RIAN: Why don't we then? We'll have a big bash however you like it in Solvang and let my mum throw us a party here. This may be the grand compromise. Everything else will fall into place.

I brighten a bit, considering this alternative. It's quintessential Rian, trying his best to please us both. Orla probably won't love it, but at least Rian is making an effort on my behalf. It only addresses part of the problem, and really, it's the least important part of the problem, but it's reason enough to stay. For now.

ME: That could work. It's a great plan, actually.

RIAN: See, there's a solution to every problem if you think hard enough. Now why don't you come over and we'll watch a movie. At least the first fifteen minutes or so of one.

I chuckle, remembering this is the era before the expression "Netflix and chill."

ME: Sounds like an amazing evening to me. Give me a bit to shower and get presentable.

RIAN: Don't take too long, mo chroí.

I smile down at my phone and hop in the shower, letting the scalding water rinse away the layers of cooking oil and potent herbs. After ten minutes of scrubbing, I'm finally more like myself. I slide into clean clothes and feel revivified.

Until I notice my phone has lit up like a Christmas tree.

Six missed calls from Orla in the span of fifteen minutes. And a whole string of texts.

ORLA: What nonsense have you put into my son's head???

ORLA: Do you really intend to marry my son five thousand miles away from me?

ORLA: I can't believe you'd do this to me.

ORLA: This isn't what he wants. Not really. You're going to break his heart.

There are a dozen messages, all variations on the same theme. I capture screenshots and forward them to Rian without commentary. They speak for themselves.

I stride over to the garment bag and unzip the dress. It looks like someone at least had it cleaned before they donated it. I see a tag with the name of the thrift store, not one I've ever frequented, and the price. She shelled out all of twenty euro for the dress yet clung to the notion that buying one to suit, one that actually fit, was wasteful. She'd probably spend five hundred euro on a dress for herself for the wedding and say what a bargain it was because she could wear it again. Hell, it would be a mercy if the spiteful old cow didn't show up in a white gown and a veil herself.

The phone vibrates again in my rear pocket.

RIAN: Yeah . . . I miscalculated. She won't go for it. I'm sorry.

ME: She won't go for it? This isn't her wedding. It's not for her to "go for" anything. She gets an invite and she shows up. Or not, if she doesn't want to. That's how it works.

RIAN: I'm her only child, Sabrina. She's all alone besides me. Try to understand where she's coming from.

ME: I have, Rian. I really have. I may have been too hard on her before, but she's crossed a line here, not me. She's not reasonable.

RIAN: I don't know what to say. I don't have it in me to break her heart.

ME: But you have it in you to break mine.

It's not a question.

Part of me wishes I could soften, but I can't. She will use every bit of energy in her body and every spark in her soul to make me miserable. She claims to want Rian to be happy, but only if she can be the only woman in his life. It isn't right and it isn't healthy.

And I can't bear to have her stupid dress in my flat a moment longer. I snatch the garment bag and double back for my leather tote before I run down to the street below. My time here is over, but I won't leave the dress behind for this version of me to deal with.

I can do that much for her.

It's early enough most of the shops should still be open. I wander the streets until I find something resembling a thrift shop. Objets Trouvés appears as if out of the ether in one of the smarter shopping streets in the city. I've been in dozens of thrift shops in Dublin, but I have never seen this one before. It does feel oddly familiar, but I don't linger over the why of it. I have a task at hand—getting rid of this infernal dress—and need to get on with it.

I feel remarkably calm. The first time I left Rian, I spent days ugly crying. Not now. I'm sure I look a fright, but I am mistress of myself. Maybe because this is my second time leaving Rian, it stings a little less. That isn't true . . . It's just the ache is familiar enough that I've learned to live with it.

I enter the shop and see a familiar woman with soft gray curls and artful laugh lines around her eyes.

The woman doesn't seem to recognize me, but she greets me with the warmth I experienced at the airport. "Hello, dearie. Got something to off-load, do we?"

I nod and hand over the garment bag. "It's you."

She chuckles, deepening the lines around her eyes. "Indeed it is, love. Who else would I be?"

I shake sense into myself. "Sorry. It's just been a bit of a day. I must have mistaken you for someone else."

"I confess, I'm nervous to hear that. I'm not sure our fair city can manage two women of such beauty and wit within its walls." She gives me a roguish wink, and I smile in return. She unzips the bag and takes in a sharp breath. "Oh, you have had a bit of a day, haven't you?"

She doesn't make the assumption that I've found the dress in an attic or that I've come across it by happenstance. As soon as she touches the lace, she knows what's happened. I can see the recognition in her face.

"It's not your time, dearie. And not your dress."

"No." I shake my head in agreement. "It's not." And despite all my restraint up to this point, tears begin to spill over onto my cheeks.

Her expression, which has been bordering on piteous, mercifully turns businesslike. "If that's the truth of it, there's no use mulling it over. Time to move forward, yes?"

I let loose a ragged breath. "I think so. Pretty sure I've got a plane to catch."

Her blue eyes meet mine, and she radiates comprehension. "I think you do, dearie." She looks the gown over once more and lifts a brow. "Someone has left a note."

"What?" I'm not surprised I hadn't noticed. I'd been too shocked at Orla's audacity to see the thick ivory envelope, nearly the exact shade of the dress, pinned to the label inside.

The woman passes me the envelope that has *Sabrina* penned in Orla's meticulous script on the front.

> Dear Sabrina,
>
> Forgive me for doing this, but you are too talented to give up your dreams like I did for Rian and his father. Despite what he may say to the contrary, Rian has always wanted a traditional wife. One that will set her own ambition aside to support his. He may seem fair-minded now, but things will change if you marry. I confess I enabled this trait in him, and he's become too much like his father. I can't bear to see someone with your spark and vivacity reduced to serving as his maid, cook, and

eventually nanny. I could think of no other way to scare you off than being the evil mother-in-law from every bad movie ever made. I hope you'll understand in time that I want only the best for you.

Your friend,

Orla

I stand speechless in the middle of the thrift shop. Could this possibly be true? Was Orla really trying to protect me from suffering the same fate she'd endured? Was Rian really as traditionally minded as she believes?

Past me would have scoffed. Rian was thoughtful. He brought over takeout when I was too tired to cook. He loaded the dishwasher. He seemed to *love* my ambition.

But as I replay the last few conversations Rian and I had, her warnings don't seem baseless. His talk about slowing down, children . . . He hadn't mentioned those things in my previous stint here because we hadn't gotten quite this far. I hadn't tried so hard to make it work. Orla had resorted to disrupting my work and buying an *inappropriate* (thank you, Robin) dress to scare me away because this time I was so invested in being more empathetic with her so things would work out between Rian and me.

The woman seems unfazed by my standing, mouth agape, in the middle of her shop like a befuddled codfish. "So what will it be—cash or store credit? Ordaithe was a grand house back in its day. I can give you a hundred euro since it's in such good condition."

I finally snap my mouth shut. "Oh no. You can have it. Just . . .

I don't know . . . make sure it finds the right home." I wipe my face with the back of my hand, suddenly embarrassed to be weeping so openly in public. But it's not like I haven't wept in front of this woman before in an even more public setting. There is no way she isn't the Ticket Agent, if a bit younger.

She pats my other hand, which is resting on the glass case where she's arranged her bits and bobs of secondhand jewelry. "I absolutely will make sure this dress finds the right bride. Don't you worry your head about that. But I have to insist you take something in exchange."

I shake my head. "No. Nothing, please. I really need to go."

She holds up a hand and grabs a green leather backpack—*my* green leather backpack—from a shelf.

"Take this for your trip then. A wee gift. It will serve you well."

I look down. "I already have one just like it."

She doesn't say anything, but I can feel it's full. I open it to find all my odds and ends. From my actual timeline.

"Best you find your way to the airport, dearie. It's getting late."

Chapter 14

DECEMBER 30, 2024
BURBANK AIRPORT

I walk slowly back up the Jetway, the green backpack hanging listlessly from my shoulder. Leaving Rian a second time, no matter how justified, has sucked the very marrow from my bones. I had loved him. Loved the life we might have had. But my vision of our future together wasn't based in reality. Orla was probably right; he wanted a cook and a maid more than he wanted a real partner. But my surface assessment of our problems was just as true: Orla was a huge obstacle. She was warning me away as much for her own sake as for mine.

With her around I never would have been the priority in Rian's life that I should have been. She was a broken woman, grasping to retain a sense of relevance. And Rian just wasn't strong enough to set boundaries with her. Their relationship wasn't a healthy one, and neither of them were ready to change their dynamic enough so that I—or anyone else—would be truly welcome in their little circle.

And he loved being catered to. No matter how much he put on

the façade of the modern man, he *liked* the way Orla coddled him and had hoped to train me to be her replacement.

I tried with Orla. I really tried this time . . . and I can move on again knowing I did better. Could I have done more? Could I have done even better? Maybe, but it never would have been enough. And perhaps I was "too much" for each of them. And that's fine. I shouldn't have to make myself less for anyone.

I hope that the version of me I left behind stays on longer at Baile Phadraig. She shouldn't let the heartbreak chase her from a job she loves. I hope she visits the rugged coasts of County Mayo and takes in the vibrant beauty of County Kerry. I hope she kisses the Blarney Stone and finds a fairy ring hidden in the green hills that sprawl outside the city. But I am glad to be back in my own time.

Probably.

"Rough crossing then?" the Ticket Agent asks as I approach her in the lounge.

"You were there." It's not a question. "At the secondhand shop."

She smiles as she shows me to a seat. "As I told you, dearie, I've had a great many careers in my lifetime, and I usually find I'm where I need to be. You couldn't leave Ireland without your pack. And I also promised you all those years ago I'd find a way to compensate you for the dress. It wouldn't be right otherwise."

I blink a few times. Am I fully grasping the situation? "So that's what this is? Payment?"

"Of a sort. And I'm pleased to let you know that your dress finally found its rightful owner after waiting in the shop all this time. Another lovely American in Dublin like yourself. I'm certain she'll come back for it soon."

A cloud passes over her face as she gets lost in her thoughts. I realize I'm not the only soul she's been charged with looking after, and that seems only right. There are a lot of people in the world who can use a little boost from fate.

"I'm glad." My heart lightens a tad. Just because it wasn't the dress for me didn't mean it wasn't perfect for someone else. Was that why Orla had been pulled toward the dress? She was a catalyst for the dress to find its way home. There *was* something truly enchanting about the gown, but it's clear the dress is meant to be part of someone else's future, not mine.

But something about the Ticket Agent's statements gives me pause. "How do you know? If you're working for the airline . . . ?" And I realize maybe the question is a little silly. Aside from the obvious reality that she's sending me on these trips to my past, there could be a more prosaic explanation, like she's still in touch with the people who bought the business from her. But I get the sense that isn't the case.

This question and a million others bubble to the surface. Chief among them is: Why am I doing this? So far it seems like a torturous exercise in reliving my own bad decisions.

"I don't think now is the right time to get into the mechanics of things, dearie. That last trip was hard on you."

"It was. I really cared for Rian." An understatement, but it says enough.

She slides me another cup of her amazing coffee. "I know you did. And he seemed like a good sort of lad. It's hard to be deceived by someone you think you know."

"Yes." I stare into the void of the deep brown liquid in the mug before me. "And his mother is . . . intense."

The Ticket Agent chuckles. "That Orla is a piece of work, I grant you. She means well enough. But she wasn't wrong about her son either. He wasn't a good fit for you."

I rub my temples, feeling the strain of the visit poking at the backs of my eyes. "I thought I had it figured out. I tried to look at her situation with more empathy. I tried being more patient. But none of that mattered because Rian was a massive jerk in nice-guy clothing."

She takes my hand in hers. "You did brilliantly, dearie. But sometimes you can do all the right things and still fail. That is one of the hardest lessons to learn."

It sounds like the sort of pithy advice my father used to give. "I wish I took comfort in that."

Her expression turns serious. "I'm not sure you're meant to. Not yet anyway. That's a gift you'll give yourself on down the road."

I find myself unable to meet more of this mystery without question or doubt. "Who are you, anyway? You're more than just a ticket agent. Do you have a name?" I'm embarrassed that I haven't thought to ask the question before now.

She laughs, perhaps because I am only now thinking to ask. "Of course I do. Many in fact."

"Should I call you by any of them?" I hope the question isn't impertinent. She feels like something of a deity or a fairy godmother in an airline uniform. But she hasn't seemed too hung up on formalities thus far.

She smiles a bit ruefully. "As you wish, dearie. I'm rather partial to Rosaline."

Rosaline. A rather romantic name, calling to mind Romeo's faithless lover, but it suits her.

"So what am I doing here, Rosaline?" I finally summon the courage to ask.

She looks at me as though the answer is painfully obvious. "Why, learning, of course. I promised you I'd repay you for the dress, and I could think of no better gift than knowledge."

"I can see your point, I suppose."

"Right. You learned to let go of your regret about how that relationship ended. No matter how hard you tried, Rian was a dolt and Orla was going to make a mess of things. She doesn't know any different. And between you and me, she isn't doing that boy of hers any favors either."

"Still?" Since she seems all-knowing, I might as well ask. "Is she still chasing his girlfriends away even now?"

She nods. "Confirmed bachelor now, even if he's the most eligible one in Dublin. He's decided he can't disappoint Orla by forcing her to play second fiddle. But truly, I think he realizes most modern women aren't as self-effacing as Orla. The real pity is that *she's* heartbroken he never married or had children, and she can't see the part she played in his single state. Nothing more pathetic than a person who can't see their own folly."

I shake my head. I should be glad to know I dodged a major bullet with Rian, and Orla too, but it's all too fresh to take any solace.

Rosaline heaves a sigh. "They're the authors of their own misfortune. And none of it is of your doing."

"I'm glad of that at least. I really thought he loved me, though."

She exhales, a bit mournfully. "I want you to remember that it does a soul no good to lament not being able to turn a heart of marble into man flesh. Those sorts of regrets will drive a person mad."

"Wise words."

"He's a fool and you're well shot of him." Resolute, she pushes back from the table. "Why don't you take another trip? I don't want you to linger overlong on what wasn't to be. Your mother has a special talent for that, and I'd hate for you to fall into the same trap."

"What do you mean?" I'm not surprised she's privy to the inner workings of Robin's mind. It's not like she works hard at keeping them a secret.

"Oh, she had a very set vision for your future. Would you like to see?"

I shake my head. "No, I couldn't live through that."

"No, no, dear. I'd never make a woman try on a gown that won't fit. But there's no harm in holding it up in front of you in the mirror. Give me your hand."

I raise my shaking hand off the table and offer it to her. I feel a swirl of colors and I see myself in high school—tall, awkward, and pimpled and dancing with Tim Espersen at the prom. Robin had badgered me into saying yes. Instead of going to the CIA in New York, I went to a culinary school on the West Coast. Instead of working in Silicon Valley, Tim founded a start-up. It wasn't going well. I didn't apply for Michelin. I got pregnant and worked in Tim's aunt's diner in Solvang. She hated me. I hated the diner. Tim and I were horrible for each other.

"That was dreadful," I finally manage to say.

Rosaline chuckles. "Indeed. Your mother missed that mark altogether. You might make a better match as adults, but I suspect you're both happier married to your work than each other."

"Too right. Listen, Rosaline, this has been . . . educational, but I'm not sure I want to go anywhere else. This has been a mistake." I stand and look around for my luggage—my actual luggage, not just my bewitched backpack. More mechanics I probably don't want to ponder. I touch my head. *Did* I fall off a ladder at Chloe's party and this is just brain trauma? But I feel no lumps or bruises.

Unfortunately, I feel utterly and objectionably lucid.

And I don't see my luggage.

Rosaline crosses to my side and wraps an arm around my shoulders, comforting in her grandmotherly way. "I know you might not think so right now, but I promise you it *will* be worth it. I just need you to trust me a bit longer."

She seems so sincere, but I can't imagine facing the plane again. It was one thing to relive most of a day in 2009 with Edward, but I lived *weeks* in the timeline with Rian and felt all of them keenly.

She seems to understand my exhaustion but won't yield. "Come now. This is a horse you need to get back on. Maybe an easier trip this time, yes?"

I look at her, pleading. "What if I just go spend a week on a beach in Hawaii, drinking rum-based cocktails and trying to figure out my future from there? I don't know if my answers are on the beach, but it wouldn't hurt to look, right?"

"That may be a good idea yet, but all in good time. I think it's time we look at things a bit differently. Instead of playing patchwork and trying to mend what you thought were your mistakes, let's see what might have happened if you'd made some different choices altogether, shall we? It might give you a fresh perspective."

My shoulders sag, but it does sound less fraught than trying to salvage relationships clearly destined to fail.

"Think of a path you didn't take, dearie. Let's try it out."

I rack my brain for a few moments. "Okay . . . what if I'd applied for the job as a sommelier in Copenhagen?" I'd talked myself out of applying for a position at The Mesmerist, an eccentric restaurant in Copenhagen, thinking the job was out of my league at the time. I'd only just earned entry-level somm certification with the Court of Master while I was in London, shortly after Dublin, and thought I should temper my expectations.

But it was an opportunity I'd wondered about. Had I sold myself short by not applying? What if I'd missed out on a stellar experience?

Rosaline gestures toward the Jetway. "What if, indeed? Let's find out, shall we?"

Chapter 15

COPENHAGEN

This is fine, this is fine.

I force myself to stop shaking, but my nerves have gotten the better of me. It was hard enough to navigate moments from my actual past, but coming to Copenhagen means muddling through a past timeline I never lived in a city I have never visited. If I am in Copenhagen, it means I landed the sommelier job at The Mesmerist. I don't just think but *know* I am in over my head.

My phone tells me the date is July 21, 2016, which fits with the timing I would have expected, directly after my stint in London. I calculate that I am twenty-nine, and it's shortly after I made the transition to front-of-house work to help round out my résumé.

It's always been amazing to me how restaurants are really divided into two worlds. The work is quite different between them, but how draining and rewarding they both can feel on the same day. I love cooking and the camaraderie of the kitchen, but seeing the faces of happy patrons is a special sort of joy I learned to appreciate in this epoch of my career.

My phone confirms that I did, indeed, land the job and that I am not expected until late afternoon. It's just midmorning now, so I need to piece together what Sommelier Sabrina would be up to before service.

It would seem Rosaline was kind enough to leave me a crib sheet of sorts: a slip of paper with my address in the city and other vital information I'd otherwise have no way of knowing, tucked safely in my backpack. I move it to my pocket for easy access. Given her talent for thinking of all possible contingencies, it's a shame there aren't more fairy-godmother types in the travel industry. They do a lot better at managing the experience than the hedge fund billionaires we have running the show now. But I suppose that's an effect of Rosaline actually caring about human beings. I find the taxi stand outside and give the driver my address. This time, I'm not taking in familiar sights but drinking them in for the first time like a proper tourist.

Ironically, my flat is in the Nyhavn neighborhood, one of the most touristy areas of the city. The "New Port" is lined with the row of easily recognized colorful buildings that grace postcards and tourism posters with *København* printed in a whimsical font. My flat is a vibrant blue above a quasi-traditional Danish restaurant that caters to the tourist crowds. It's the sort of place I'd avoid under normal circumstances, but as they're literally neighbors, I'd probably make a point of visiting a couple times a month. Especially in low season when they need the receipts. A glimpse at the menu at least looks promising.

I climb the stairs to the flat, hoping that Rosaline hasn't made a grave error in her instructions. But given that she hasn't steered me wrong yet, I trust that this apartment is either mine or, at a minimum, where I'm supposed to be. I find a likely looking key on the metal key ring in my pack. The key ring is heavy and made of silver-toned metal in the shape of a daisy, which is both the national flower of Denmark and very reminiscent of a Michelin

Star. On the back it's engraved: *Velkommen hjem, Sabrina. Fra Nikolai.*

"Welcome home, Sabrina. From Nikolai."

Who on earth is Nikolai? My Realtor? The engraving is a little too intimate for a corporate gift of that sort, though. *Welcome home, from Smith Realty* purchased in bulk? Okay, sure. But the personalization of it makes it feel like one small step below jewelry. Curiouser and curiouser, but I likely won't find the answers to this mystery in the hallway.

I poise my key to slide it in the lock, but before I turn it, I hear indistinct clattering inside. I pause. Someone is inside. Before assuming I'm being robbed, I pull the paper from my pocket and double-check the address Rosaline provided. I am indeed at the right place.

The most likely explanation is a roommate. Probably this Nikolai? I look down at my hands and see they're ring free, which is a relief. I do *not* want to navigate being thrown into a marriage without the benefit of a courtship to learn the person's ins and outs.

Despite my frugal nature, I have avoided having roommates since culinary school. My erratic schedule doesn't exactly make me the easiest person to live with, and I find the solitude of my own place helps me to cope with the hectic pace of restaurant life. And with my luck, I'd end up with a cheerful morning person who insists on banging and crashing about while I'm trying to catch up on sleep after dinner shifts that drag into the wee smalls.

But if I do have a roommate, their name would have been useful information for Rosaline to include in her notes. A quick scan of the paper confirms that this bit of trivia—who the hell is on the other side of my apartment door?—wasn't worthy of inclusion on her list of fun facts about this version of my life.

We'll have to discuss this omission later.

I take a calming breath. I can't stand out here all day like a marginally sentient gargoyle. I steel my resolve and turn the key. The first thing I notice is a waft of something coming from the kitchen. Something delectable. Notes of thyme, cloves, and bay leaves fairly dance on the air, and I am drawn to discover the source of the luscious aroma by my most primal instincts.

"*Hej.* You're just in time. Come taste what I made." The man, who I have to assume is Nikolai, stands in the archway of the kitchen, his cheeks reddened by the heat of the stove. He is tall, in the grand tradition of our people. Like me, he's blond and his face bears the trademark chiseled features of the Danes, but currently his are tempered with a warm smile. He's dressed in black slacks and a white tee, the standard uniform for anyone who works in a kitchen, with the understandable omission of the chef's jacket, since he is at home, I assume.

And he seems very pleased to see me.

I return the smile almost reflexively. I don't know the nature of our relationship, so I don't know if he's expecting a hug or a kiss on the cheek or . . . even the lips? So I opt for a stilted wave hello from the entryway. Bashful and awkward—always a winning combination.

He gestures for me to follow him to the table in the kitchen where two places are set. And by set, I don't mean he just tossed some forks and knives in the middle of the table for people to grab as needed, as I was guilty of doing for informal meals on my own turf. He'd set the table like he might for important company. The plates and linens are various patterns of cobalt blue and white, with splashes of yellow to add visual interest. Nice dishes, heavy flatware, crystal glasses. A bouquet of fresh white daisies with some yellow dahlias mixed in for a pop of color graces the center of the table.

I shoot a glance at my surroundings. The flat is the epitome of the ineffable Danish word *hygge*: The loose translation is "homey, cozy, and welcoming but without excessive clutter and fuss." And it's not just an aesthetic; it's a whole way of life. My dad embodied it. He had the uncanny ability to make anyone feel at home, wherever he was. I feel the same vibe here and am not sure what to make of it.

The color theme from the table linens is echoed in the living room, but the effect manages to not be too matchy-matchy. Two indigo throw blankets are draped artfully on the creamy-white leather sofa. Three decorative pillows in coordinating blue-and-white patterns, all placed strategically, break up the sleek lines of the minimalist furniture. Three pillows, not twelve.

I'm stunned by the realization that in this timeline, I really own throw pillows. Those decadent, unnecessary throw pillows that have niggled at the back of my brain for months now. Well, I am at least throw-pillow adjacent, which is almost the same thing.

The whole place is airy and bright and . . . *hygge*. And I have no idea how I can afford even half the rent here.

The kitchen is a marvel of Danish functionality, equipped with every convenience a chef might ever desire. And it's evident Nikolai is a chef of the first order. He pulls out a chair for me and sets a magazine-worthy plate at my place. The main is thinly sliced guinea fowl that has been roasted in a Riesling sauce, pungent with the aromatic herbs that greeted me at the door. He's paired it with a mushroom-risotto cake so perfect, I wonder if he didn't arrange each grain by hand, and a small pile of sesame snap peas with carrots and red peppers adds a dash of color.

He sets his plate next to, not across from, mine, and I'm not sure how much I should read into it. His body language seems relaxed, so it's safe to assume I didn't move in last week, but I can't tell if his feelings are romantic or not. Copenhagen is an eye-wateringly expensive city, so it's not shocking I'd need to share rent. Especially for a flat directly on the canal. He doesn't reach over to caress my knee or make any other sort of familiar gesture, so I just try to mirror his ease.

I sample the guinea fowl and fail to restrain a moan of unbridled bliss. It is possibly the best thing I have tasted in my long and storied career. That includes Edward's gingerbread *espuma*, my curried Créole sauce, and the astounding meal I splurged on for my thirtieth birthday at Le Bernardin in New York. I'd dined alone that night, but the food had been company enough.

"Good?" His hopeful eyes are fixed on me. I realize instantly that he's not fishing for a compliment but asking for real feedback. Colleague to colleague. It's clear he values my opinion, and I can't help but soften a bit. Apparently, the way to my heart is by appealing to my professional sensibilities. How romantic of me.

I reward him with a smile. "You got the herbs just right, and the sear on the bird is spot-on. Well done." I sample the mushroom-risotto cake and the peas and offer similar accolades. Every note is perfection, and it all works beautifully together. I make my praise specific because it's clear he's a serious chef who isn't just after a pat on the head.

I want to ask him questions about his work, but these are things that I, as a roommate, would know already. "I think it's ready for a specials menu." Seems safe enough. I can't ask if he'll audition the dish. He might be head chef somewhere. He's certainly talented enough, if on the young side, to have climbed so high on the ladder. Though I'm not particularly adept at guessing ages, I can't imagine he's much older than thirty. Thirty-two at the most—a few years older than me, but not many.

"From your lips to Chef Bjørn's ears." His smile is a rueful one.

Key bit of information unlocked: Chef Bjørn is the renowned head chef at The Mesmerist. The brains and talent behind one of the most unique restaurants in the world. So Nikolai and I are colleagues; he in the back of house and I in the front.

"You don't think he'll consider it?" I think back to my insecurities in Ireland and hope I can disabuse him of any similar line of thought.

He shakes his head. "Bjørn has a concept, and the chefs are just there to execute it."

I want to reach over and pat his knee to console him but refrain. This man may be Copenhagen Sabrina's bestie. Or boyfriend. I have no way of knowing. But I *do* know he's my colleague, so I'll let him take the lead on physical contact. Anything as tedious as landing in an HR hearing does not seem like the wisest use of time travel.

"That seems like such a waste of talent." And it is. I totally understand that Bjørn is a sort of wunderkind in our profession and he is entitled to focus the kitchen's efforts to support his vision. But the chefs who work under him aren't robots. They are world-class chefs in their own right. By not incorporating their ideas and creativity, he's leaving a tremendous resource untapped.

It's something Éugenie Rosier understood when she brought Maison Ortense into prominence. Every set of hands in the kitchen is an asset, and none of them should be taken for granted, and she'd imparted that lesson to Joëlle.

But Bjørn "knows better" and the result is disaffected talent like Nikolai.

"I can drink to that." He pours me a scant glass of Riesling, left over from the sauce, to go with the meal. "A half glass before service won't dull your palate."

I accept the wine, but my stomach lurches. I am going to have to fake an entire six-hour dinner service as sommelier. I *am* a fully trained sommelier, but it has been years since I used those skills in any real way. After Dublin, I apprenticed as a sommelier at a posh hotel in London, learning the service end of the trade on the floor and cramming in theory courses around my shifts. I honed my tasting skills whenever the opportunity and my budget allowed.

It is possible to spend thousands of dollars on wine to prepare for the blind tasting part of the exam, but I tried to do it on the cheap when possible. It took a year, but I got my Certified Sommelier designation, the lowest of the three tiers, from the Court of Master Sommeliers. Advanced certification would have taken another couple of years, realistically, but an attainable goal if I'd been so inclined. Earning the title Master Sommelier is a lifetime endeavor, however, and far beyond the level I needed to bolster my résumé.

When an opening for a sommelier at The Mesmerist had come available in my original timeline, I'd been torn. It was the sort of thing that garnered notice on a résumé, but I wasn't sure it was the kind I wanted. "She's eaten *there*" carries some street cred in the industry, but I had wondered if "she worked *there*" might be a double-edged sword. I would have the clout of having been selected to work at one of the most unique restaurants in the world, but would people wonder if the eccentricity of the place might lead me to make odd choices as a sommelier?

The Mesmerist is something of a legend in the industry, but it's as much a theater as it is a fine-dining establishment. It has two Michelin stars, but when I'd been considering my options, it seemed too far removed from the rest of the restaurant world to give me transferable skills. I'd skipped applying altogether.

In my original timeline I instead went to Boston, not a Michelin city back then, and worked as a beverage manager for an upscale white-tablecloth steak-and-seafood place. Their wine list punched way above their weight class by the time I had my way, and the chef had accepted the challenge to bring the food up to par with it. That job wasn't the most exciting entry on my résumé, but I was proud of leaving that restaurant better than I'd found it.

But it had been taking the safe route. I've spent more than a little time wondering if I was too cautious with my choices in this era of my life. But at the time, the idea of applying for a position at such a prestigious restaurant with only basic credentials in hand felt presumptuous. Rude, even. Yes, I'd done well on the sommelier certification tests and had stellar recommendations, but there had to have been dozens of other candidates with far more experience and much better pedigrees than I could boast vying for the job.

I can't imagine how I stood out among the applicants, beyond having a modest working knowledge of Danish, thanks to my father, that other foreign applicants might not have. I am intrigued by the art and science of the sommelier's world, but I feel less secure in my ability to identify the varietals, vintner, and vintage of a wine from a few sniffs and a sip than I do in any other element of the restaurant business.

A saucier's work is nothing short of alchemy, it's true. Their work takes patience, skill, and a good sense of timing. But all those things can be learned at the stove by dint of hard work if one has the drive. A true sommelier, though? Those are born, not made. One can study the books, travel to the vineyards, and taste every wine in creation, but the nose and the palate of a gifted sommelier can only be honed—not forged from nothing.

And while I don't consider myself a total loss when it comes to the art of wine and drink pairings, I'm nothing like a master of the craft.

I raise a glass to him. "To the finest chef in Nyhavn, even if Bjørn can't see beyond the end of his nose."

Nikolai snorts with light derision but raises his glass to clink against mine. "At least we will have some fuel to get us through service."

"This is more than fuel—it's art." And I mean it. Were he newer to the craft, I wouldn't be concerned about his creativity getting stifled. Learning to bring Bjørn's fantastical creations from concept through execution is akin to years of advanced culinary training, and it would be invaluable experience for an entry-level or intermediate chef. But Nikolai is ready to lead. I can tell this from a few bites. Even more important, I sense he has the even temperament that would make him run one hell of a good kitchen.

He wraps an arm around me in a quick embrace. I don't hate it. "That means a lot coming from you."

I take his gesture to mean he's comfortable with a bit of touch, so I gently knock my shoulder against his. "Far be it from me to withhold praise where it's due. You're talented."

He knocks shoulders with me in return. "I owe a lot of it to you, you know. Lessons in exchange for rent has been the best bargain of my life."

Ah, that explains how I'm able to afford this place. But how is *he* able to afford it for both of us on the salary of a sous-chef? He may only be a *chef de partie* for all I know. But have I really been that instrumental in his cooking?

Just then, a sleek black cat with a small patch of white on his neck, akin to a priest's collar, hops onto the table and curls up in the empty space to my right as though he's claiming his rightful place. He shows no interest in the food but is more interested in being part of the family.

Nikolai rolls his eyes. "Spoiled Pjuske. Don't try that when *Farmor* comes to visit. She doesn't believe kitties should join us at the table. Even handsome boys like you."

I parse the Danish from the sentence. One word is easy: *Farmor*—paternal grandmother—must be referring to Nikolai's own mother. I wonder if she visits often and hope she's kinder than Orla or Robin, but I'll reserve any judgment for now. That Nikolai speaks to the cat as he would his own toddler is ridiculously endearing.

I mentally scan my limited Danish vocabulary for the more obscure term, and remember that *pjuske* is something akin to "fluffy" but has the connotation of "disheveled" as well. A misnomer of the worst sort, given that he is the most elegant creature I've ever beheld. His fur is suited for the dress code of a society cocktail party. And a red bow tie on his collar to boot. Pjuske blinks slowly at me, so I reward him with gentle scritches under his chin. "Pjuske? For this refined gentleman?"

I realize I've misspoken. This version of me likely would have known the story of the name. Thankfully it doesn't seem to faze Nikolai.

"You didn't see him when I found him. He was nothing but skin, bones, and matted fur. No one would have been able to guess how dapper he would become in time. Hard to believe he lived under my bed until you came along."

I can't control my countenance. Copenhagen Sabrina would know Pjuske's story, and Nikolai will think I'm a nutcase. But it doesn't make sense. I am hardly a cat whisperer; I've never even considered owning a pet before. Shuffling a cat or a dog from one job to the next, one *country* to the next, is a larger headache than I'd want to take on.

"I know you don't believe me, but until the day you moved in, he wanted nothing to do with mankind. You showed him people are worth trusting."

Pjuske, as if to illustrate his point, climbs into my lap, takes one turn before settling in, and purrs like an outboard motor. Despite the coziness I feel here, I still feel waves of tension dispelling as I absorb the cat's vibrations. He is the very embodiment of trust and affection. For reasons I can't define, the threat of tears pricks the corners of my eyes.

I snuggle the cat closer. "I'm glad you were able to keep him."

Nikolai reaches over to scratch between Pjuske's ears, and he, too, is rewarded with the slow blinks that denote trust and affection in a cat. "Yes. It took a little convincing for my parents to allow him here, but in the end, he does less damage to the property than holiday renters. Speaking of which, Dad says he'll be by shortly to see about the tile in your bathroom. Having this place on Vrbo for so many years took a bit of a toll."

The place looks pristine to me, but I haven't seen the whole flat yet. "Oh, that's great. Thank you."

More key information unlocked: The flat is owned by his family, which I hope means a steep discount on rent. I feel marginally less guilty about the arrangement now. Though I do wonder if I should offer to help with the cost of any repairs since it seems I'm not paying rent.

Also key: Nikolai referenced *my* bathroom, which implies we don't share one. And if we don't share a bathroom, I think it's safe to infer our sleeping quarters are separate as well. So I have to assume we're not an item. If we are, it's still early days and we're taking things slowly by sharing only the common spaces of the flat, like the kitchen and the living room. An unusual arrangement, but it will be easier for me to fit in than if I were trying to be an impostor in a committed relationship that's had months to develop.

And I do feel like a bit of an impostor in my own life.

Nikolai crosses to the fridge and produces a miniature *Jordbærtærte*—strawberry tart—that is simply the strawberriest thing I've ever tasted. The dark chocolate and marzipan can't compete with the berries, and it's like they decided to accept their role as support flavors. Dad used to wax poetic about summer strawberries in Denmark, but it wasn't just the rose-colored glasses of youth and nostalgia that fueled his description. They really are juicier and more flavorful than any specimen I've tasted before.

Pjuske sniffs at the confection out of curiosity, but astonishingly, he doesn't attempt to sample Nikolai's handiwork. It's like he understands the rules he must follow to be allowed table privileges.

"You have to charge me rent," I declare at length. "I can't think of what else I can teach you." I don't break eye contact with the dessert, as though I'm afraid it will wander off my plate.

He laughs and places a hand on my knee. "Never. And my parents wouldn't hear of it. They could never charge the daughter of their favorite old school chum."

I exhale. They knew Dad? I want to pelt Nikolai with questions. How had they known him? For how long? Longer than I had, obviously, since they had to have met him before I was born. I shove down a small pang of jealousy that they'd been able to know him in his prime while I had not. I don't remember him speaking of his life here beyond the typical childhood reminiscences and lavish descriptions of the restaurant scene. He hadn't mentioned any friends so dear they would offer his daughter free lodging.

And I just happen to work at the same restaurant as their son? The coincidence seems remarkable that I would stumble over these people on my first-ever trip to my father's homeland. Deep down, I know that the connection to my father is exactly why I've stayed away.

For years I've wondered if every tall, blond man would remind me of Dad. Would I feel his stoic presence in the storied, historic buildings of the old town or his vibrant energy in the brightly colored façades of the trendy neighborhoods? Would I look for him around every corner and feel that familiar ache when I realized it was just another stranger?

But clearly there are people here who aren't strangers. They are friends I never knew I had.

Chapter 16

It isn't perfect, but it will hold." Oskar Rasmussen, Nikolai's father, stands in my bathroom, arms akimbo, surveying the four tiles he'd replaced with the precision of an accomplished craftsman. There had been some hairline cracks in the existing tiles I probably never would have noticed if they hadn't been pointed out to me, and Oskar had insisted on making the repairs himself. He looks remarkably like his son, just with more white around the temples, stylish tortoiseshell glasses, and the stubbly beard of a retired man who has gleefully given up daily shaving.

"It looks better than new. Thank you so much. I'm happy to—"

He holds up a hand before I can finish my sentence. "*Nej.* I could not look myself in the mirror if I took a single krone from Jannick Sorensen's daughter. And the damage wasn't caused by you."

"Dinner then." I shoot him the best imitation of my dad's "I'm not accepting no for an answer" look. "And soon."

He holds up both hands in mock surrender. "I will never say no to a meal cooked by you and my son. I don't think there is a flat in Copenhagen with more culinary talent under its roof."

His expression is one of pride, but the tinge of grief there is unmistakable.

I can't come out and ask outright, but I can test the waters to see if my hunch about the root of his sorrows is correct. "I'd be nowhere without my dad's influence. He was the one who shoved me into the world of fine dining."

Oskar barks a full-bellied laugh. "I've no doubt my old friend Jannick was persuasive, but the way I understand it, all he had to do was lead the proverbial horse to water. You drank from the waters eagerly enough." A cloud passes over his face. "Before the accident he wrote to me to tell me how proud he was of you."

I place a steadying hand on the cool marble of the bathroom sink. "You kept up correspondence all these years?" Dad had been in the States for almost twenty-five years before he passed. I can't imagine not seeing letters posted from Denmark in the hundreds of times I fetched the mail in my eighteen years at home.

Oskar shakes his head. "*Nej*. Both of us were stubborn, but he was the better man of the two of us. He wrote to me when you went off to culinary school in New York. Something about you going off and seeking the dream he and I shared must have inspired him to reach out. We only had the time to exchange a couple of letters before he was taken from us."

This feels like a fresh confession, so Copenhagen Sabrina apparently hasn't pressed the issue. I wonder why . . . And while there is no way I can contain my curiosity well enough to allay this conversation, I do hope there isn't a reason why the Sabrina native to this timeline has been more circumspect. But I press anyway. "You and he wanted to work in the restaurant business?"

A smile tugs at the corners of his lips. "Yes, we had a grand vision of opening a restaurant together: La Mer Grise. We were going to be spoken of in the same breath as Escoffier and Carême."

I chuckle at the idea of my father at the height of his youthful bravado. "So why didn't you?"

The merry twinkle in his blue eyes dims a bit. "Ah, a tale as old as the gray sea itself. We quarreled. Over a girl, naturally."

I don't want to derail his soliloquy with a question, so I just offer an encouraging, "Oh?"

He gestures toward the living room where Nikolai and his mother are conversing on the sofa over coffee. "Yrse. For me, it's always been Yrse. I can't say I'm sorry she chose me, but I *am* sorry it cost me my dearest friend."

"That's so sad." I can't think of anything more profound to add. If Dad was willing to leave Denmark and everyone he knew and loved because of Yrse, whom I met briefly earlier as she assisted Oskar in the tile repairs, he must have loved her beyond words. Which seemed to be the only way he was capable.

I had always thought Robin was the end-all and be-all for him. From my perspective he'd certainly loved her like she was the only woman in the world, and he was lucky enough to have been chosen from among billions of eligible suitors. To know there had been love before her shouldn't be surprising. He was a grown man when he'd met her, after all. But it was still jarring to think of his life here and all the secrets it held.

Oskar shakes himself from his reverie. "Well, if your father hadn't gone to America, you wouldn't be here now. And I know in my soul your father had no regrets on that score. I'm only sorry he wasn't given the time to come back and introduce you himself as he planned to. He said in his letter that he hoped to surprise you with a trip for your graduation."

"He did talk about bringing me here. I was always sorry we

never got the chance. And it seemed wrong to come here without him." I had wrestled with the worry that feeling his presence here would be too painful, or worse, that I wouldn't feel him at all. The pain of losing someone so dear is awful, but no one tells you how much worse it is when you realize how much the pain has dulled. It's like losing them a second time.

"I should have reached out after the accident. I suppose I let my grief get the better of me, and I couldn't bear to write to your mother as I should have done. I am sorry for that. But perhaps you were meant to meet us now, after you have had time to adjust to your loss a little more."

Oskar is probably right. Meeting him, Yrse, and Nikolai so soon after Dad's passing might have been too much to process. They carry a bit of him in their hearts, just as I do.

I cast my eyes downward and will the tears not to fall. As many do-overs as Rosaline might allow, the life in which Dad survived his fall and we came here when I was fresh out of culinary school wasn't one I'd ever get to see. The life where Oskar was a beloved avuncular figure in my early adulthood. Where Nikolai and I would have entered the culinary trenches at around the same time. I might have stayed here in Copenhagen instead of meeting Edward in New Orleans. Nikolai and I might have built each other up, rather than Edward and I flinging insults at a Christmas party. Life might have been very different.

Oskar wraps an arm around me. "I don't mean to upset you, *min skat*." I flinch at the endearment my father used so often. "But, selfishly, having you here is a chance to make a few things right. And it is a joy to see you and Nikolai share the flat your father and I shared as young men. It feels like life has come full circle in a way."

I return his embrace. I can see why Dad had felt a kinship with this man. And more things start to make sense. Dad had been grieving his friendship with Oskar and his unrequited love for Yrse so much that he couldn't bring himself to talk about them. And if Oskar's reactions are any sort of metric, leaving them behind had been the hardest sacrifice of his too-short life.

He'd loved so deeply, he'd had to leave. Whereas me? I've never stayed anywhere long enough to make the sort of human connections I'd miss. Have I been too scared to love anyone as much as I loved my father?

I circle back to Oskar's previous statement. "This was Dad's flat too?" I hope this isn't something Copenhagen Sabrina should already know, but I get the sense she's kept Nikolai and his family at arm's length. Her pain is a bit fresher than mine, after all.

He nods, not acting as though this is old hat. "It belonged to his parents, and they left it to him when they died. It may have been in the family for a few generations before that, too, though I can't be sure. Yrse and I bought it from him so he'd have the funds to get a start in America. It was the only help he would accept from anyone. But I've considered this the Sorensen home my whole life. I thought about selling it a time or two, but I could never bring myself to do it. Closest I could do is rent it out, and we see what a mess that was." He gestures to the repaired tiles that, in all honesty, would have been fine for quite some time as they were. "But to see you back here does my heart good."

I swallow back so many words. It's hard to imagine this place that has been updated with so many modern conveniences being my dad's boyhood home. His parents' home. Who knows how many of my ancestors lived and died within these very walls? But rather than feeling haunted by the ghosts of generations past, I feel . . . at home.

"Are you two making porcelain for new tiles in there?" Yrse's voice, rather lyrical and her English more accented than her husband's, floats into the bathroom before she herself enters it.

Despite decades of marriage, Oskar's face brightens at the sight of his wife. "All finished, *min kærlighed*. Just reminiscing about old times with our Sabrina."

She smiles and wraps an arm around me. "*Meget godt*. Having her here is like having a bit of Jannick back with us, is it not?"

"Exactly so." Oskar's voice is husky. "But we sentimental old fools are probably boring her socks off."

"Not at all. Quite the opposite. It's wonderful to hear about him from other people who loved him." I squeeze Yrse back. She radiates kindness, and it's plain to me why Dad would have been smitten with her. She actually looks a bit like Robin, but without the barbed tongue.

I realize it *has* been a long time since I got to reminisce about Dad. Robin changes the subject, Brian clams up, and Chloe was young enough that she didn't get to relate to him on an adult level. She remembers trips to Disneyland and being hoisted on his shoulders at parades, not long conversations about sustainable restaurant management and the virtues and limitations of the farm-to-table movement. I love gabbing with her about the early childhood memories, but Chloe and I just can't connect about him on quite the same level.

We return to the living room, where Nikolai is pouring more coffee and has added a platter of butter cookies to the coffee table. Made from scratch, no doubt. And though I am still stuffed from lunch, I have to sample his handiwork, which is obviously incredible.

We chat for a solid hour about everything and nothing. More than a little about Dad and their shared experiences at school and the two years shortly after. Like Dad, Oskar had avoided the restaurant business. He'd become a watchmaker, like his father. It wasn't his passion, but he enjoyed his work. I think neither of them could face their old dream without the other, but both were thrilled to see their children go into the industry they'd intended for themselves.

In this instance I don't mind the vicarious living. Nikolai and I have come to the field of our own volition. His rapport with his parents is easy, and I find mine is too. Rather than being distracted counting down the minutes until I can excuse myself from their company, I am enjoying the conversation and being in the company of people who share this connection with me.

I'm sad when Nikolai looks down at his watch and declares, "We should leave for service soon." Odd, given how anxious I usually am to dive into work. I exchange hugs with his parents, who look pleased when Nikolai casually wraps an arm around me as they turn for a final wave.

Chapter 17

As I step from Nikolai's black Škoda, the ground feels unstable beneath my feet. A bit too literally. I force my wobbly knees into submission and fight the sensation, summoning every bit of bravado I keep in reserve. I will have to act with all the self-assurance I was able to muster in New Orleans or Dublin . . . but without any firsthand experience to guide me.

I'm shocked when, instead of going to the kitchen, Nikolai goes behind the bar. It's worse than I thought. He's not a chef whose talents are being underutilized—he's a bartender whose talents aren't being utilized *at all*. It takes every bit of my resolve not to go into the kitchen and tell Chef Bjørn what a fool he is right to his face.

The expression on Nikolai's face is somber as he sets to polishing glasses and dusting bottles before service. He does look up at me and smile with a "good luck" before returning to his preservice checklist. His words don't feel so much encouraging as they do cautionary. He's wishing me luck because I'm going to need it.

The Mesmerist is in the industrial part of the city, not terribly far from the airport, so I have an exit if things go disastrously wrong. We're earlier than necessary for our shift, and for this I am grateful. I'll have at least a few minutes to familiarize myself with the wine list and the layout of the place in peace. I hope I can gain my bearings before the rest of the staff comes in and wonders why I am bumbling around like a new hire on their first day. Though effectively, that's what I am. Under normal circumstances, this would be fine. I've been the new kid in town so many times that it comes with a dose of adrenaline I find pleasant, in a demented sort of way. What I don't like is feeling incompetent when I, in the eyes of my colleagues at least, have several months of experience under my belt and should be well up to speed.

Within moments I realize there is no hope whatsoever of getting my bearings. The restaurant is divided into several distinct areas: The first is a dark foyer where guests are greeted with an amuse-bouche and a beverage by a server who more closely resembles a mime than someone in food service. Next, they're led into a breathtaking lounge where bottles of wine are stacked to the ceiling in a labyrinthine series of plexiglass cubbies so complex it reminds me of a thriving beehive. This is where Nikolai will be stationed for service, and I am grateful I'll have access to him if I need help. I *hate* depending on colleagues to bail me out, but this may have to be one of those times.

The lounge alone nearly gives me the vapors. Even if I could somehow memorize the wine list—and it is *vast*—how would I be able to find a specific bottle among the thousands on display? I've read about this place and watched several videos, but seeing it firsthand is something no human recording device can replicate. There are two more areas, but I can't bring myself to contemplate those just yet.

I stay in the lounge, which is where I will first greet my guests. The servers are now buzzing about like gray-clad worker bees, trying to ensure the tables are ready for inspection. There is no menu, as such. Naturally, allowances are made for allergies, all noted in a computer system that is likely sophisticated enough to run the entire European nuclear program. But the typical guest at The Mesmerist comes in expecting to eat what they're served for each course. I use the term *course*, but in reality, they are more like "encounters" with various food concoctions.

It's sort of like an endless flow of tapas, but most offerings are even smaller than the Spanish small plates. The typical dish is one or two bites and is engineered with more thought behind it than the construction of the Brooklyn Bridge. Fifty of them over the course of six hours. Per guest. Fifty guests per night at staggered intervals. Twenty-five hundred dishes served per evening, not including any extra beverages. The amount of labor—just on the service side alone—is mind-boggling.

Behind the main bar in the lounge, I find a grid with an employee schedule, complete with names and job titles, including mine and Nikolai's. At least he's lead bartender. He *should* be sous-chef or the *chef de partie* in charge of pastry. His guinea fowl was incredible, but his tart and butter cookies are what remain emblazoned in my memory.

When Nikolai's head is turned, I snap a photo of the directory with my phone so I can reference it later if I need to. I also learn I am not *the* sommelier, but one of several on duty tonight. I glean from the website that the guests can choose a "sommelier experience," which means those opting for this expensive package will get near-constant attention from a sommelier over the course of their evening. This explains how I was able to land the job: They needed far more of us on staff than the average restaurant. I make sure my Certified Sommelier pin is affixed securely to my lapel and endeavor to take a deep breath.

I study what I can and let the relief wash over me when I discover there are various beverage flights that can be purchased. For wine, there are three tiers that range from expensive to large mortgage payment, as well as "mixed" flights that include cocktails, beer, and nonalcoholic beverages. A surprising number of fermented beverages like kombucha are available, which is certainly on trend, but I would think these would be difficult to pair well with many foods without overpowering them. I cross my fingers and hope to persuade my guests that one of the wine flights is the way to go. It removes most if not all of the guesswork and should lead to the best possible experience.

I locate all the wines on the three tiers and find that Chef Bjørn has even indicated which glasses he wants used for each segment of the meal. I begin to believe I might not embarrass myself entirely. The odd patron will want a cocktail, which Nikolai will manage, and there will be guests celebrating special occasions who will want champagne. Easy enough. Unless an emergency causes us to retool the menu on the fly, which seems unlikely given Chef Bjørn's reputation for precision, I feel like I can manage the service. Maybe.

A truly good sommelier would be able to go off the cuff in a place like this and love the challenge of it. Few restaurants have lists this comprehensive or pairings so unusual. They would know the wine list and the planned menu frontward and back and take an active role in the theater of the place. They would help weave the story that Chef Bjørn is trying to tell. And that monumental task is one I am not equal to. The best I can do tonight is fake it.

And I *hate* faking it.

The general manager, whose name I gather from the roster is Svend Madsen, walks in. He's every bit the tall Nordic man one would expect to see on a Danish tourism poster. I do a stealthy Google search on him and learn he is *very* prominent on the Danish food scene. He's in his late fifties but looks twenty years younger. Blond with chiseled facial features, and wearing an expression without an ounce of humor, Svend looks little removed from his Viking roots. Only a pristine navy pinstripe suit takes the place of crude garments of leather and homespun wool, and his hair is cropped short rather than left to grow wild. Despite his impeccable attire and grooming, it's all too easy to imagine him in a rough-hewn horned helmet out of a Wagnerian opera.

"Are you ready for service?" His words are growled more than spoken, but in perfect British English. It feels more like he's asking my competence to serve in the armed forces than to pour a few glasses of wine. Has something in particular set him off, or is this just his usual sunshiny disposition? I refrain from smiling, figuring American ebullience would only irritate him further.

"Of course." I speak with more confidence than I've earned, but I sense he isn't the sort to look at any sort of equivocation with anything other than hostility.

He nods and moves along, presumably to the kitchen, but not before his steely blue eyes shoot me a glare that feels like it will bore a hole in the very fabric of my soul.

Nikolai leans closer to me from across the bar and stage whispers, "Once again you survived the Madsen death glare. Well done."

I smile, despite my nerves quaking as I see on the clock behind the bar how close we are to opening doors. "What can I say? I'm made of stern stuff."

"Danish hardware with American programming. A formidable combination." He sends me a wink from behind the bar, and I have to stifle a laugh. Given the quiet atmosphere, it feels like trying not to giggle in church. His expression turns more serious. "If you don't mind me saying so, you seem a little off tonight."

"I *feel* a little off, to tell the truth." Honesty is the right choice. If I confess to feeling a bit wonky, it'll cover any missteps I make. And I know I'm likely to. And a bit of sympathy may lead to a discreet helping hand if I fumble.

"You know the list better than anyone here. Why so edgy?" He's prodding, but out of concern. It doesn't feel like he's trying to uncover the mask of an impostor. Even if that's exactly what I am.

"Svend 'Death Glare' Madsen doesn't help my nerves." It's a convenient excuse and has the benefit of being at least part of the reason I feel like I am walking into an important final exam for which I am wholly unprepared. "And I don't want to incite his ire by botching anything."

Nikolai snorts in derision. "You'll incite his ire even if you don't. Just do the job and try not to throw a glass of pinot noir in Madsen's face before the end of the night. That's as good as it gets here."

I decide to make light. "Right, red wine would stain, and I don't want to foot a bill for a new suit. Pinot gris it is."

He nods, his expression deadpan. "That's what makes you management material."

It's my turn to snort in derision. It would be several more years before I make the jump to GM, and it's not like that was a glowing success.

The banter has me feeling a little lighter, and I want to kiss Nikolai on the cheek for his help. But I refrain because I'm sure Svend has strict rules about displaying any sort of human emotion while on duty. The first guests should be arriving in twenty minutes, and I try to commit as much of the wine list to memory as I can. It's probably futile, but a few scraps of information are better than none.

My study is interrupted by the sound of heavy footfalls on the marble floor. I look up to see Svend making a beeline in my direction, his eyes laser focused on me. I close the thick leather wine list and put all my energy into screwing a neutral expression on my face.

"We have some important American influencers coming today. From *YouTube*." He says the word with such disdain I worry it'll permanently affect their website traffic. "Chef Bjørn wants them accommodated; whatever they want is on the house."

YouTube influencers? Is that really necessary? The question hovers on my tongue, but I don't speak it. The restaurant only opens the reservation portal quarterly, and they sell out in minutes. With heavy, nonrefundable deposits too. Comping a table of YouTubers when we don't need to scare up business seems like a waste of several thousand dollars to me.

The question must be telegraphed on my face, though, because Svend answers it immediately. "Chef believes it will help increase visibility with a younger demographic. He is constantly concerned with remaining relevant."

This is a fair point. Fine dining has historically been a hobby of the "upper middle age" set. I've found the regular clientele in places like these are generally late in their careers or early in retirement and finished raising their kids. They have the money, the time, and the energy reserves to travel in style. The problem is that with uncertain economic times and fewer secure jobs to be had, younger Gen Xers and Millennials aren't poised to take over the void left when their Boomer parents begin to weary of chasing reservations at the new hot spot in town and dressing to the nines. But that, heretofore, hasn't been a problem at The

Mesmerist, which is hip enough to draw in the young elite who can foot the staggering bill.

Svend continues, "As for me, I want their visit to be as unobtrusive as possible. You will be their sommelier for the night and will stay with the table the entire evening."

His subtext is clear: *You're the American in-house. You'll babysit your idiot countrymen and make sure they aren't a nuisance to the other—paying—guests.* While it will be somewhat of a relief to have only one table to contend with, it will be an exercise in always being on hand without hovering, which is maddening for all involved.

I meet his gaze, unflinching. "I wonder if they wouldn't rather have a sommelier who *isn't* American. They might prefer a more authentically Danish experience."

"This is the best possible arrangement." He speaks in declaratives without room for nuance. He probably thinks it conveys a commanding presence, but it mostly serves to make him seem like a petulant child. Of course he does have authority in this situation, but he lacks real leadership skills.

I narrowly avoid rolling my eyes. "As you wish."

"Their manager confirmed they will be here in fifteen minutes." He walks off without further conversation.

Manager? They're important enough to need a manager? I always envisioned "influencers" as being goofy teens with hand-me-down iPhones doing stunts and overly tanned twenty-three-year-olds giving makeup tutorials. Clearly the world of internet stardom is beyond me.

He returns through the great doors that separate the lounge from the restaurant's main room, hopefully to share his sour disposition elsewhere.

Nikolai, whose hands are busy wiping away nonexistent smudges off pristine glassware with a stark white linen cloth, shakes his head after the doors close behind Svend. "Sorry about that. They must be pretty high profile if Chef thinks they're VIPs, though. It'll be a good chance to show off."

I try to force a smile, but showing off is the last thing I'm qualified to do in this situation. I take one last steadying breath and hope I don't make a fool of myself.

I have just enough time to do recon on our influencers. I'd hoped it would be one of the dignified YouTube channels with decent production values where cultured travelers trot the globe to feature the best of the best in fine dining and local hidden gems. The kind that provides legitimately valuable information for the jet set and travel/food escapism for the mere mortals who, if they ever did manage to save up for plane tickets to Denmark, would have to eat bread and cheese from the supermarket or try their luck with food carts for the duration of their stay.

I admit to watching too many of those videos in my own spare time, justifying them as industry research. But this is nothing like that at all. Their channel is devoted to adventure travel and "exotic experiences" aimed at a much younger demographic.

Among their extensive catalog of videos, I don't see a single video dedicated to a restaurant or food at all. This sort of video seems totally off-brand for them. Why would someone as famously discerning as Chef Bjørn feel the need to give free table space to this sort of influencer? But then I see they have six million followers, more than twice my favorite foodie channel's subscriber base. The temptation to welcome them makes sense now—but I share Svend's apprehensions.

At the appointed hour four young adults—two men, two women—dressed stylishly in all black appear in the lounge. Svend appraises their attire and gives a look of restrained approval as he leads them to me. And I admit, they look perfectly appropriate for the venue. Fashion-forward but minimalist . . . which is how I'd describe most of Denmark, really. Not that I've had the time to see much of it beyond my flat yet.

They were greeted with a glass of peach kombucha and little crackers made of caramelized seaweed in the foyer . . . and now I am on duty. I'm poised with a wine list and a spiel about why any of the wine flights would be the best possible choice for them, but they are far more invested in filming than they are in anything I might have to say.

"We're actually here at The Mesmerist, *the* premier dining experience in Copenhagen!" the shorter of the two women screeches into the high-end DSLR camera held by a wiry-looking man, who seems either anxious or overcaffeinated. Or very likely both. Svend shoots me a murderous look. *Keep them quiet. Your job is on the line.*

Fabulous. If I flub this up, it will make for a very serious blip in my future. To work at a restaurant of this caliber without leaving with a good reference in hand is career suicide.

The taller brunette woman and the man without the camera squeeze into the frame and wave. They finally take their seats while the cameraman takes a wide shot of the lounge before turning back to the table. He focuses on the darker-haired woman, who gives a toothy grin to the camera. "Oh my god, guys! You wouldn't believe this place. The entryway is even extra. And this kombucha is incredible. They need to carry this in the States." She swirls her glass of bubbling kombucha for the camera. It resembles champagne, and the effect under the light *is* stunning.

Sadly, she doesn't seem to understand the difference between a small-batch home-fermented kombucha and one mass-produced for sale in a big-box liquor store. Worse, her voice can be heard all the way in Sweden.

I introduce myself to the table before Svend explodes. They seem only mildly interested in my presence and seem utterly bored by my discussion of the wine flights. I finally address the elephant in the room. "I'm thinking it might be best if you take footage and do the voice-over in post? The sound quality will be better, and it will be less obtrusive to the other guests trying to appreciate their meal."

The blonde woman pierces me with a withering glare. "This is what we do. Voice-overs lack spontaneity and authenticity, and that won't resonate with our fan base. Our manager said this was cleared with your people." She speaks with the sort of vocal fry that makes me itch. How anyone can stand to listen to her on videos for more than a few seconds is beyond me.

Svend is glaring at me with equal intensity. Bjørn might have approved this intrusion, but Svend has not. And as their designated handler, I will catch hell if these people continue to speak like they're projecting their un-miked voices to the back of a stadium-sized theater.

I make a mental note for any future work in management: Make sure front and back of house are on the same page and don't put the staff in the middle when their visions clash. It's a crappy place to be as an employee.

But now is *not* the time to act like a mid-level employee, and I summon my managerial gravitas. "All the same, if you could keep your volume down, it would be appreciated." I shoot her back a glare of my own. Not withering, just businesslike. Svend is right that we can't have a comped table ruin the atmosphere for those paying good money for a once-in-a-lifetime experience.

They roll their eyes and give the wine list a cursory glance. They all order the mixed-beverage flight, which contains wine as well as beer and cocktails. They're constantly recording, but their commentary *has* gotten quieter. They accept their beverages without a second glance, which doesn't surprise me. They don't seem to be the sort who would know a prized vintage Châteauneuf-du-Pape from a boxed wine and only care that it gets them buzzed.

If I were less ethical, I'd be tempted to serve them two-buck chuck to see if they'd notice. But alas, we have nothing like cheap wine in-house, and I feel compelled to give them what they order, even if they aren't paying for it.

We survive the first several encounters in the lounge without further incident. They are louder than what Svend would prefer, but I sense that's true of any guest not eating in reverential silence. The moment has come for us to transition to the next phase of the evening, and the influencers follow me to their next table.

My breath catches at the sight of the main room, which is massive and domed, like a planetarium. Projected on the ceiling are images that reflect something about the entrée that is about to be consumed. The messages are sometimes literary, sometimes political. Often about conservation and sustainability, which I admire. All manner of exotic ingredients in jars sit along the wall, giving the place more of a laboratory feel than a restaurant, which doesn't seem wholly inappropriate.

The cameraman, whose name I learn is Devon, takes sweeping shots of the domed room, and I can't blame him for being in awe of the place. The women—the blonde is Jane and the brunette is Riley—give their commentary in appropriately hushed tones, as if recording in a church. Though the atmosphere is closer to that of a modern museum than a place of worship, the quiet veneration still feels appropriate.

One of the first dishes is shaped like an ear, meant to represent how big tech is listening in on, and commodifying, everything we say. It's actually made from pork and vegetables, but it's human-looking enough to be very off-putting. The pictures of ears all over the domed ceiling make the effect even more surreal.

"Oh god, I don't know if I can do this." Riley looks at her plate and whimpers. She motions to Devon to stop recording, and he obliges.

"You have to. It's content." The other man in the group, Brandon, has been mostly silent for the majority of their visit, only speaking when spoken to, and looking rather sullen except when he knows the camera is pointed at him.

From my quick study of their videos, I gather he's more of a stuntman than a foodie, and this is definitely not his wheelhouse. I cringe at his use of the word *content*. As though an amusing reel on social media is the height of what this six-hour dining experience can aspire to.

"Suck it up, Riley." Jane, while the camera is rolling, claims to be "BFFs" with Riley, but that doesn't seem to translate to life off camera. Perhaps that's why they record so much of their lives—their friendship wouldn't tolerate it otherwise.

"No, it's gross." Her voice has gone up several decibels, and I take a few steps closer to the table, ready to intervene.

"It's just like eating bacon." Brandon slices off a small corner of the earlobe and eats it as a pledge of good faith. He glances down at his plate once the flavors have registered. "It's actually the best thing I've tried here so far. Savory and just a bit crunchy."

Riley has gone fully chartreuse. "Ewww, you're gross, Brandon."

Devon, who looks far more haggard than the others, pleads with her. "C'mon, Rile, I need this on film."

"No." She slams her napkin on the table and glares at Devon with such intensity, I worry the camera he has angled at her will melt. Heads have turned in their direction, and the patrons are beginning to look peeved at their antics. Svend, who has been circulating the room, catches my eye. His expression is nothing less than murderous. I intervene with all the professionalism I can muster.

"Hi, we can absolutely clear this for you." In a regular restaurant I'd offer a new entrée on the house, whether she deserved it or not, just to keep her quiet, but I'm unsure what the policy is here when everything is so carefully orchestrated. I opt for something that *is* in my gift. "Would you like another glass of the kombucha you enjoyed so much?"

"Just get this away from me!" She is full-on shrieking now, and the projections of ears all over the dome seem to be setting her off even more.

I clear the plate, handing it discreetly to the server who began rushing toward the table at the sound of the patron's distress. As realistic as the ear looks, I'm not surprised the server seems prepared for this outcome.

Riley seems calmer now that the offending dish is no longer in front of her, but she is clenching her eyes and covering her ears to avoid looking at those in front of every other diner as well as the images of ears of all shapes, sizes, colors, and—I'm sorry to say—volume of ear hair swirling around on the dome overhead.

As obnoxious as Riley and her group are, I feel bad for her.

A meal out, especially one that costs more than most people's monthly take-home pay, should be a pleasant experience. I'm all about food pushing boundaries, but I'm not in favor of a thousand-euro-plus dinner sending a patron into a panic attack.

Svend finally crosses the room to my side, incandescent with rage. He's trying to intimidate me with his piercing stare, but I don't cow under his gaze. I'm not the wet-behind-the-ears kid chopping vegetables at La Fontaine Mirabeau anymore and I won't act like it.

"What is the meaning of this?" he hisses.

I gesture in the direction of the cowering Riley, who is still in sensory-deprivation mode as the ear mosaic is still very much in full swing.

"She is bothering other guests." He discreetly nods in the direction of some patrons who are looking askance at Riley's over-the-top reaction. Not good. But even more upsetting to me is the absolute indifference of her fellow influencers, who have continued filming as though all is perfectly well. They keep Riley carefully out of the frame and do nothing to comfort her.

I respond to Svend with the same venom he's been hurling at me. "What would you have me do? Kick her out? That's under *your* purview, not mine." He looks affronted that I've lumped in bouncer duties with those of general manager, but it really *is* his duty more than that of a sommelier.

He takes a step closer, his blue eyes flashing like jagged ice. "I told you to keep them under control."

"That's nice for you. If you haven't noticed, she is an adult human with her own free will. I have done as much as I can to defuse the situation. I don't like having them here any more than you do. If you don't like her behavior, bounce them and take the heat from Bjørn when they pan the place for all six million of their followers. But that's on you. It's. Not. My. Job."

For the briefest moment he looks as though he's impressed by my defiance but then regains his composure. "We'll be revisiting your attitude later."

I don't respond. Because, in fact, we won't be discussing anything later. There is power in knowing I can leave this at any time. But it occurs to me that this always has been and always will be the case. I can leave any unpleasant situation at any time.

And it's probably a good thing I haven't taken advantage of this too often in my past; there is a lot to learn from sticking around even when things are hard. But in this scenario, there is nothing to be gained from letting myself be disrespected by someone like Svend. Or by staying at a restaurant whose vision I can't entirely get behind.

If I were to write this place up in The Anonymous Epicure, and it's more than tempting, I'd have to say it might be worth the experience if you have a few buckets of money lying around to burn and you run in crowds where eating here may get you some bragging rights. But for us mere mortals? We're better off eating in restaurants where the chef thinks about the guests—and the food—over the spectacle of the meal.

Chapter 18

Off so soon?" Nikolai rushes after me as the restaurant begins the process of shutting down for the night.

"Oh, you bet I am." My table of YouTubers has departed with only Riley offering me thanks before they left. I've managed to evade Svend, but I know my luck won't hold for long. While I feel a bit guilty for not trying to figure out what my end-of-service duties entail, I don't feel much like waiting around for a lecture.

I can imagine Svend all too clearly as the washed-up off-off-off-Broadway director in half-moon reading glasses, gripping an ancient clipboard, salivating at the opportunity to berate the cast and crew after a performance to help fill the void in his sad little life. He radiates the sort of bitterness that only years of rejection can produce, and I wonder, with as much disinterest as I can muster, what has gone so terribly wrong in his life.

Maybe *he's* even more in need of a cosmic do-over than I am.

I almost feel sorry for him. Almost.

Nikolai looks around and sees that no one is looking for us. He grabs me by the crook of my arm, and we walk purposefully toward the door, under the misguided notion that if we can't see Svend, he can't see us. Like we fear a fate similar to that of poor

Orpheus and Eurydice from Greek mythology, and don't dare look back.

We clear the restaurant, all but sprinting toward the staff parking lot until we reach his Škoda.

"He was in rare form tonight," Nikolai says once we're on the road. He doesn't head toward the city and our flat, which is fine by me. A setting where the air doesn't fairly crackle with my father's boyhood memories will make it easier to breathe. "The influencers, I suspect."

"Good. I'd hate to think that was his good side." This is not the sort of thing Copenhagen Sabrina would say. She'd be well acclimated to Svend and all his moods by now. But Nikolai knows I'm "off" today, and I can't bring myself to care. "It's not like I can control their behavior."

"I'm sorry you had to take the brunt of it tonight. It's not right." His eyes are focused on the road, but he glances over at me from time to time.

"No. He's the worst sort of GM. He's the kind that conflates bullying with leadership skills, and I can't stand it. He is the face of every toxic workplace I've ever encountered."

Chef Jerome at Hotel Esmeralda immediately comes to mind.

The result of his bullying was Edward, who in turn became a bully himself.

Such sad little people. People who have claim to legitimate talent but whose overinflated sense of it overshadows their work. Maybe Svend is a failed chef himself, and GM at The Mesmerist is the best he could do. And though he isn't legally obligated to make his bitterness everyone else's problem, he manages the task as though he is. At this stage of his life, he'd do better to retire early and take up fishing. That way the only person he'd make miserable is himself.

We sit in silence for a good half hour or more, and I appreciate the calm. There is something about Nikolai's presence that is comforting in a way I haven't experienced with anyone else. With Edward, I was always on edge about saying the wrong thing.

Nikolai pulls over to an overlook by the coast, adjacent to what appears to be a massive bird-watching preserve. The bustle of the city feels a world away, though I know it's not all that far. Nikolai seems to know I need solitude without my saying a word.

He really is incredible. I've only known him a few hours, but I hope Copenhagen Sabrina can see what a catch he is. If she wants to date, she could do a lot worse. But maybe this Sabrina, like me, has been too focused on work to consider jumping back into the dating pool. For her, it's been three years since Rian. For me, it's been both eleven years and a matter of hours. I am in no headspace to offer this version of myself any sort of advice.

Nikolai shuts off the engine, grabs a pack from the back seat, and gestures for me to follow him. A sandy strip of beach is just across the street, mostly empty given the late hour. He offers me his hand, and I accept it. We walk by the sparkling gray waves, still illuminated by the last rays of late-summer sunset. I imagine Copenhagen must be dreary during the short daylight hours of winter, but there's something to having a sunset that lingers past ten at night.

We wander a few minutes, and I find it hard to concentrate on anything other than his hand in mine. He must be thinking the same thing, because he pulls our joined hands up and places a featherlight kiss on the back of my hand.

"I have wanted to hold your hand for a long time, but I've been afraid to rush things. I hope you don't mind . . . I just wanted to comfort you as best I could."

With a shaking breath I repeat his gesture and kiss the back of his own hand. "Not at all."

With his free hand, he tucks a loose tendril of my hair behind my ear and caresses the side of my face. "I'm glad." His tone is a bit husky. He is clearly besotted. But not with me. With Copenhagen Sabrina. I have to try hard to remember this.

We stop at a particularly pretty stretch of beach before the last rays of sun give way. From the pack he produces a huge blanket, which we spread over a large swath of sand. I make to sit facing the sea, but he stops me before I execute my maneuver.

"Face north tonight, not south."

I raise a questioning brow.

"Trust me. The show is coming from the north tonight."

We lie on the blanket, facing north as Nikolai urged. Within moments the sky is a sea of rippling gray waves. It's as though the sky and sea have changed places for the night, and I can't restrain a gasp. "What . . . what is this?"

"Noctilucent clouds. A trademark of our northern climes. The understated cousin of the Borealis. My dad once told me this is what inspired the name for the restaurant he was going to open with your father. On nights like this, they'd go out as far from the city as they could to enjoy them."

I whisper, "I don't blame them. This is the most beautiful thing I've ever seen."

"La Mer Grise. 'The Gray Sea.' It's fitting." He nods.

"I like that it would have had a special meaning for them. I can imagine what an amazing restaurant they would have built."

"So can I. But I can't find it in my heart to regret the outcome. The world would be a much duller place without you."

His hand finds mine again, and I love the feel of his fingers laced in mine. "I think the same about you, Nikolai."

He is silent for a moment before he finds his next words. "Trust me when I say these words are costing me dearly. I think you need to leave The Mesmerist, even if it means leaving Copenhagen. Madsen will personally see to it that your career is stunted."

"Why does he have it out for me?" I can't help but ask. I've had conflict with managers before, but I am generally well liked by my superiors. To be loathed by a boss like this is a wholly new experience for me.

"Because you intimidate him. You dance circles around him in every aspect of this business, and he can't stand it. You see contempt and rage when he glares at you? All I see is inferiority and envy."

"How pathetic."

"It is. And it boils down to this: Madsen won't stand to see you promoted in-house. So no chance of getting any managerial experience. And even if you tripled the alcohol receipts single-handedly, he wouldn't give you a good reference to go elsewhere, especially anywhere in Copenhagen. The longer you stay, the harder it will be for you to find a new job. You have *weeks*, not months, before this becomes a hole in your résumé."

An ache sears my gut. He's speaking truths I don't want to hear. "You're right, though I hate it."

"I wish things could be different." He doesn't bother to conceal the emotion in his voice. "But you want Michelin, and this is not going to get you there."

Copenhagen Sabrina has told Nikolai about Michelin. This is . . . big. And a tad scary. Edward had been the only person I'd confided in, and that came to a no-good outcome. The number of people who know my aspirations has now doubled, which should be more than a tad scary. It should be terrifying. But I can't picture Nikolai ever using information I shared with him in confidence as emotional blackmail the way Edward did. He is a different caliber of human being.

I snuggle closer to him to brace against the lowering temperatures and the nip of the sea air that coils around us with every flutter of the breeze. He mirrors my gesture and I love feeling the warmth of his flank against mine.

At length he breaks the silence. "I'm sorry that coming to Copenhagen was a mistake for you."

I sit up on the blanket. "I don't think it was, Nikolai. Professionally, things weren't perfect, but I do think I was meant to come here now. If only for a short while. But what about you? You're far too talented a chef to spend your career as a bartender."

"Don't worry about me, *min elskede*. I'll be fine."

"I *will* worry about you. I worry about any talent being underutilized. And when that talent happens to be in the possession of someone I care about, I'll worry as much as I like." Feeling emboldened, I reach over and caress the side of his cheek. He closes his eyes, as if to tell me he's savoring the moment.

I lie back down, and he takes me in his arms. We stare up at the gray-blue waves overhead, listening to the soft lapping of the ocean behind us, and lose ourselves in the beauty of the night. I have no idea why I needed to come to Copenhagen, and I know I'm not meant to stay much longer. But for the first time, I really wish I didn't need to go back.

Chapter 19

DECEMBER 30, 2024
BURBANK AIRPORT

Well, how was it, dearie?" Rosaline greets me with enthusiasm that could only be the product of far too many cups of caramel-laced coffee. "I should think visiting your father's homeland was a thrill." She escorts me to our little table where a fresh cup is waiting for me.

How many cups have I had in this timeline, and should I be concerned about caffeine poisoning? I don't feel jittery, though, and my pulse seems normal, so I indulge in a few sips.

"I'm happy I went." Noncommittal and true. "I'm pretty sure I was right to choose Boston over The Mesmerist in my original timeline, but I still wish I'd had time in Copenhagen before I went back stateside. Does that make any sense?"

"A lot of sense. And now you've had the chance to see what that decision would have brought, dearie. And I hope there were things of use to you there?"

I no longer have to wonder what that life might have looked like, which is the most incredible sort of cosmic gift, but she must know this. I consider a more concrete answer. "I met a general manager who made me realize I was far better at that job than I gave myself credit for. That's something."

"More than a *little* something if you ask me. You've rarely given yourself the credit you deserve." She reaches over and pats my hand affectionately. "I'm glad to hear you speak well of your own skills."

I squeeze her hand in return but laugh at her praise. "He set a pretty low bar. 'Avoid bullying junior staff' is just basic decency."

She rolls her eyes a bit at the thought of Madsen's antics. "That seems to be a lesson many in the upper tiers of the kitchen hierarchy haven't learned. Yet here you are, with twenty or more working years ahead of you, with that lesson etched on your heart. I'd say it's reason enough to be proud."

"Well, when you put it that way . . ."

She gives an authoritative nod. "I *would* put it that way. I'm glad you put your time to good use."

I don't tell her how much use. My last few hours with Nikolai at the beach, solving all the woes in the culinary world into the wee smalls. Holding each other close, knowing our time together was short. A goodbye at the airport that was more tearful than I'd expected.

And there was all my dad's history I'd gleaned from chatting with Oskar and Yrse. I'd only known them for hours, but I would miss them all dearly. All of it felt like fundamental bricks in the foundation of my life that had been missing.

And they still are.

I didn't make the choices Copenhagen Sabrina did, so my life is going to have different consequences.

Rosaline calls me back to the present. "A penny for your thoughts, love?"

I begin to offer up a glib quip about them not being worth

nearly so much but think of something more prescient to ask. "Am I actually changing my history with all this, or am I just immersed in an interactive display of the blooper reels of my life?"

Rosaline chuckles, but her tone invokes some gravitas. "I wouldn't be so presumptuous as to claim I understand how all this"—she gestures vaguely toward the Jetway—"works. But I will tell you that while I do believe there is an optimal destination for each of us, the path there is never ever a straight line. And mistakes don't exist. Not in matters like these."

I wish I were fully convinced she's right, but a persistent weight presses on my heart and causes a throbbing at my temples the more I try to contemplate it. "It seems like going to Boston immediately after London *was* a mistake. But so was Copenhagen, at least professionally. How can both paths be wrong?"

"Nothing simpler, sweet girl. Sometimes you're *meant* to take a wrong turn. Now when a person makes a whole string of them right in a row, I begin to fret, sure. But if you listen to the most successful people in the world—presidents and prime ministers, artists and inventors—not one of them will say they never took a misstep in the whole course of their lives. Often those driven to do great things make the most spectacular messes, to own the truth. And it's often while wading through that 'dark moment of the soul,' praying for a sliver of light, that they find their greatness."

"That makes a lot of sense," I admit. "I just don't know what it means for me."

"You'll figure it out. Now tell old Rosaline. What would you say has been your 'dark moment of the soul' thus far? I know you want to say the death of your father, but that was something that happened *to* you. It impacted you, but it was entirely out of your control. What I want you to do is think of a hard moment over which you had more agency."

I understand the distinction. Nothing has affected me more in my life than my father's death, but I *had* been a passive participant in it. I'd been three thousand miles away and not even aware he was gone until it was too late.

I reflect a few moments more and finally say, "Probably when I was let go from Maison Ortense."

She nods in sympathy. "Ah, that has been hard on you, hasn't it?"

"It wasn't fair." I hope I don't sound like a petulant teenager, but at the moment, that's exactly how I feel.

"No, dearie, it wasn't. And if it were in my power to make it right, I would. But fortunately, you *do* have that power. And the opportunity to use it, thanks to me." She nudges me with an elbow.

"Let's do it." I feel a surge of adrenaline. I've thought about all the things I could do differently on repeat since I left . . . It has only been a couple of weeks since I left, yet it feels like a lifetime.

Rosaline leans closer. "Might I offer you a bit of advice?"

This is the first time she's offered, so I nod enthusiastically.

She takes my hand in hers. "Trust your gut. You have it in you, but you have to believe in the talents you've worked so hard to cultivate. Promise me you won't be afraid to shake things up."

I nod again, determined. "I promise. I want Joëlle to get her star. On my watch."

She smiles brightly. "Well then, Sabrina Fair, go chase the stars."

Chapter 20

PARIS

And just like that, I'm back. Paris. *The* Michelin city.

The city I loved as deeply as I loved any man, and which broke my heart just as thoroughly as any of them. Sure, loving Paris is a little cliché, but I can't help myself. It is the center of the world I've been dreaming of my whole adult life—and quite a few years before that too.

I am in the living room of my one-bedroom apartment in the tenth arrondissement of Paris, eight blocks from the restaurant, which is in the second, right in the beating heart of the city. The apartment is small, of course. It's Paris, and the real estate is some of the most expensive in the world, but it's a cozy place to fall after a long shift.

I peek in my room and look at the old comforter I'd gotten from a secondhand shop. It's antique gold–colored satin and probably fifty years old, but unspeakably soft. It cost me all of fifteen euro, and I'd had to run it through the washer at the laundromat three times to get the musty smell out of it, but the sight of it brightening the tiny bedroom always cheered me after a difficult service. I donated it back to the thrift shop before I left, but that act had been more painful than I'd thought it would be. It's nice to travel light, but it's also hard leaving little treasures behind all the time.

I'm unreasonably glad to see it on my bed. Just a few weeks ago, I told myself that keeping it would be silly and impractical. It would have taken an entire extra suitcase, and the resultant fees, to bring it to the States, and I couldn't justify that. I look at the silly blanket, and all it represents, and think maybe I was hasty to bail on Paris altogether. Leaving town is always my first impulse when it's time to move on, but I could have stayed and found another job here, or at least somewhere in France. Possibly a great job, where I wouldn't have to start from scratch for once. I have a comical vision of shoving the massive gold comforter in an oversized Ikea-style shopping bag and schlepping it on the Métro to grace the bed in my new flat.

Which, admittedly, wouldn't possibly be as nice as this one. As a perk of the job, the restaurant investors subsidize the rent because they want the GM close at hand. They wouldn't go so far as to secure an apartment in the same neighborhood as the restaurant, where rents are drastically higher, but it's far better than having the GM living within their means an hour away. It's a good compromise, and I love it here. Leaving this space behind was a real blow, second only to the job loss itself, but I was given no choice. Even if I could afford full rent here, which I can't, the investors handle the lease, and it was their prerogative to pass the flat on to the next GM.

And they will do it again if I fail a second time. Which I don't intend to. If I have to leave Maison Ortense and this flat again, it will be for Michelin.

Rosaline is right. I have to trust my instincts and fight for Joëlle and her star. Her predecessor, Éugenie Rosier, is a legend in the Paris food scene. She is now enjoying a much-deserved retirement in Èze on the Côte d'Azur and hopefully eating copious amounts of seafood she prepares leisurely in her own kitchen, pleasing no one's palate but her own.

It's important to note, Michelin stars belong to the restaurant, not the chef, though it's often hard to divorce the two. When Éugenie retired, Michelin stripped the third star from the restaurant. It's not meant to be punitive, but rather, it provides the opportunity for the new chef to prove their mettle. Especially in the common scenario where a restaurant passes from one generation to the next in the same family. The younger generation deserves the chance to prove they aren't riding on anyone's coattails.

Which Joëlle is not. She took everything Éugenie taught her and has run with it. I can't speak as to why Michelin hasn't given her the third star, but it can't be due to her food. We can't even be sure Michelin has sent an inspector since she took over, given the volume of restaurants they have to review every year and the limitations on their staff.

As Joëlle herself often says, a third star is a little bit like your ninetieth birthday—never promised. It doesn't matter how much you think you've earned it by doing all the right things; it still might not happen. None of that matters to the investors, though, and I'll have to make them see that she deserves a fair shake.

I finally check my phone and realize I'm about three months back in time. Two and a half months before Joëlle and I are let go. Not much time to right the ship. It's early morning yet, but I am expected at the restaurant in two hours as preparations begin for lunch service. No, I'll go in now to reorient myself and draw up a battle plan. I'm going to stay in this timeline until I catch up with my own if necessary. Anything to have another chance to help Joëlle earn her star.

I dress in what I've dubbed my "work uniform." Before I

started in Paris, I invested in seven single-breasted pantsuits in tones of black, charcoal, and navy, which I alternate. They're all designer, all purchased on consignment in the US where I can find clothes that accommodate my height, and all professionally tailored to fit me like they're bespoke. I restrict myself to three pairs of sensible low-heeled pumps in coordinating shades of black, gray, and navy as well. I do have one suit in brown that I favor for fall, and a red one for my sassier moments, but I generally stick to the basic seven to take one decision off my plate before service.

It's not quite as restrictive as Steve Jobs' black T-shirts and blue jeans routine. I mix up camisoles and accessories for a bit of fun, and to blend in with the fashionable crowd, but I organize it all on Mondays when the restaurant is closed so it feels like one medium decision instead of a dozen smaller ones. I had thought, and still think, the practice leaves me with just a scrap more bandwidth for work.

Today is a Tuesday, and it would appear my black suit with large brass buttons is up for the day, along with a cobalt-blue satin shell that makes me think of the throw pillows in Copenhagen with a little pang, which I force myself to push aside.

Just as I'm about to head for the door, my phone dings and I retrieve it from my pocket that I'd had tailored to be large enough to serve a purpose beyond annoying me with the promise of a pocket and delivering nothing but disappointment.

JOËLLE: Can you meet the fishmonger? I've had a bit of a problem at the dentist. He's due in twenty minutes.

I remember this moment vividly. She'd gone in for a routine cleaning, and the dentist noticed one of her fillings was loose.

He decided to jump into giving her a crown before asking if her schedule would permit for an invasive procedure. Thankfully for the dentist, he sedated her enough that she didn't murder him for gross misconduct.

She had been miserable all service, poor thing, but this time I can be prepared to take over as much as I need to. Three months ago, I'd jumped right in to meet the fishmonger because she wasn't comfortable enough with her sous, Girard, to delegate the task to him. I know now *this* is a key problem to solve. If Joëlle can't trust her sous to do something that is vital, yes, but ultimately not all that challenging, there is a fatal problem in the kitchen. Either she needs to gain trust in her sous, or he needs to be replaced. I'm fine with whichever outcome will best serve Joëlle and the restaurant.

ME: Consider it handled.

I just don't tell her how. She doesn't need the stress while she's in the dentist's chair. And it may have more of an impact for her to see after the fact that he has succeeded in following her directives. I wouldn't have tried this before, but it's time to be more hands-on in matters of staffing.

I bring up Girard's number, pull up the messaging app, and begin to type.

ME: Hey, are you free? I've a bit of a work favor to ask of you.

His three dots appear instantly.

GIRARD: Of course, Patronne. Anything.

I roll my eyes at his nickname for me. *Patronne* loosely translates to "boss lady," and while most people use the term unironically, I can't help but feel a trace of condescension in it from Girard.

ME: I need to accept the seafood order in about twenty minutes, but I may be running late. I don't want to keep an important vendor waiting, so would you mind going in and seeing to it? I'll forward you the invoice so you can check everything off.
GIRARD: Isn't that Joëlle's job?
ME: Usually, yes, but she asked me to do it as a favor this once because she has a personal appointment she can't miss. I should be there before he leaves, so I just need you to get the process started.
GIRARD: Of course. Will be at the restaurant in ten.
ME: You're a lifesaver.
GIRARD: I know.

I groan. Ego was never the problem with that one. I forward the order invoice to him, tuck my phone in my pocket, and grab my trusty backpack. I root inside for my keys and find that I'm still using the daisy key ring from Nikolai. This is huge, but I don't have the time to process it all just yet.

Girard has a good eye and confidence enough to perform the task, but I hail a cab anyway. Girard is young to be promoted to sous, but so, too, had I been in Dublin. He is talented and ambitious, but despite this—or maybe because of it—Joëlle is wary to hand over the reins to him in any meaningful way. As GM I'll have to find a way to foster this relationship or save everyone's time and end it for them. Joëlle is as talented as it gets, but she needs the best possible team if she's going to have a successful run as head chef.

The problem with any hierarchy is that when someone higher up the ladder moves on, too often everyone underneath gets shoved up a rung, whether they're ready or not, because it's always easiest—and cheapest—to find new entry-level people. But it remains that while someone can be a perfectly competent station lead, they may not be at the point in their professional development where they're prepared for the responsibility of sous-chef.

When that's the case, it's easy enough—in theory—to hire an experienced sous from outside an establishment. But when people feel the promotion they earned has been outsourced, it can lead to friction in even the best-run kitchens, so efforts are made to promote from within. Sometimes the result is that a chef thrown into the deep end proves their worth spectacularly. Other times, they drown and the kitchen suffers.

The taxi drops me off about twelve minutes after the vendor was scheduled to arrive, which is ideal. Girard has had enough time to show that he's capable, but I'm there early enough to intervene if anything is amiss. And nothing can be amiss if Joëlle is going to earn her star. Flavors have to be complex and original. Ingredients must be unique and inspired. There is no room for a single entry on the menu to be anything less than stellar.

Girard is deep in an animated conversation with the seafood vendor when I enter the kitchens, shooting me a glance as though I am intruding on some kind of private meeting before he forces his expression back into a neutral one.

"How's it going in here?" I pretend I didn't notice the look he'd cast my way.

"Perfectly well. Everything appears in order." His tone implies that he has everything under control with subtle undertones of "I'd prefer you didn't interfere." But interfering isn't just my prerogative, it's my duty.

I take a cursory look over the order and find that everything is, as Girard promised, in order. As I hoped and expected it would be, because if the second-in-command can't handle a simple delivery, he has no business being sous. I hope Joëlle will gain some trust in him for this.

"Joëlle won't be too long, but she emailed me instructions for the specials, which I'll get to you. Can you handle starting service?"

He nods, the corners of his lips tugging slightly upward. He is going to be at the helm, at least temporarily, and I expect he's excited for the opportunity. I'd never led a service the entire time I'd worked back of house, but being a head chef was never my goal. I know it *is* Girard's dream, and it must feel to him as if he's making an important milestone. And he is, if he can pull it off.

"You've got this." I don't flash him a bright smile as I might have done in an American kitchen, but rather just a ghost of a grin that I hope he finds encouraging.

I retreat to my office where I run the financial side of the restaurant. I'd taken a number of restaurant accounting classes in culinary school for this very reason. Tracking vendor payments, general expenses, and payroll is drudgery, but it's a necessary part of the trade. While I don't want to make a career out of spreadsheets and databases, the ledgers tell the story of a business, and there is a lot to learn from them.

I fire up my laptop, which is connected to a large monitor that makes the hours of staring at columns of numbers more bearable on my eyes. I launch Restaurant365 and lose myself in the ledgers for a bit before I hear a smart rapping at my office door.

"Entrez." As our staff comes from all over the globe, English is the de facto language in the kitchen, but I do try to observe the niceties in French when it seems practical. Not for the first time am I glad that I took French in high school despite my mother and the counselor trying to tell me Spanish would be more useful.

Joëlle comes in, her delicate face looking swollen and her deep brown eyes looking frazzled. Her usually perfectly slicked-back brown hair is unkempt from her time in the dentist's chair. The last time I saw her, when we were unceremoniously fired, she looked similarly discomposed, which was not the way she preferred to present herself to the world. She was one of the few people I'd considered a friend over the course of my career, and I spent more than a little time worrying that she blamed me for our dismissal. I want to hug her and apologize for something that hasn't even happened yet, but before I even have the chance to disabuse myself of that notion, she leans over my desk.

"Did you approve the order for bluefin tuna?" The dental work and her strident tone have made it hard to parse her words.

I blink, uncomprehending. "No, I asked Girard to handle the seafood order. I wanted to see if he was up to the task."

She throws her hands up in frustration. "Either the seafood vendor pulled a fast one or Girard changed the order. There is a massive cut of bluefin out on Girard's prep station. At least a hundred pounds, Sabrina."

I curse under my breath and check my email for the final delivery invoice from the seafood guy. The PDF is waiting there, showing an added line item for the tuna and a very bloated total due. Girard has committed a screwup of the first order. We're a high-end place, but this is astronomical, even for us. Bluefin is rare, and usually a restaurant has to commit to buying the whole fish—all five hundred pounds or more of it. This isn't quite *that* disastrous, but we can only flip so many tables in a service. We have three days *at the very most* to serve one hundred pounds of the most expensive seafood on earth before the quality starts to turn. Even if every table ordered bluefin—and was willing to pay market price—we'd still lose money.

I mumble another curse and lead Joëlle out to the kitchen where Girard has his head down focusing on a skillet.

"So you were just going to spring a new dish on us without warning?" I don't bother with a preamble. "And spend close to *ten thousand euro* of restaurant funds without asking?"

He looks up from the skillet, his eyes flashing. "Neither of you will listen when I suggest something."

"*Petit éspece de—*" Joëlle growls, then winces from the effort. I put a hand on her shoulder to keep her from creating a workplace-hostility incident that could get us in trouble.

"Setting the menu is Joëlle's prerogative, Girard. If you want to audition a dish, you do it the right way."

He looks at me with all the disdain of a surly teen. "I saw an opportunity and I took it. The fishmonger offered me the chance to split a fish with another restaurant, and I couldn't resist. Bluefin is rare to come across in a smaller quantity." The arrogance rolls off him like a cheap cologne. "Taste this and you won't be upset anymore."

He offers us each a portion, which Joëlle refuses due to her dental work, but she smells and assesses the plating. She meets my eyes, and I can tell she's not particularly impressed. Not for what we'll have to charge per plate. The saucier has done some good work with a pesto to accompany it, and it looks pleasing enough. I sample it and find it—fine? While Girard's fate rests largely in Joëlle's hands and is yet to be settled, I decide we'll be firing the seafood vendor. This is decent tuna but not worth a third of what he charged us.

"This was an opportunity you clearly weren't ready for, Girard. There is a lot wrong here, and that's why we don't add new dishes on the fly like this. We have to calculate a price point for every new entrée. And that price point needs to make sense. You bought bluefin at *three times* the market rate when he should have been offering you a *deal* to split with another house. We're going to have to charge three hundred euro a plate just to break even."

His lip curls in a sneer. "You don't think people will pay it?"

I stare at him, unflinching, and he has the good graces to appear intimidated. Precisely the effect I'm after. "Not more than once. Sure, it's well prepared, well seasoned, but it's not anything gobsmacking. Specials in a restaurant vying for a third star have to be better than flawless, especially for the cost. They have to be art. This is *not* art; it's barely adequate."

This is the worst insult I can hurl at him, and I'm fully aware of it as the words escape my lips. He tosses a dish towel down on the counter with a flourish. "What does an American know about food? What would you have me do? Drown it in ketchup?"

Joëlle emits a low, guttural growl and I restrain her before I find myself bailing my head chef out of jail for assault less than an hour before service. I take a step closer to Girard.

"Leave this kitchen. Now. You'll be paid in lieu of notice and get whatever severance you're entitled to by law if you go quietly. If you don't, I'll report you for a *faute grosse* and you won't get a cent. And we'll win. I'll go after damages too, given what you committed us to with this damned fish. And if I hear of you badmouthing Joëlle or this restaurant, I'll be sure you never work in the industry again. In Paris or anywhere else. Not even Chez McDo will have you. Do I make myself perfectly clear?"

He looks at me, furious, but knows I am well connected enough that I speak the truth.

He removes his apron and throws it on the floor, glaring in my direction and Joëlle's. "You'll never get a third star with this one at the helm, you know. Éugenie's genius was a fluke, and she was daft to leave Joëlle in charge just because she's a woman. Her legacy will be destroyed within six months." He storms out with a rude gesture and without a backward glance.

Joëlle looks at me in wordless horror. Whether she's struck silent by the sudden departure of her sous or in too much pain from her dental work, I can't say. She isn't at her best, and it would have been an appropriate day for her to lean on her second-in-command. That's his job, after all, to keep things running when the head needs support.

She will have to lead the kitchen for the services, despite feeling miserable, and I'll have to fill in where I can. It's too late to shift everyone up a rank, and I'm not sure we want to pull some people upward if they aren't ready. Clearly we made that mistake with Girard.

"We can do this, Joëlle." I pat her on the back, and she's as tense as cellophane stretched too tight over a bowl. I pick up Girard's apron off the floor, don it over my clothes, and begin cleaning up his mess, resisting the urge to grouse. After a few attempts at re-living my own life, I'm finding that cleaning up messes left behind by others and sometimes—okay, especially—myself is tedious work.

Chapter 21

What in the hell do I do with all the damned tuna?" Joëlle moans almost to herself.

"Whatever you want, so long as you can pull it off in a hurry." I gesture to the plate I'd sampled from before scraping it into the bin. "Something better than that, at least."

"Low bar," she mutters and gets to work.

Her brow is furrowed in concentration as she contemplates the fate of the massive cut of fish she needs to make palatable in a hurry. Because of Girard's blunder, we'll take a bath on the cost of it no matter what. Her job is to minimize how long and soapy it will be.

And she has approximately fifteen minutes to figure out how to do it.

Right now, I need to alleviate some pressure from the room. "Listen, don't worry about the price point. If we sell at a loss, so be it. Just do the best you can, and we'll recoup the money elsewhere. It's not an insurmountable problem."

Her shoulders lower by a couple of inches, and her breathing deepens. I hope it's enough reassurance to get her through service.

She barks out orders, wincing every time she opens her mouth, to Thérèse, the *chef de tournant*, or swing chef, who is now her acting second-in-command along with me. Thérèse is capable enough, a sort of Jane-of-all-trades who suited the role of swing cook to a tee, but she's overwhelmed by the magnitude of the sous job. She can handle it for today, but she needs more time at every single station before she's ready to move up.

As I dice and prep, I mull over the talent at our disposal. Our saucier, Yann, is just coming into his own, and I sense he would be loath to switch before he really finds his footing, even for a promotion. And given the promise of his talent, I don't want to risk disrupting his progress there. But as the senior *chef de partie*, he would naturally be next in line for sous. I'll have to finesse that one. Finesse, it seems, is always key to the role of manager.

I can see now that we've been so careful to respect Éugenie's legacy, we have been afraid to change *anything* in the year and a half Joëlle has been in charge. It's as if we're afraid to insult Éugenie by making the most minor staffing changes, when major ones are clearly called for. And this all has to end now.

Yes, Éugenie left tremendous shoes to fill. I amuse myself by imagining those shoes as size 13 Louboutin stilettos, encrusted with crystals and sporting the famous red soles. Hard to fill and even harder to walk in. She made a mark for herself on the Paris restaurant scene, possibly the world's oldest old boys' club.

And hard as it is for me to give him any credit, Girard was right that Éugenie had wanted to pass on her legacy to another female chef. But she hadn't singled Joëlle out just because of her gender. She is brilliant in her own right and ten times the chef Girard is. He just can't accept that he was legitimately passed over for a more talented chef who happens to be female.

Reinstating the third star would be a coup not only for Joëlle but also for Éugenie. It would prove that she'd chosen her successor well and had left her legacy in capable hands. I don't think

Joëlle's kitchen is in dire straits the way Edward's in Denver must be, but there is a lot more to do than I allowed myself to believe even a few weeks ago. And Girard clearly wasn't the asset I'd thought he was, but we know this now and can regroup.

A mantra repeats in my head: *I cannot screw this up. I cannot screw this up. I cannot screw this up.*

So I will chop, dice, fry, and sauté everything in sight until I drop. Whatever Joëlle needs to have a stellar service.

"Okay, Chef. Try this." Joëlle speaks softly, I assume because it's less painful for her.

She places a plate before me, and I examine her handiwork. Rather than the pesto Girard had paired with the fish, which didn't really make a lot of sense to me from a flavor perspective, Joëlle seared the bluefin in a toasted sesame crust that adds interesting texture and a nutty flavor that enhances, rather than competes with, the tuna. I revise my assessment of the quality of the fish. It's not worth what the vendor charged us, but it's decent bluefin. The fishmonger might not be fired after all. The dish is way above par, especially given the constraints Joëlle has been put under. She's done marvelously, just as Éugenie knew she would.

I wolf-whistle to get everyone's attention, not caring that it makes me look like an oafish American. "All right, we have a sesame-crusted bluefin tuna as the special. Probably for the next three nights." I turn to the waitstaff who are gathered for the pre-service orientation. "It's going for two-twenty-five, and I need you to peddle it like your lives depend on it."

Aveline, our Franco-American sommelier, is at my side, peering over Joëlle's shoulder. Joëlle offers her a small portion so she can get a feel. She's lost in thought just a moment, then her eyes come back into focus. "Top-dollar food, top-shelf wine. Pair it with the Sella & Mosca Vermentino or *maybe* the Domaine du Cassis rosé if they want something creative."

She's very much an all-business American, but with the French elegance that comes imprinted on the DNA. And she has a nose for wine unlike any other I've seen. She's a gem, but we can't afford to pay her for full-time work at the rate she deserves. The chances that we'll lose her to a better opportunity are basically 100 percent, so we need to make the most of her expertise while we have her.

I pat her shoulder. "Spot-on. Urge them away from anything less. I don't want people pairing this with thirty-euro bottles of house Chablis."

Aveline gives me a curt nod, and I know she understands the assignment. We're going to lose money on the fish, but the profit from the wine will help offset it.

Joëlle is instructing the *poissonnier* on how to portion the fish and store what we can't use for service in vacuum-sealed bags in the coldest part of the fridge. He's working at such a rapid clip to keep the quality of the fish from degrading that I worry for the safety of his fingers so near his fish knife. His movements are a blur, but with the poise and control of a dancer. Like Aveline, he's an absolute keeper. Joëlle sets me to work trimming green beans to be served in a brown butter and toasted almond sauce that will play off the flavors of the toasted sesame.

"Patronne, I need to tell you something." Our expo, Nadia, speaks in hushed tones. The tones a manager ignores at her peril. There is a situation in the front of house, and it is her job to communicate it with the back if it isn't something she can resolve on her own. I shoot Joëlle a look and she nods, ordering one of the other prep cooks to fill my station.

I guide Nadia to my office, where I close the door and look at her expectantly.

"It seems that before his departure . . . Girard"—she speaks the name like an expletive—"called one of his friends from *The Guardian* and got him a table. He was sure his tuna would be a sensation and wanted to get coverage."

"Of course he did." I rub my eyes and, once again, stifle a curse. Nadia is fantastic at her job and can spot a critic from a hundred paces, so it must be true. Girard must have phoned *The Guardian* before the fishmonger even took his leave. He was so certain his dish was going to be a sensation, he couldn't bear not having the press on hand to commit his greatness to the historical record. What a conceited, pompous arse.

"I thought you'd want to know, but I didn't want to throw things off in there, *vous savez*?" She gestures back to the kitchen with her thumb.

I can only imagine Joëlle's state if she finds out a critic is in-house on the day she's had to prepare a new dish on the fly. Of course she's a professional and will do everything to keep her cool, but even the calmest, most collected chef has a limit to the chaos she can swallow in one service and still keep performing at peak.

I do *not* want to test where that level is. Our eyes are on that all-important third star, and while Michelin may boast about being independent and not at all influenced by other reviews, the inspectors are human. The company may be impartial, but if a restaurant as high profile as Maison Ortense gets panned in a major paper, no inspector alive will not have their opinion colored by it. And a glowing review would hurt nothing.

"You're absolutely right. Great call." I massage my temples for a moment, formulating a plan. "Okay, Joëlle's tuna is damn good, so make sure he orders it. You take that table personally, not anyone else. Whatever he wants, put him at the front of the line back here. Just don't comp or discount the ticket, or he'll know we're wise to him. And above all, make sure he knows Joëlle is at the helm and Girard went home unexpectedly. The last thing we want is her accomplishments being attributed to him."

"Got it." Nadia actually clicks her heels together before she spins to leave. She is the finest expo I know, and the first among the keepers.

The more I consider it, the more I think most of them are keepers, save perhaps a couple of the newer prep cooks who don't seem to have the motivation I'd like to see. The place really is an embarrassment of riches, talent-wise. For the most part it's just a matter of moving the square pegs back into the square holes where they belong and hoping there is a comfortable slot for each of them that will allow their talents to flourish.

I have visions of creating a massive bulletin board, the kitchen hierarchy laid out on masking tape, a pushpin at each space, and the name of each staff member on index cards ready to shift and move into place. Joëlle and I are at the bottom, the rest shuffling into their correct places in the rows above. Most would put the head chef and GM at the top, but I prefer to think of us as the foundation of the place. If we aren't solid, the proverbial building will collapse.

Blank cards for the spaces we need to fill.

This will be a project for Joëlle and me on Monday, when the house is closed for rest and cleaning. For now, we have roughly one hundred pounds of very expensive tuna that needs our attention so we can seduce our patrons—and one persnickety Parisian food critic.

Chapter 22

Nadia flips the sign from Open to Closed, and the entire staff looks ready to pass out. It has been twelve long, grueling hours from the beginning of lunch service to the end of dinner, but we pulled it off. More than that, the sesame-crusted bluefin is a smash hit, and the man we were fairly certain was the critic for *The Guardian* left smiling . . . a rare enough trait for a Parisian.

If tomorrow goes as well as today did, and I have no reason to believe it won't, we'll be able to off-load the entire massive cut of fish with only a minimal ding to the restaurant's finances. The sort that we could offset with one splashy Valentine's Day tasting menu with a good markup.

I take solace in knowing that if Michelin had been at the service, they wouldn't have withheld points for the quality of the products or our price point. Joëlle has risen magnificently to the challenge, and I am immensely proud of her.

"Patronne, can I have a word?" Joëlle looks dead on her feet, and her hard work hasn't helped her swelling. I consider telling her to go home and rest and that we can handle her concerns in the morning, but she looks troubled enough that postponing the matter might keep her from sleep.

I usher her into my office, where she flops unceremoniously in the chair opposite my desk. I take my usual spot and pray she's not about to quit on me after a service that, while successful, was more than a little harrowing.

"We need a new sous." She croaks the words, exhaustion and pain coloring every syllable. "Soon. And I think we need to hire from outside the house."

I lace my fingers and exhale. "Agreed."

She sits up a little straighter. "I expected more of a fight."

I hold my hands up in surrender. "Joëlle, it is your kitchen, and I want you to have the best possible team under you. I freely admit that I overestimated Girard's value to the staff, and I'm honestly glad we learned what he is capable of. And while I think promoting from within is generally the best practice, I've been racking my brain all night trying to figure out who could take over for Girard, and I'm frankly at a loss."

She blinks. "Merci, Patronne."

It's clear now that it's not only *my* instincts I need to trust, but hers as well. As Éugenie always said, it's a poor chef (or manager) who doesn't use all the talent at their disposal to its best advantage.

"Do you have any contacts? Anyone you'd like to bring in?"

She shrugs. "Most of the people I'd want have other positions, unfortunately. I'll have to do some digging."

The daisy key chain in my bag flashes deep in the synapses of my brain. "I might have someone we could consider. No promises, but he's talented."

Her eyes look pleading. "*Je t'en prie*, not another oh-so-talented genius chef whose ego can't fit in the kitchen."

I shake my head. "No, quite the opposite. Brilliant, but he doesn't see it. Maybe you could help him with that if it works out."

She looks dubious, as though a male chef with an *under*inflated ego is some sort of mythical creature. After a beat she finally says, "*D'accord*, but on a trial basis."

Naturally, she wants to vet him herself, which is absolutely her right. I extend my hand for her to shake. "You have my word. Now go get some sleep."

I put her in a cab myself and retreat to my office before I head home. This idea may not work at all, and I'll have to tell Joëlle this unicorn of a chef is otherwise engaged, but it's worth a shot. She doesn't need to know the particulars of this bizarre experiment I'm living.

I pull out my phone and look in the contacts. Sure enough, Nikolai is listed there along with his parents. I look at my messaging app, and it appears we have made good on our promise to stay in touch. For years. Not daily, but it seems that we check in multiple times a week.

I read through a long string of our correspondence, which ranges from the banal to the heartfelt. It looks as though we've shared our wins and frustrations, our hopes and disappointments without fail since I left Denmark. We've met up a handful of times, and I find a few selfies of us in various European cities. He's offered suggestions for my blog, which is thriving, and I've been encouraging him along as well.

And I am delighted. Somehow, notwithstanding this itinerate lifestyle of mine, I have managed to forge a friendship that has lasted. I'm only sorry that I've missed out on so much of it. And I've learned, for better or for worse, my time travel is having an impact on my "real" timeline, though I think that term is disingenuous now. All of these timelines are now, more or less, mine.

And there is one realization that horrifies me. He's still at The

Mesmerist, though finally working in the kitchen as a vegetable prep cook. Svend has since retired, thank the stars, but Nikolai is still being underutilized.

I should feel sorry for Nikolai, but the emotion pumping through my veins right now is rage. How dare Bjørn not see that one of the best chefs in his sphere of influence is being wasted pouring, chopping, and dicing? I don't know if Nikolai is just getting off his shift or at home catching up on sleep, but I don't care if he's awake. I'm texting him anyway, and it can be the first thing he sees in the morning.

ME: You're coming to Paris. You're going to be the new sous-chef at Maison Ortense. Ask your parents to take Pjuske for a couple weeks and pack some stuff in a bag. I need you here ASAP.

Amazingly, his three dots appear.

NIKOLAI: Are you insane?

A truly interesting question given my recent habit of time travel. I still haven't ruled out the possibility that this is all just the result of a traumatic brain injury at Chloe's party and that I will wake up in a hospital room in my own timeline, three days of my life unaccounted for. I hope that's not the case, but coma dreams this lucid don't seem all that probable.

ME: Never saner.

Fine. The veracity of that statement is questionable, but it's true enough in this context.

ME: You need to be doing more than peeling carrots. This is where you belong.

NIKOLAI: I'm scheduled to work . . .

ME: And how many times have you ever called out? I am asking for you to give it a shot for two weeks. If you hate it, you can go back to Bjørn.

His three dots appear and disappear repeatedly, so I busy myself hunting for flights, pleased to see available flights for under a few hundred dollars. I'll buy the ticket myself, so as not to incur another charge for the restaurant after the bluefin incident. I don't wait for him to make excuses.

ME: There is a 7 a.m. flight tomorrow . . . Well, later this morning . . .

NIKOLAI: You mean . . . less than seven hours from now?

ME: Yep. You could be sous-chef in a two-star Michelin kitchen by 10 a.m., traffic permitting. Are you really gonna say no? Don't give me any excuses about sleep—you can nap on the plane.

NIKOLAI: Do you really think I'm ready?

I don't dignify this with a response. Yet. I purchase the ticket and forward it to his email.

ME: Check your inbox, dweeb. You were ready for this eight years ago.

I take the regional train to Charles de Gaulle and stand sentinel at the passenger-arrival area, just beyond baggage claim, a mere quarter of an hour before Nikolai's flight is due. Impeccable timing, and I'm armed against my scant night's sleep with a coffee strong enough to dissolve the glaze on the dingy subway tiles. All good omens.

Nikolai emerges through the frosted automatic doors, and I realize, a little too late, that I don't know how to greet him. A hug? Parisian air kisses? A firm handshake seems a little formal . . . But he takes all the guesswork out of it when he stops in front of me, discards his luggage, picks me up in a bear hug, and does a full 360-degree twirl before he sets me back down.

I am fairly certain that no one has tried that with me in approximately twenty-eight years. At the age of nine I'd surpassed most adult women in height, and I'd been sure the days of twirling were over. Apparently not.

I take his carry-on backpack while he manages his larger wheeled case, and he takes my hand as we wend our way to the taxi stand. Once inside, he pulls me close and pelts a soft kiss on the curve of my neck.

He breathes in and lingers a moment. "I love the way you smell of coffee . . . and vanilla . . . and gardenias? Jasmine?"

I think of the scent profile of my perfume and chuckle. "Four out of four. Well done." Ironic that my mother, who willfully misunderstands me because she refuses to accept that I won't morph my entire personality to please her, was the one who unearthed my signature scent. She wanted the dutiful daughter who stayed in Solvang, married a nice boy in tech, and had kids for her to show off on Facebook to all her friends but whom she was simply "too busy" to visit. She also wouldn't mind if I'd find a way to lose about six inches in height. Eight if I really wanted to make her day. Anything to make myself smaller.

I'm rewarded by another small peck on the cheek and one on the back of my hand. It's as adventurous as he dares in the back of a taxi. And I'm glad for his restraint. But it makes me surprised that I couldn't detect any trace of a formal romantic attachment in the whole litany of text messages we've shared over the past eight years. I may or may not have read the entirety of them while trying—and failing—to sleep last night. It felt more like snooping than perhaps it should have. I mean, the phone I have in my possession right now is the actual phone I have waiting at Burbank Airport under Rosaline's safekeeping.

And the woman he knows and cares about is . . . *basically* me. If it weren't for the decision I personally made to try for the job at The Mesmerist, Paris Sabrina wouldn't have known Nikolai existed. And I have a hunch he might be the secret ingredient that Maison Ortense has been needing.

"Are you really sure about this?" Nikolai looks an impressive shade of kelp green as the taxi slows and we exit onto the pavement in front of Maison Ortense. It's a gracious old building in true Haussmann style: ivory façade with ornate iron scrollwork. And for someone who has been shoved behind a bar instead of being allowed to shine in a kitchen, I imagine it's a little imposing. His vibrant blue eyes linger on the red plaque with two Michelin stars that so resemble the daisy key chain he gave me.

I tug on his arm so he's forced to break eye contact with the infernal plaque. "There isn't a doubt in my mind that you will impress everyone in there. Including me."

His usual rosy complexion has gone pallid. "But what if there are doubts in mine? I've never been more than a line cook. What if I can't keep up?"

"The hardest part is the timing. I will be at your elbow helping you with pacing all night. Consider me your link to the expo for the night. Training wheels. And Joëlle will be at the helm. You have it in you to follow her lead."

He lets loose a shaky breath. "I suppose."

"Go on and suppose all you like. I *know* you can handle this. A hundred kroner says you stayed up memorizing the menus and recipes I forwarded you and you've got them all committed to memory." I arch a brow at him, daring him to contradict me.

He offers a grudging nod. "I did. Joëlle has done well with the bluefin. It was a smart choice, given the time constraints."

I drag him through the doors. "That she has. And we have to do it again today. Better, if we can."

He screws on a neutral expression, and he does an admirable job of not looking terrified as we enter the kitchen. Most of the staff are in the very earliest stages of prep, though several, like Yann the saucier, had to be in more than an hour ago to get things simmering long before service. All heads swivel at my arrival. That used to intimidate me, if I'm being honest, but I find it natural now. Joëlle and I are the captains of this ship, and this is our stalwart crew looking for some leadership. And now I know I have it in me to provide it.

I smile but not too broadly. "Bonjour, chefs."

They look up, most setting down their utensils as though they've been called to attention. "Bonjour, Chef," they reply in chorus. That never gets old.

"I have a new sous-chef for us today, imported from Copenhagen especially for you all. I know you will treat him with the courtesy and respect you did his predecessor."

There is a failed attempt to hide a snort of derision somewhere near the butcher's station. Perhaps that's setting the bar too low.

I'm beginning to see Girard wasn't held in as high esteem as I'd previously let myself believe.

"Better still, you treat him with the courtesy and respect you'd like to receive, were you in his shoes." The smirks disappear from faces. "I am counting on you to show him the ropes today. Show him not just how we do things at Maison Ortense, but how we wish to see them done moving forward. Can you do that for me?"

The eyes staring back at me are a little wider now. I don't know if I've impressed them, but I've certainly shocked them. They answer, "Yes, Chef." In unison.

And I hope they can keep up that cohesion for the rest of the service.

Chapter 23

"*Bon travail.*" Joëlle holds up her hand toward Nikolai in a high five gesture. She is, for the first time in recent memory, smiling while at work.

Nikolai returns the gesture and beams at her. I've never seen anyone more natural in the kitchen. From the moment he was placed in front of a stove, his nerves dissolved like a pinch of salt in boiling water. He not only kept pace with Joëlle and the rest of the staff but is also encouraging them to up their game. Already. He didn't need me by his side to excel; he just needed me out of the way.

And from the look on Joëlle's face, she's ready to offer him a job for life.

And to sweeten the pot? We sold out of the blasted bluefin before any of it went bad. Nikolai had suggested a second special: a bluefin tuna tataki appetizer. Elegant little bites of sesame-seared tuna with elaborate garnishes that would allow a table to sample the tuna without committing to it for their main dish. Nearly three-quarters of the tables ordered it, and the profit margin was even higher than Joëlle's dish.

Nikolai's plane ticket is quickly becoming the best three hundred bucks I've ever spent.

Nikolai and I finally escape the kitchen and opt to walk the eight blocks back to my flat. It'll be cramped, but I could hardly ask him to foot the bill for temporary lodgings for a two-week trial period. He's been to Paris a few times but generally the more touristy parts of the city. He's as enchanted as I am to stroll into the "real" neighborhoods where average folks live and work.

"You were amazing today." I pull my coat tighter around me against the autumn air that is just beginning to take on the fangs of winter.

He takes my hand in his. "I don't know what to say other than thank you for the opportunity. It's been like living a dream."

I turn my head to look at him. "Nikolai, why? The Mesmerist will never use you to your full potential. If you'd left and found a job at even a middling restaurant back when we first met—one where they'd utilize your skills and invest in you—you'd be a head chef by now. Vying for stars and all the things."

He looks up at the sky, where all the actual stars have been obscured by the low-hanging clouds of fall. "I don't really care about the stars, though I know plenty of chefs say that without meaning it. I just want the chance to create and experiment. To feed people."

"And that is a reachable goal for someone with your talents." I squeeze his hand. "All I know is, Joëlle looked ready to propose marriage back there, which I doubt her poor boyfriend Paul would appreciate. But I think it's safe to say she'll want to offer you the job at the end of your trial period. If she can wait that long."

He looks serious, taking a pause to gaze at the city enrobed in the soft glow of streetlights. "It doesn't seem real."

I fight the smile tugging at the corner of my lips. "I am more familiar with that sensation than I ever cared to be."

His voice is low and strained. "What if today was a fluke?"

I roll my eyes. "First of all, it wasn't and you know it. How often do you practice at home?" I know from the historical record of our text messages that he develops new dishes at home All. The. Time. He keeps careful notes of all his recipes in dozens of leather-bound notebooks. His parents, friends, and neighbors are the best-fed people in all of Denmark.

"Three or four new recipes a week. Sometimes more when I'm feeling particularly creative." He looks almost sheepish at the admission. Like it's an indulgence to spend so much time cultivating a talent he's not being paid to use.

"Precisely. You could probably plan five years of seasonally appropriate menus from your notebooks without breaking a sweat. My one worry was how well you'd manage a team, and you're a natural at it. You applied everything you learned at The Mesmerist along with what you've taught yourself at home to your work today, and you nailed it. Everyone noticed how good you are."

"I loved it," he confesses.

I lean over and brush a kiss on his cheek. "I could see that. And you deserve to have a life you'll love."

We stop in the middle of the sidewalk, and he leans his forehead against mine. "You know that I could be handed the keys to my own restaurant tomorrow. The restaurant of my dreams. And it would be a good life. A great one. But it wouldn't be a life I would love if you aren't in it."

I free my hand and wrap my arms around him as he wraps his around me. It doesn't matter that my perception is that I've only spent a day or two in this man's company. The lived experience of every version of me that has spent time with Nikolai feels imprinted on my soul. I had loved Rian. Naive me had thought I loved Edward.

But Nikolai? Nikolai is home.

What if all the feelings of sadness and regret that came bubbling to the surface at Burbank Airport were just the universe telling me I'd missed meeting the person I'm meant to be with?

And for some unfathomable reason I was granted the gift of making it right.

As much as Michelin, Joëlle's star, and the restaurant world are important to me, being with Nikolai is an opportunity, a choice, a life I don't want to botch either.

I let out a shaky breath. "Let's make it work."

The version of me who has spent eight long years as pen pals with Nikolai has been dragging her feet. I know myself in any timeline well enough to know I've always worried that a serious romantic entanglement would have the potential to derail all my plans. And those plans matter, a lot. But I realize, as the other versions of myself aren't quite able, that love doesn't have to mean forsaking everything else in life. Quite the opposite, really. The right partner is an asset in attaining all those external goals. The right partner is a cheerleader—nay, an entire hype squad—for the person they love.

I know Nikolai is mine. He has sent me novels' worth of texts over the past eight years, cheering me on as I moved from post to post.

And I want to be *his* hype squad too.

He swallows hard against threatening tears. "You mean it?"

"I do." I wipe away the few tears that have managed to escape their confines and compose myself. "It may not be easy, and it may have to look different from the average relationship, but I want us to be together."

And for the second time in my adult life, he picks me up and twirls me. Because every woman, even a Viking warrior, loves a good twirl now and again.

"It's here, but I couldn't bear to read it." Nadia appears at the open door of my office with a copy of *The Guardian*, open to the food section, held against her chest like a beloved teddy.

I expected the review would be printed today but had hoped to keep it under wraps until after service so it wouldn't derail morale if it's less than glowing. No such luck. Thankfully no one is within earshot except Joëlle, Nikolai, and me, the three of us gathered for a preservice confab.

Joëlle makes to grab for the newspaper but thinks better of it. She looks to me. "No, you read it."

I suppress a giggle. Like many chefs, she's a tad on the superstitious side. As if somehow my reading the words in her stead will magically transform a poor—or worse, a mediocre—review into a positive one. I motion for Nadia to close the door. If the review is a clunker, I don't want the rest of the staff to hear about it until we can't conceal it any longer.

Like Joëlle, I'm trembling at the thought of what the review might contain, but I keep it on the inside so I don't get their nerves more rattled than they already are. I scan the article, processing quickly so I don't let the anticipation get out of hand. I read aloud:

> Chef Joëlle Durand is proving herself a more capable replacement for the great Éugenie Rosier than might have previously been thought. While she is young, her talent is a formidable one. Her work with bluefin was exceptional, especially given that it can't be a medium she's worked with extensively. Chef Durand shows a great nuance for flavor and

has created a more-than-satisfactory experience. Special nod to the pastry chef who prepared the best tarte au citron I've had in recent—and not so recent—memory. Maison Ortense is worth the visit.

"Merci à Dieu." Joëlle clasps her hands and presses them against her lips. Her first review as head chef is better than anyone might have hoped from such a notoriously cranky reviewer.

I shoot her a glare from across my desk. "Don't give Him all the credit." I gesture toward the ceiling. "Reserve some for yourself. You pulled off a miracle with that bluefin." And it *was* nothing short of a miracle. It turned out so well, I have refrained from murdering the fish vendor with my bare hands.

Joëlle and Nikolai's cooking has been amazing, but their heroism in the ledgers is the sort of triumph the public will never see. "You should be proud. Your first major review as head chef is a big deal. We'll frame the review for display in the entryway, and you should keep one for your portfolio too."

"*Oui*, Chef. I will need a few minutes before service if you don't mind." She is so elated that I worry she is going to levitate right out of her chair.

"Let me guess, off to the nearest *tabac presse* to buy up every copy of *The Guardian*?"

She nods. "My mother and brother will want copies . . ."

I hand her ten euro from petty cash. "It's on the house. Reserve one for Étienne, too, since his tart was called out."

She nods and bounces off like a nine-year-old sent to a candy store with a hundred-dollar bill.

But just as soon as she disappears, another figure takes her place in my doorway. Two figures actually. Messieurs Phillipe

Grandin and Fabrice Martin, who lead the investment group that owns a controlling interest in Maison Ortense. Nadia and Nikolai make a hasty exit from the office, knowing the financiers always have to take precedence.

The men remind me of a modern-day French equivalent of Laurel and Hardy. Grandin is tall, wiry, and given to nervous fidgeting. Martin is a short, rotund sort of man who wheezes even when sitting still. I didn't care for them in my original timeline, and I don't find my opinion of them much improved. But investors are rarely my favorite sort of people.

"Well, well, it seems Mademoiselle Durand is pleased with herself." Grandin cranes his head, presumably to watch Joëlle's exit from the kitchen, then closes the door behind him. He and Martin take the seats Nikolai and Nadia just left, looking as grim as pallbearers. But this isn't so very different from the way they look at any given moment, so I don't let it fluster me.

"As well she should be. She's just received a wonderful review from *The Guardian*." I pass the paper across my desk, but they leave it untouched.

"We've come to discuss the matter of your unceremonious dismissal of Girard Bodin. This was not a matter you brought before us, and we would not have sanctioned it if you had." Grandin laces his fingers, looking very much like my middle school principal who loved giving wayward students long lectures about how disappointed he was in their conduct. Spoiler: No one much cared about his disappointment.

"I wasn't aware that staff changes were under your purview." I endeavor to keep my tone even, but I am only marginally successful in my attempt. "It was made very clear to me that all decisions concerning hiring and dismissal at the rank below the chef de cuisine were to be my responsibility, in conjunction with Chef Durand."

"Technically speaking, this is true. But we firmly believe that a chef as young and inexperienced as Mademoiselle Durand will benefit from the support of a talented chef like Chef Bodin." Grandin's tone is so obsequious I feel a tinge of green around my gills.

"I believe you mean *Chef* Durand." I don't bother to correct him with any sort of tact. "Messieurs, perhaps you weren't aware of the costly and egregious error Girard made concerning *one hundred pounds* of bluefin tuna. I'm sure I don't need to tell you the enormous cost he committed this restaurant to the very first moment he was given the smallest taste of a leadership role. It was my duty to dismiss any employee who makes such a large, unsanctioned purchase with restaurant funds. He is lucky I didn't report him to the authorities."

Martin shifts uncomfortably in his seat. "Chef Bodin approached us about the matter. He expressed a great deal of frustration at not having more creative license in the kitchen. More of a say in the running of things."

I lean forward and don't break eye contact. "He was a *sous-chef*. It isn't his place to have a say in the 'running of things.' His job is to follow Chef Durand's orders and see to it that the rest of the kitchen falls in line. A task at which he failed miserably time and again. And as for a lack of 'creative license,' he could have auditioned dishes for Chef Durand and myself at any time. He only chose to do so once, and it was woefully below par."

"That is not how Chef Bodin frames things." Grandin speaks as though the matter is settled.

I barely restrain myself from growling. "That may not be how he frames things, but I am telling you how things *are*. His value as a member of staff was minimal. He fell short of the mark as a leader and, to be direct, wasn't even an adequate follower. Chef

Durand did not let him take over more responsibility because she didn't feel he was equal to it. His actions on Tuesday morning proved her concerns were valid. The only reason we kept him on as long as we did was because Éugenie Rosier designated him to take Chef Durand's place as sous when she was elevated to her current role."

Martin had cast his eyes downward, but now he summons some resolve. "It was not Madame Rosier who appointed him as sous-chef, Mademoiselle Sorensen. It was the board. We would have preferred him to take over from the start, but we allowed Madame Rosier to pass on the baton to the successor of her choosing as a courtesy for her years of service to the restaurant."

"How gracious of you." My tone drips with disdain that I don't bother to conceal.

"Quite." Sarcasm seems to be lost on Grandin. "Be that as it may, we feel that Mademoiselle Durand has been given an adequate opportunity to prove herself and has not met the goals we set as a benchmark for her success within the allotted time. The board is of the considered view that the time has come for Chef Bodin to take the lead."

"You promised her two years," I remind them.

Martin chimes in. "We do not feel three months will make much difference, and we'd prefer to have Bodin at the helm before the busy holiday season."

I pause a long moment, my stare enough to make Grandin fidget. "No, you're worried three months is just enough time to make all the difference in the world." I point to the newspaper. "She's getting noticed and you don't *want* her to succeed so you can replace her with that miserable little slimeball."

It occurs to me they may well have somehow persuaded Michelin not to send inspectors. Wealthy men have connections, and

Michelin inspectors are spread thin. They could spin it so nicely too. *"Chef Durand just needs some time to get her footing. Why not come next year to give her the chance to settle in?"* They couldn't risk her earning back that star. And they had hired me because I was new to the rank of GM, American, and wouldn't have connections in Paris that might sway things in her favor. Like friends at *The Guardian*.

The game is rigged, and we were never going to win. They never would have let us.

"Purely conjecture on your part, of course." Grandin sniffs as he passes me a folder with what I presume are my walking papers. "You'll note there is a healthy severance package if you 'go quietly,' as your people say. And you have until the end of the month to vacate your lodgings. But if you say anything to the press or make any sort of public spectacle, we reserve the right to withdraw any remuneration beyond the wages you are due."

This had *not* happened in my original timeline because we had been kept on for the full two years of our contract. The review had made them nervous. I thumb through the pages and one of the names of the signatories leaps out at me. I look back up at their dim-witted faces. They look expectant, as though I will jump at their generous severance. I clear my throat. "Well, you have been thorough. I hope Chef Bodin is waiting in the wings somewhere. Service is in two hours and Chef Durand and our new sous, Chef Rasmussen, obviously won't want to interfere with his *vision*."

The pair of them blanch. Martin finally finds his voice. "Certainly, as preparations for today's services have already begun—"

I sign the document and close the dossier before they can rescind the offer, my eyes shooting daggers. "You forget, messieurs, that we are not handing in our notice. You have dismissed us. Effective immediately, according to the agreement I just signed. For us to work another two services would put us *all* in a legally awkward situation. It says here"—I tap the dossier with my index finger—"that we are ineligible for any further wages for services performed. You cannot ask for labor without promise of fair compensation."

"Well, I don't think—" Grandin blusters.

"Clearly you did *not* think, messieurs, or you would have handled this matter with a bit more delicacy. And you might have thought to obfuscate that Georges-Luc Bodin is one of your investors. Who is he? Girard's father? Uncle?"

The two men have been rendered mute. I take no small pleasure in this. Clearly I've hit the rusty old nepotism nail square on its ugly, corrupt head, and it will take me only a few seconds with my phone's internet browser to uncover the link between the investor and Girard.

Grandin finds his voice first. "You will be paid nothing if you make a statement."

I smirk. "Oh, Monsieur Grandin. I wouldn't debase myself with something as crass as a public spectacle."

Grandin exhales and Martin's jaw unclenches.

I lean closer and lower my tone to its very depths. *"I won't have to."*

Chapter 24

"I can't believe it. *Connards.*" Joëlle is picking at her pastry but feeling unequal to eating it. I don't blame her.

After pushing past Grandin and Martin, I'd grabbed Nikolai by the arm, direct from his station, and went to track down Joëlle. I broke the news on the sidewalk in front of the *tabac presse* where she'd been buying papers. I hated to shatter her blissful morning, but delaying the truth wouldn't soften the blow when it landed.

Thus, we all agreed to let Girard sink or swim on his own and started walking until we ended up at Angelina. It's one of those places that's so good you don't blame the tourists for swarming, but locals rarely go because of the crowds. But today is drizzly and decidedly off-season, so there are empty tables at the ready. And I've always thought bad news is easier to bear with a ready supply of chocolate and baked goods. They were happy to accommodate us in the far back corner at my behest. It's a nice, secluded spot for a good gripe fest.

I've never had time to sample their legendary hot chocolate before, and it has been a huge gap in my Parisian experience. I make a note to buy several boxes of their cocoa mix to take home on my way out.

But how long will I be in Paris? Will it be stupid to buy it just to donate it in two weeks when I'm kicked out of my apartment? Will it be worth hauling it wherever I land? I sag in my chair with the weight of having to move on yet again. It's the same weight I'm feeling in my own timeline. It's not that I want to stay still. I love the idea of traveling all over the world for Michelin. I just also want the luxury of a home base. A home base with throw pillows, my satin comforter, and a majestic black cat.

It's not about settling down so much as having a soft place to land.

I reach over for Nikolai's hand, and though he only worked one full day at the restaurant, he's just as sad as Joëlle and I are.

He presses his lips to the back of my hand. "I knew it was too good to be true."

I pull my hand back. "Nikolai Søndergaard Rasmussen, enough of that. This is one restaurant opportunity out of millions. And I mean that literally. You could get a job in a great kitchen tomorrow without help from anyone. You don't have to go back to The Mesmerist. I'll be mad if you do."

He shakes his head. "I know I can't go back now that I've had a taste of a kitchen like Maison Ortense. But it's . . . terrifying, you know? Trying to find something new. New doesn't always mean better."

"And a bird in the hand doesn't mean squat if it doesn't feed your soul," I counter. "I want you to make a list of ten restaurants anywhere in the world where you want to work, and we're going to make a game plan. This very afternoon."

"Yes, Chef." He actually gives a mock salute. Apparently, I've become bossier than I used to be, but in my defense, it seems to be getting some results.

"And you, Chef Durand?" I cock my head and look her square in her deep brown eyes that are doing a remarkable job of keeping back tears, though I know she's struggling with it. "What's the plan?"

"I have been unemployed for forty-five minutes. Can you let me catch my breath?" Her words are those of a surly teenager, but she looks more sad than petulant.

"No. You have a dazzling review running in a major newspaper. Today. It's in every newsstand in the city." I pull the paper up on my phone and hold it up for her to see. "Your face is on the front of the Lifestyle section of their website. That publicity will be buried tomorrow. Not forgotten, but it won't be front and center either. Put your feelers out *today* while you're fresh on everyone's minds."

She shrugs. "Won't they wonder why I'm looking for work?"

"Let them wonder. Why would a chef with such promise, one who is so well liked and respected, be let go hours after a triumph like this?" I waggle my phone for emphasis, the website still glowing. "A bit of bad gossip for Maison Ortense and its investors is just what they deserve. They can't rescind your severance because you're job hunting. And you'll have me as a reference."

She looks pensive, so I decide to break the somber mood. "Champagne," I declare, trying to spot our server and make eye contact. "This is an opportunity for better things, not a setback. And we're going to act like it."

The waiter, bless him, makes no reaction to my ordering a bottle of champagne at ten in the morning. The French really are wonderful about that sort of thing. Though purists may turn up their nose, I opt for a rosé, because nothing, and I mean nothing, screams celebration like pink bubbles.

Not surprisingly, the champagne improves the mood at the table. "What about you?" Nikolai asks once he's downed a quarter of his glass. "You've got all our lives figured out. What's next for the great Sabrina Sorensen?"

He's circumspect in front of Joëlle, which I appreciate. She is too deep in the industry to know about my hopes for Michelin. And Nikolai is close enough he can't *not* know. Because that crazy lifestyle would affect him too, if I'm ever lucky enough to get the job. And right now, he's showing he can be trusted with my dreams.

And it's true. I'd always planned on applying to Michelin when I was at my zenith. When I had managed a restaurant they deemed worthy of their highest honor. But as Rosaline told me not long ago, the right path in life is rarely the most direct. Is it time to apply? Should I just stay here and live out my life until I catch up with my timeline?

My spidey-sense tells me that as soon as we hit that moment, the one where I first met Rosaline in my timeline, the window for this cosmic redo will be over. That's not all that long from now—less than three months. I could easily just pick things up from here and move on with this life. It does seem like a reasonable option.

Is there anything I would do differently? It's a loaded question. I've seen iterations of my life that I thought I could improve, and with one exception—the one sitting at the table and holding my hand as if I might flee—none of the changes were really for the better. Edward is never going to change. Orla helped me see that Rian was a gargantuan mistake. And, well . . . that third star was just not in the cards for Joëlle and me. I'm just able to see these points in my life from another angle. I can't say I have fewer regrets, but maybe I understand them a little better.

It makes them lighter to carry, and that's not nothing.

"I do have some thoughts," I tell Nikolai at length and brush a kiss against his cheek. "I'm going to apply for lots of jobs. Ones that excite me. Ones that will work for *us*. I want to open as many doors as I can, and then I'm going to let fate sort it all out. If the universe knows better than I do what's best for my future, I'm going to listen."

Both Nikolai and Joëlle look at me, gobsmacked. They know me well enough to know I am *not* one to let my future just happen to me, as though I am a passive participant in my own life. I am the author of my own story, and I *make* opportunities. I don't just find them. And usually? That's a solid approach to life. But this once, it's time to slow down and see where I feel pulled to go next. Right now, it's what feels right. But there are some things I need to do before I let the chips fall where they may.

"Who are you, and what have you done with Sabrina?" Joëlle looks only half kidding.

"Oh, I'm still here. And I'm going to give the universe as much material to work with as I can. We all are. We aren't going anywhere until we've drawn up lists, made calls, and set ourselves up for one hell of a next step. And once we do that, I'm going to De Gaulle. I've got some loose ends to tie up."

Nikolai's eyes widen. He's waited eight long years for me to commit, and to him it looks like I'm preparing to bolt yet again. I take his hands in mine. "I need you to trust me. I won't be gone long."

His face relaxes by a few degrees, but he still looks skittish. I absolutely need to be transparent with him. And I'll tell him everything. Soon. And hope he doesn't think I'm a total looney tune by the end of it.

But I have to let the events unfold first. It feels like speaking it aloud might jinx the whole thing. But he needs as much honesty as I can give.

"Listen, I may need a few months to settle some things, but you have my word we'll ring in the new year together. Deal?"

He looks solemn, and we shake hands as if sealing a business deal. Which suits me fine, as this is a promise I take every bit as seriously as a multimillion-dollar merger.

For several hours we monopolize the table in the far corner of Angelina, phones and laptops blazing until we've made some significant progress on next steps.

And I send one very important email.

Chapter 25

DECEMBER 30, 2024

BURBANK AIRPORT

Rosaline greets me at the Jetway. For the first time since I met her, which was somewhere between an hour and a lifetime ago, she looks surprised.

"I wasn't sure I'd be seeing you again, dearie. It seems like you got quite the handle on things."

We take our places at the usual table, but I don't bother with the coffee this time, amazing as it is. I'm geared up enough without it. "I think I do. But I want to talk to you before all this"—I gesture to the lounge—"goes away at the stroke of midnight, so to speak."

Rosaline looks dreamy a moment. "Cinderella *was* a charming lass."

"What?" I sputter.

Her eyes focus back on me. "Never mind that now, dearie. What is it you want to talk about?"

I want to press but know I won't get anywhere. I might as well get the information I came for. "I couldn't change the outcome in Paris. Why was I allowed back?"

"You may not have changed the decision of your investors, but you were able to gain an understanding of the situation that helped you respond differently. Which, it seems, you did."

I nod. "The game was rigged. There's no sense in counting it as a loss if we never had a shot at winning."

"Right you are. It's a bittersweet lesson to learn, but life isn't always fair. The best we can do in times like these is regroup and move on. And you, your young man, and Chef Durand have done just that. Which is why I'm surprised you came back to me."

This is fair. And I'd considered just watching my life unfold. And it's tempting to look at my phone and see how it's all gone, but I can't dismiss the feeling that I have the power to fix one more thing before I go back to the regularly scheduled programming of my life. "I do think I've left one thing undone, and I'd like one more hop if you'll let me."

Her expression is serious. "Just remember, you've done some good work so far. I'd hate for you to undo it all."

With Nikolai's appearance in my life in Paris, I know for certain my actions during these jumps backward are indeed having an impact on my actual life, so I am worried about this too. I've made some serious promises to him. Promises I fully intend to honor.

"I need to go back to New Orleans." I speak the words with reluctance. I feel like a ten-year-old going for a flu shot. Old enough to know it's necessary. Too old for tantrums. Young enough to still be cranky about it.

"Are you sure, dearie? I would think that chapter is closed for you, what with young Nikolai waiting for you."

I shake my head. "I'm not going because I want to reconcile with Edward. But I do think I can leave that chapter of my life in better shape than I found it." I turn her words back on her. "Do you trust me?"

She pauses a moment. Long enough to show she's giving me the respect of a considered response. "I do, love. You've got a good brain in your head and a strong beating heart in your chest. And you've the good sense to make use of both. Godspeed to you."

I board the plane for one last jump backward and will myself to have the same confidence in my choice as Rosaline does.

Chapter 26

NEW ORLEANS

Once more, I'm back at Hotel Esmeralda. This time, rather than channeling a diatribe to throw at Edward's head like a Ming vase, I stand back and watch him sidle up to his friends as I've seen him do twice before.

"Honestly, she's a glorified dishwasher and she acts like she's actually got some talent just because Jean-Rémy said a few nice words. She's delusional."

His back is to me, but like my first time in this situation, I don't draw attention to myself. I ignore the titters of laughter from his friends—people I had thought were my friends too—and work my way back into the crush of the crowd. It isn't long before I find the objective of my search: Cecil Granby. As I hoped, his face lights up at the sight of me.

"Ah, there she is, the prettiest lady in all of Louisiana. I don't suppose you have space left on your dance card for the likes of me."

He is so over the top it actually works. I decide to respond to his Cajun charms in kind. "Oh, for you, Mr. Granby? Always."

In an impossibly debonaire fashion, Cecil gestures to the band, whose members immediately switch to a slower-paced ballad. The man really is something out of a cartoon, but the softer music will make conversation far easier.

"Now, darlin', you can tell old Cecil. You are dying for the chance to come work for me, aren't you?"

I pretend to blush. "Mr. Granby, it would be an honor, but I'm not ready for a place in your kitchen just yet. After a year or two more under Jean-Rémy? Perhaps."

In a year or two I'll be long gone from New Orleans, but Cecil doesn't need to know that.

The corners of his mouth perk up. "Very wise of you, my dear. It's often tempting to jump at an opportunity, but sometimes it's prudent to wait until we're ready. But don't you worry yourself. If you're working under Jean-Rémy, I know you're using your time wisely, and I'll hold a space for you."

I beam at him. "That is so kind of you, Mr. Granby. Though if you're looking for new talent, I wouldn't pass over Edward Fairbanks over a few bland appetizers."

He twirls me on the dance floor and smiles indulgently when I'm back in his arms. "You're loyal, Miss Sorensen. I like that about you."

I return his smile with a high-wattage version of my own. "Oh, it's Sabrina to you. But it's not just loyalty. He was just a little off his game today. I heard through the grapevine that Jerome put him on brunch shift, and he's taking it hard. He hasn't even told me directly, so I think he must be pretty upset."

Cecil looks sympathetic. "Brunch service is a grim fate. But I suspect my old friend Jerome knows what he's doing."

I flash Cecil a conspiratorial look. "Oh, he knows exactly what he's doing, Mr. Granby. He's taking his best, most promising young talent and shoving him out of the limelight so he can't outshine him. I honestly think he's threatened by Edward."

Cecil pauses a moment to consider this. In his heart he must know Jerome is capable of this. "You really think so?"

I let him pull me in closer. "You know Jerome far better than I do. Do *you* think that's his style?"

Cecil's sigh is reluctant. "I can't say it isn't like him. An unfortunate trait of his."

I lean in closer and purr in his ear. "You know what the sad part is? I think Jerome's antics are getting inside Edward's head, which is precisely what Jerome wants. I've eaten Edward's food many times, and he's never had an off day like this before."

Cecil hems. "So you agree it wasn't up to par?"

I shake my head emphatically. "Not at all. The chef I know would have been able to do better than that in his sleep and blindfolded. He needs a new kitchen before Jerome destroys what's left of his confidence altogether."

Cecil appears pensive. "I am looking for a new sauté chef who will train under my sous with a thought to replace him in a year or two. He might consider it a step backward."

"Better a dishwasher in a happy kitchen than the head chef in a miserable one." Edward's insult bubbles into my thoughts, but I push it away. Those words no longer deserve my headspace.

"True enough. You're wise beyond your years, Miss Sorensen."

I stifle a snort. If he knew I was a thirty-seven-year-old, seasoned industry veteran dragging as a twenty-three-year-old thanks to a sort of fairy godmother who inexplicably chose to set up shop at Burbank Airport, he'd probably have me committed. "You have no idea, Mr. Granby. But I do appreciate you considering Edward. You won't be sorry."

"No, I don't believe I will be. Not if he's as good as you claim he is. I'll give this young man of yours a call in the new year. Miserable or not, I won't deprive old Jerome of a staff member until the holiday crush is over."

Honorable. Even staff poaching has its etiquette. I plant a kiss on his cheek. "That means the world to me. Thank you."

"You've warmed the cockles of this old man's heart, darlin' girl. I just hope I can whisk *you* over to my kitchens before long."

I flash him another smile. "It's impossible to say what the future holds. But I am grateful to you."

The song ends, and he kisses the back of my hand with a practiced elegance. Did he attend something akin to the Rhett Butler Finishing School for Southern Gentlemen? More likely, he was a charter member of the organization. I can see Cecil eyeing Edward from across the room, assessing. In a few weeks he is going to offer Edward the job, and it might be just enough to keep Edward from becoming the disenchanted young man who insulted the woman he claimed to love, or later, the acerbic, bitter, middle-aged chef who'd lost his passion for his work without realizing it.

The world might just have one less bully in it. Because he was shown kindness when he needed it.

Edward doesn't really deserve this effort from me. The tongue-lashings I gave him—both times—were warranted, really. Not a single word was untrue or unjustified. But they served no purpose other than to make myself feel better about what he'd said. But apart from the initial satisfaction of letting him have it, I never felt peace or catharsis from either exchange.

But by quietly pushing him toward a terrific opportunity that might change this toxic cycle in his early career, I might improve the trajectory of his life. And even if it doesn't change the outcome for me, at least I can leave this epoch of my life knowing I did my best to leave things in the best shape I could.

I exit onto the street, ready to depart for the airport. I need to get back to my real life and figure out where things have led.

"Sabrina, why are you out here?" It's unusually quiet out in the humid streets of New Orleans, and Edward's voice splits the chilly night air like a church bell.

"Getting some air." True enough.

"Yeah, it's packed in there. Are you ready to come back in?" He has his eyes on the door. He doesn't want his absence to get noticed.

I force a smile. "I don't think so, but you should."

He has the good manners to look confused. "What do you mean?"

I take a step closer and kiss him on the cheek. "I want only good things for you, Edward. Take care of yourself."

Comprehension floods his face. "Listen, Sabrina, I—"

Part of me wants to hear his apology, but I hold up a hand to silence him. "It's okay. For a long time it wasn't . . . but . . . it just doesn't matter, Edward. I meant what I said. I want good things for you. I just hope you'll be on the lookout for them."

He stares at me, baffled. I'm not ashamed that I'm a bit proud to have him at a loss for words. On cue, Jean-Rémy exits onto the street and makes a beeline toward us. "Everything okay here, folks?"

"Um . . . yeah. I guess so." Edward's words are strained as he tries to make sense of things. "Do you need a ride home?"

I don't love the idea of being trapped in a car with him, trying to find some oxygen in the air poisoned with awkward silence. I shake my head. "No, it's okay. A walk will do me some good."

Edward seems ready to protest. My apartment's not particularly close and it's getting rather late, but Jean-Rémy interjects before he has the chance. "Don't worry, I'll get her home safe."

Edward thanks him and turns to me. "I'll call you tomorrow?"

I shake my head. "No need, Edward. Get back in there. Your friends are waiting."

And now he knows I heard what he said. Which is good. He needs to understand that it's not me, it's him, to spin the old maxim on its head. His posture is slightly slumped as he turns for the door, but he's trying to keep it together. And that's fine. He's experiencing the consequences of his actions and should feel bad.

"You okay, Princess? I think I know a breakup when I see one." Jean-Rémy wraps his warm arm around my shoulders. "Though I should be mad at you. I came out here to give you what-for since you're leaving us to work for Cecil Granby, and now you've deprived me of the fun of a good lecture. I can't give you an earful thirty seconds after you dumped a fella."

"Man, the NOLA foodie rumor mill is fast. And, as usual, wrong." I choke back a laugh and a sob all at once. "I was actually trying to persuade him to hire Edward."

He gestures for us to start walking in the direction of his car. "And then you broke up with him five minutes later?"

I loop my arm companionably in his. "That's the beat of it."

He shakes his head. "I don't understand you kids these days, but that was incredibly nice of you."

I squeeze his arm with mine. "A parting gift, you might say."

He chuckles. "An awful nice one."

"Well, the good news is that it didn't cost me anything more than a dance. And if it means his future is a little brighter because of it, so much the better." And I hope it works out for him. I have to believe that Edward really is a good person who just spent too long in a toxic environment. Maybe if his course changes, he won't bring as much of that toxicity to his own kitchen when the time comes. But that's on him now.

We reach the car, and I rest my head against Jean-Rémy's shoulder for a long moment, breathing in the whiskey and cigar smoke–laced New Orleans air. "I'll be fine. It was inevitable, really."

He squeezes me a bit tighter. "Of course you will be. I'm gonna teach you how to carve a Christmas goose for the dinner service tomorrow. You'll be too busy to be sad."

I smile. A new station is Jean-Rémy's love language. But it won't be me who's there tomorrow. Not this version of me. I've done what I came to do, and I'm ready to go back.

I let him drive me back to my place. He puts the car in Park but leaves it idling. "You gonna be okay?"

I clutch my evening bag to my chest. "Yeah. Maybe not tonight, but very soon."

"That's all I can ask for." He presses his lips to my forehead. He had been like a surrogate dad to me so soon after losing mine. That Jean-Rémy would be gone in such a short time seemed brutally unfair. And I want to do something about it. There is probably something in the rules about this, but if there is, Rosaline hasn't said anything about it. The old saying about it being easier to ask forgiveness than permission creeps into my brain.

I swallow hard, finding a lump in my throat heavy with tears. Not for Edward, but for Jean-Rémy. "Listen, can you do me another favor?"

He looks at me, his face etched in concern. "Anything, Princess. What's wrong?"

I take his hand. "This is going to sound crazy, but when was the last time you saw a doctor?"

His eyes roll up, as if calculating a complicated sum. "Lordy,

I can't say for sure. Maybe eight years back when I had a flu I couldn't shake? I was missing too many shifts and couldn't let it slide anymore."

It was basically what I expected. Jean-Rémy considered himself like an old car that you don't take to a mechanic if it's still running. "Will you please see a doctor? Just an annual physical."

He bumps my shoulder. "Aww, old JR is just fine."

I press where past me wouldn't have. "Please do it. You work long hours and eat rich food for the job. Melisse depends on you."

Pulling the Melisse card is a dirty trick, but this is worth it. I have no idea what happened to her, but I certainly haven't seen her name in any programs for the New York City Ballet since he passed. And I've made a point to look when the notion strikes, though I've only met her a few times in person.

He exhales slowly. "All right then, if it means that much to you. I can't see it would do any harm. There isn't much sense in pretending I'm twenty years old anymore."

I plant a last kiss on his cheek. "Thank you."

Color rises in his cheeks. "Well now, if a visit to the doctor gets me a kiss from a pretty lady like you, I'll make a regular habit of it."

I smile, this time deep from my soul. "See that you do. And thank you, Jean-Rémy. For everything."

He waits until I'm safely in my building before he drives away. I watch him from the entryway window until his car is gone from view. It's the last time I'll see him—again. There is something awful in knowing someone's fate, and I'm glad I hadn't known the first time. But I'm grateful in no small measure that our goodbye was what it should have been all those years ago.

Chapter 27

DECEMBER 30, 2024
BURBANK AIRPORT

The Jetway feels different now. The glow is less vibrant. The sheen on the wood paneling is dulling, almost before my eyes. The magic is fading.

Rosaline is waiting for me as usual, and she, too, looks as though she's growing fainter. She must be getting ready to go on and guide the next lost soul back to their rightful path. My time is up, and I am ever so grateful to have my time with her, but I will miss Rosaline all the same. Her wisdom. Her warmth. Her coffee.

That loss will sting.

"Well done, dearie." Even her voice is growing faint. I take her in my arms while I still can. She isn't quite as warm as a person should be, but she returns my embrace with all the magic she has left. She whispers in my ear, "I couldn't be prouder of you."

"Thank you." My words are choked by tears I refuse to wipe away. I've earned them. She hands me an ordinary-looking claim ticket for my luggage and escorts me to the door of the lounge where my future awaits. I turn to give her one last hug, and she's already gone.

I linger in the doorway just one moment longer, and I hope the next person to benefit from her guidance knows how lucky she is.

I summon my courage and find myself back in the hustle and bustle of the airport. The inter-holiday crowds are thickening, and I no longer have the luxury of solo travel on my private retro-jet. More's the pity, but the environment will fare better if I join the rest of my fellow men and fly commercial like I've always done.

I feel a moment's panic—just briefly—when I realize I have no idea where I'm supposed to be going. But it passes when it finally occurs to me to look at the claim ticket. My bags are checked through to Paris. That's a start, at least. I tuck myself out of the way and riffle through my green backpack to examine its contents. I'll miss being able to trust that the bag has everything I need, but I'm more than capable of packing it for myself now.

The contents are much the same, and I retrieve my phone. The lock screen shows a digital boarding pass. I'm headed to San Franciso on a plane that boards in fifteen minutes, then my flight connects to Paris after a short layover. Before I close my pack, I notice some additions. A thermos of coffee and a jar of caramel, all covered in tape that reads *TSA Inspected and Approved*. Rosaline left me a parting gift of her own, and I blow a kiss heavenward in thanks.

I get to my gate just as the doors open. I'm booked in an aisle seat to San Francisco and a window seat for the long-haul flight. Aisle for an easy off to make the connection, and window to rest against for the long haul. Either Rosaline knows me *that* well, or I'd booked this ticket for myself. I'd like to think it's the latter. I'm ready to be in charge of my own life again.

I'm one of the first to board, so I have several minutes to piece together the last three months of my life before I'm obligated to put my phone in airplane mode. Before I'm able to dig through my texts and emails to see what has happened since Joëlle, Nikolai, and I left Maison Ortense, there is a ping on my phone.

NIKOLAI: Have a good flight, min elskede. My flight will get in just an hour before yours. Will meet you at the taxi stand?

Like an idiot, I smile at my phone screen as though Nikolai can see my face. I don't have to scour my phone to know I haven't botched what really matters.

ME: I'll be there, darling. 😘

NIKOLAI: I made reservations for dinner. I hope you don't object.

In truth, I would rather spend the night in, but going out for New Year's Eve is a grand tradition, so I can't object too much.

ME: Sounds great. Where are we going?

NIKOLAI: Chez Éugenie, of course. Joëlle is delighted we can make it. She's hoping you'll reconsider the GM job.

I click away from the texts for a moment to read through my emails. I search for those sent to Éugenie Rosier on the day of our dismissal from Maison Ortense. Her reaction to the dismissal was exactly what I'd hoped for. Pure and unmitigated fury. She had taken an obscure little restaurant and turned it into a Parisian icon within two decades, and she wasn't the sort that would tolerate a boardroom full of bean counters trying to tell her they knew better than she about how to pass on her legacy.

Éugenie owned a minority control in Maison Ortense. Not enough to overrule the board, but a substantial enough portion that when she pulled her funds from the endeavor, it caused a cascading series of financial disasters for Maison Ortense. Because Éugenie was an investor, my email was in no way a violation of my severance agreement. And Éugenie was well within her rights to divest from Maison Ortense to open a new restaurant, named in her honor, where she would have more control over how her legacy is carried out. Joëlle is at the helm, and she's already getting noticed.

And Éugenie was not bound to silence in the way Joëlle and I were, so her very frank discussions with *The Guardian*, *Le Monde*, and even Michelin about her displeasure with the board's decision to dismiss such a talented chef and manager could not result in any legal action against her. A quick search tells me that Girard's first three months as head chef have not gone particularly smoothly. A text from the saucier Yann tells me Girard has gone through four sous-chefs already and that Yann himself will be leaving to work for Joëlle.

Joëlle sent me a link to an article outlining the impropriety of the board's actions. Georges-Luc Bodin is, in fact, Girard's father and the driving force behind the board's decision to push Girard for the top job. Every member of the board, especially Georges-Luc, is being investigated for their misdeeds, and there has even been some question as to the legitimacy of Girard's culinary school credentials from the great Alain Ducasse Academy. The exposé predicted Maison Ortense would fold within another two months. Our revenge, it would seem, has been brutal, swift, and complete. And so very civilized. All we really had to do was let the natural consequences play out.

Well done, us.

The question remains, *why* would Nikolai say I have turned down the GM job? The seat belt sign comes on so, uncharacteristically, I spring for the on-flight internet so I can keep hunting.

I can't imagine any version of my life where I would turn down that job . . . unless . . .

Upon closer inspection it appears there is a new email account on my phone. The first three were there when I'd left:

- Personal, for friends and family
- Professional and career stuff, but not tied to a specific job's email server
- Commercial, the one I use for shopping, newsletters, and anything else that will result in undue spam

But there is a fourth in place of my usually corporate-branded email for wherever I'm working, which in the past was always labeled with the name of the restaurant, like Maison Ortense or Baile Phadraig. Now, however, it's simply labeled:

- Work

I click on the account link, and it requires a face scan to access it. There are only a few messages, dating back only a few weeks. Most of it to do with the onboarding process for my new job.

As a Michelin Guide inspector.

My hands shake as I scroll through the messages, and my brain is trying very hard to process what I'm reading. I was hired three weeks ago, and my six-month apprenticeship in Paris will start in the second week of the new year. And I've successfully negotiated setting my home base in Copenhagen when I begin as a solo inspector in July. In the meantime, I'm living close to my old apartment in Paris.

In just over six months I'll be living with Nikolai and Pjuske in our flat in Nyhavn. The peaceful little place with an airy kitchen, a purring cat, and honest-to-goodness throw pillows. As a housewarming gift, I'll buy us a proper set of pots and pans that don't come from a thrift shop. I all but drool at the thought of our very own Mauviel copper cookware. And when the time comes, I am hauling my satin comforter to Copenhagen, even if it means the extra suitcase. Even if Pjuske claims it as his own and I never get to use it again for fear of inciting his wrath.

Because, finally, I'll have a place to call home.

Epilogue

SIX MONTHS LATER

Chloe's reception is *not* held at the Oak Room of the Laerke Inn, but rather a chic little marina club on the coast after a breathtaking ceremony on the beach. The walls of the club are lined with her ersatz food stalls, and the guests are raving. Accessible options like tacos, street corn, and crêpes of every possible variety are available, as well as more adventurous choices like Chinese dumplings and shawarma from the Middle East. The best part is there is not a discernible scrap of seafood in sight and Chris is in no danger of spending his wedding night in the ER.

Robin stands at the periphery of the reception, shaking her head. I'd been worried she'd try to make some sort of scene, but so far we've been lucky. She didn't show up in mourning weeds or find a moment to object to the wedding like they do in movies. Nothing so crass. She's dressed in an appropriate mother-of-the-bride dress in her signature robin's-egg blue (pun fully intended, though she'd never admit it) and she looks beautiful—stunning, really—without overshadowing Chloe, who is swaying to the music in her new husband's arms in a cloud of lace and tulle.

Reluctantly, I break free from Nikolai's embrace, walk up beside Robin, and place a hand on her shoulder. I force myself to use a conciliatory tone. There aren't any magical redos anymore, though I'm actually more worried that Robin will wish for one when she looks back on today. "Please don't do this. Not today. Chloe will see you."

She doesn't shoot me her usual daggers, but she doesn't soften her glare either. "I don't see why it matters. Clearly she doesn't care what I think, so she won't be offended if I don't approve."

Instead of pulling away, I wrap an arm around her. "You know she cares what you think. Probably more than she should. But that doesn't mean you're always going to get your way."

She stiffens under my touch. "It's not her I'm upset with. Not really." She twists out of my embrace, and her cold steel-blue eyes lock with mine. "How could you convince her to gang up against me?"

Of course this is my fault. I set my teeth but do not growl—no matter how desperately I might wish to. "I did you a favor. If I'd stood aside and let you steamroll her, she would have resented you for the rest of her life. She deserves to do as she likes for her own wedding. Especially since she and Chris are footing the bill. Can't you understand that?"

She purses her lips in response.

I keep my blood pressure in check. Barely. "Listen, Robin, I can only imagine how hard it is to watch your nest empty out, but you're helping your cause here. I don't want to see them cut you off because you stomped on their toes one too many times."

She crosses one arm over the other. "It's all the same nowadays. A parent can't express a simple opinion without an adult child crying about *boundaries*." She spits the word like it's gone rancid on her tongue. "Next thing you know, they won't even take your calls, and you find out about the birth of your grandchildren from a second cousin who's still allowed to follow them on Instagram."

I refrain from pointing out that she never "expresses a simple opinion." She proclaims gospel and expects us all to fall in line and live it. The Book of Robin. But if I point out a truth that pointedly, I'll lose her. Instead, I adopt a tone of concern. "That's precisely the fate that awaited you if I'd let you have your way. Chloe might tolerate your intrusions now, but Chris won't be as accepting."

I can envision how things would play out. Chloe adores Chris, so when Robin oversteps at some point in the not-too-distant future and Chris holds up a mirror to the way Robin treats her, Chloe won't hesitate to go low-contact.

And that's the way it should be when two people love each other.

I think of my own experiences with Rian's mother. I'd done my best to hold up that same mirror, but he'd refused to look. It hurts now knowing that he hadn't cared enough for me to take my side, but as I see Nikolai making small talk with my great-aunt Carlotta, I know I'm better off.

Robin chooses not to respond to my premonitions of their future falling-out, so I change my tactic. "I'm honestly curious: You didn't commandeer Annabelle and Brian's wedding. Why do you feel the need to take over Chloe's?"

Her pinched expression slackens by a minute fraction. "That's not the same at all. The mother of the groom's responsibilities are . . . different from those of the mother of the bride. Annabelle has living parents, so I couldn't very well . . . influence things . . . the way I ought to be able to do with you girls."

I almost snort. *Influence things*. That implies the bride still maintains a measure of agency, which would not be the case if Robin got her way. Six months ago, I probably *would* have given my very best snort of derision. But as fun as it would be in the moment, it won't help reach her.

I lean a little closer to her. "Who planned your wedding, Mom?"

Her eyes widen. It's been a long time since I've called her that. She looks out at the guests milling about, every face but hers smiling, and her eyes grow misty.

Whenever Chloe, Brian, or I asked about pictures, Dad would describe the day as though Walt Disney himself had been summoned to design the perfect day. Blue skies with only decorative fluffy white clouds and melodious birdsong filling the air. One could almost imagine little woodland creatures carrying the train of Robin's gown. Dad's over-the-top descriptions were so entertaining, none of us realized the pictures never materialized.

In perfect Robin fashion she blinks the mist of nostalgia away. "What wedding? Your father and I *got married*. A simple affair at the courthouse. No fuss, no reception. No pictures. Not even a cake."

There is no mistaking the regret in her voice. I knew Robin had been young: twenty-two and fresh out of college. Dad had only been in the States a year when he met her and was working low-paying odd jobs, trying to establish himself in his new country.

"Your grandfather had just passed, and there wasn't much money," she continues. She'd lost her father too young, just as Chloe, Brian, and I had. He just hadn't had the means to plan ahead the way Dad had done to ensure we'd be taken care of if something happened. More likely, Robin had insisted on better savings and life insurance so the same thing wouldn't happen to her again and, by extension, us.

"That must have been hard." I want to wrap an arm around her again, but I know she wouldn't respond well to it.

She doesn't seem to register that I spoke but continues to reminisce. "I borrowed a hideous dusty-rose dress from a friend of mine. It was the most bridal thing we could come up with since I was the first of my friends to be married. Your grandmother didn't know why we wouldn't wait a few years so we could save up and 'do things properly' as she called it. But we were kids. Impetuous and in love. I'm pretty sure she was shocked—and secretly delighted—that your brother had the good manners to wait until a full year after the wedding to make his appearance."

Now I do laugh. Robin's mother was a formidable woman, even more so than Robin herself. I can't imagine she'd have looked too kindly on her daughter having a seven-month baby.

"Do you regret not having a big wedding?" I try to push gently. It's only a matter of time before she closes up again.

She shrugs, noncommittal. "If I had a magic wand? Sure, I'd give us the money for a nice to-do. I wish we'd had *real* pictures. Not the snapshots your uncle Phil took with his old Kodak. Lord, we were so broke, I'd had to save up for the roll of film and save again to develop it." A smile actually flashes on her face for the briefest of moments.

I lower my voice another degree. "Why have you never shown us the photos? We asked a dozen times when we were kids."

She exhales deeply. "Pride, I suppose. I keep them hidden in a shoebox in the hall closet and made your father swear never to show you kids. It was a shabby little affair, and I confess I felt a little ashamed." A shadow passes over her face. "Your father had promised me a grand renewal ceremony for our twenty-fifth anniversary, but you know how *that* turned out."

She didn't have to say it—his accident happened shortly before their twenty-fourth and the party never happened.

I swallow back a whole pile of platitudes that rise to the surface. How Dad probably thought their little courthouse wedding was perfect. How the important thing was that they ended up married. How lucky they were that they had found each other. All those things might be true, but it didn't mean that Mom hadn't suffered a loss, and minimizing it wasn't the way to help her move forward.

"I'm sorry that never happened for you. It would have been beautiful." And I have no doubt it would have been. Mom did have fantastic taste, even if it wasn't mine.

She doesn't look at me but keeps her eyes on the mingling crowd. She affixes a Plasticine smile to her face, and though I know it doesn't go any deeper than her lips, I am grateful she's making an effort. I see a sparkle in the corner of her eye, and I'm terrified all this Dad-adjacent talk will make her sob in front of our nearest and dearest. She would never forgive me.

"This Nikolai of yours seems like a nice man." It's the closest thing to a compliment she's paid me in . . . perhaps years?

"Thanks. I think he's pretty great too." He catches my eye just then and I offer him a little wink. He raises his glass of champagne in our direction. To my credit, I don't dismiss Robin to go find a corner where I can lock lips with him like some lovesick teenager. I *want* to. Badly. But I am an adult and this is, after all, my sister's wedding.

Robin finally turns and looks at me properly. "Promise me you won't push him away unless he gives you good reason to?"

I blink furiously. That she added any sort of caveat is progress.

"I plan on keeping this one around." I discreetly gesture to the ring finger on my left hand. I'd kept it bare until today, but when Nikolai and I leaked the news to Chloe, she insisted I wear my engagement ring on her wedding day. Dad had always said that love was the best sort of good luck, and she wanted as much of it surrounding her on her special day as we could all muster.

So I wore the princess-cut diamond in an antique setting with the little amber side stones that I admired while we were wandering the streets of Copenhagen. I'd just moved back to our little flat in Nyhavn after my apprenticeship in Paris ended a couple of weeks ago, and he couldn't wait to pop the question after I spotted the ring. He secreted his way back to the shop later that day, bought it, and surprised me with it later that night over one of the top-ten meals I'd eaten in my career, and not just because it came from Nikolai's kitchen.

Nikolai and his father opened La Mer Gris two months ago to great fanfare, and I know they'll find themselves the recipient of Michelin stars in no time, without my influence or interference. They won't need it.

It is amazing that eagle-eyed Robin hasn't noticed my ring. I tend to be oblivious to this sort of thing, but Robin can usually spot a newly sported engagement ring from a hundred paces. She was one of the main reasons I'd hesitated about wearing it before I got Chloe's blessing.

Robin glances down at the ring and raises one brow. "Does it signify what a ring on that finger usually does, or is it some new feminist fad of yours?"

I don't take the bait and smile sweetly. "I hate to turn traditional on you, but Nikolai and I are indeed getting married. We're thinking next fall to let the dust settle from this shindig." And to give ourselves plenty of time to adjust to our busy careers.

She clears her throat and speaks in a low tone. "Well, be sure to send me an invitation. I'll do my best to come if I'm welcome." The expression on her face isn't passive-aggressive. She's genuinely not sure she's included.

I want to say, "Of course you are, especially if you behave," and it's about what she deserves. But I summon something from the well of grace deep within that I have often neglected where Robin is concerned. "Nikolai and I want to have the wedding in Copenhagen, in the church where his parents were married."

Her face falls slightly, but it's more traditional than she ever thought she'd get from me, so she tries harder to control her face. "How nice."

"I was also thinking of having a reception in Solvang for the people who can't travel to Denmark. Since I'll be overseas, I was hoping you might be able to help."

She lights up, legitimately. "Really? I sort of expected you to be the eloping kind."

The truth is, I might have been, if only to avoid Robin's drama. But I think part of me would regret not having a wedding, much the same as Robin regrets not having one. "Would you be able to save a date at the Laerke Inn for Christmastime? We could do a whole Danish Christmas theme."

"Of course." She clears her throat, and I can tell she's winning the battle to keep tears at bay, but it's costing her. "And I promise not to be *too* opinionated. I was wrong about Chloe and the food."

I finally summon the courage to wrap my arm around her again. "For that, I'm inviting you to come wedding dress shopping with me." I hope I don't come to rue this moment, but *not* giving her the chance would be worse. "We can go to Whitby's." It's a bridal salon in the area she's gone to for formal dresses for ages that she considers the last word in fashion.

In a flash she's all business. "No, that won't do at all."

And the lump of dread is back, and it feels worse than the time I overdid it on fondue at the Restaurant Hôtel de Ville in Geneva. I take a deep breath and force my voice to remain even. "I thought you'd prefer it." And my armor shoots up. She's going to make a comment about my height and general build. Whitby's isn't exactly known for being size inclusive.

She's crossed her arms and is tapping her foot as she does when she's deep in planning mode. "For a reception dress perhaps, but coming all the way out here for fittings would be murder for your gown."

I blink. She's absolutely right. And for once she's thinking of what might be best for *me*. "That makes sense. Good thinking."

She beams, actually beams, at my affirmation. Her eyes are glazed over in thought, but she returns her focus back to me. "I have a better idea. Let's meet in the middle at Kleinfeld's. I know it's still across an ocean, but no place will have a better selection, and you have to go to New York often enough for work. And they can have the dress shipped to Copenhagen directly. No one could manage it better."

For a moment my mouth gapes open and closed like a fish gasping for air. Mom and I had watched the earliest seasons of *Say Yes to the Dress* when I was home from college. It was one of my fonder memories of a time that was overshadowed by the loss of my dad. I hadn't thought she remembered.

She squeezes my hand. "I know Kleinfeld's isn't cheap. The dress will be my wedding gift, if you'll let me."

I squeeze her hand back. "On one condition. You let me take you to dinner and a show when you come to the city."

Tears sparkle in her eyes. "You have a deal."

As a pledge of good faith, I pull my phone out then and there and snag a dress appointment on the Kleinfeld's website for next week. Nikolai has to go back tomorrow, but my flight isn't until next week. And conveniently, I have a layover in New York, so delaying the second leg of the trip back to Copenhagen by a couple of days won't be hard. Mom promises that when she gets back to her computer, she'll make a reservation for The Plaza using her credit card points that have been accumulating for years. I'll work my magic with dinner reservations when I get back to my room. I am, not for the first time, grateful for my behind-the-scenes connections there.

I do one more quick search on my phone and find that Melisse, Jean-Rémy's daughter, is starring in *Swan Lake* at the Lincoln Center when we'll be in town. I snag the best available tickets, snap a few photos of the party to cover my rudeness a bit, and stow my phone. The rest can wait. But going to see Melisse would have made my Jean-Rémy happy, and I love knowing that. His absence at my wedding will be felt. Dad's will be excruciating. But those are the sorts of regrets we can't do anything about. Either we can let the pain take us under, or we can learn to carry it with whatever measure of grace we can conjure from within.

I see my brother sitting at the bar, his eyes fixed on Annabelle, who is recording a video fifteen feet away, completely oblivious to her husband or anyone else. She's fully glammed out and is easily the second prettiest woman in the room after Chloe. Any prettier and she'd be in poor taste for trying to outshine the bride. Brian is holding a bottle of beer and looks mopier than I've ever seen. Probably because Annabelle is five seconds away from chastising him for drinking something as lowbrow as cheap American beer.

I decide to risk his ire and cross the room to where he's rooted and brooding. He holds one hand up in my direction, keeping the other firmly fixed on his bottle. "I'm not getting into it with you. Not here. Not tonight. Maybe not ever."

We haven't spoken since Chloe's engagement party the year before. Not in any meaningful way. Not because I've gone "no contact" with him or he with me, but because we've grown so far apart there isn't much to talk about.

I put one hand on my hip. "I wasn't planning on fighting with you, dipwad."

He fights a smile at the insult I favored when we were kids, and which Robin *loathed*. I order a sidecar from the bartender before turning back to him. "I *did* come to see how you're doing."

A shrug.

"You're not happy." It's not a question; it's an observation.

Another shrug. "Who is?"

I don't let him deflect. "No one is *all* of the time. But you deserve to be happy *some* of the time. What gives?"

His shoulders sag and he takes another swig of his beer. "Annabelle is so focused on having an Insta-perfect life, she forgets I'm not Insta-perfect."

"Instagram is all a veneer. It's the highlight reels of a life when the rest of us are living the bloopers." My job precludes much of a social media presence, and I'm not sorry about it. I content myself with passive lurking and the occasional comment on friends' content. The only place I post much is in a few select book groups, and never about food or work. The Anonymous Epicure went out with a whimper, out of necessity. I can't blog and work for Michelin, and announcing my retirement from Substack might have caused busybodies like Edward to start digging into my identity and whereabouts. Ghosting seemed the smartest option.

"Not for Annabelle. She wants to *live* the highlight reels every day. She actually cried the other day when she realized she was out of homemade puréed carrots, and I suggested going to the store for Gerber. You'd have thought I suggested feeding Bailey cyanide." He's staring at his hands now. I sense I'm the first person he's confessed this to. "It's hard to live with, I can't lie."

I'm grateful for the interruption when the bartender brings my drink. "I bet it is. I assume you've tried reasoning with her?"

He laughs into the neck of his beer bottle. "Yes, and she wanted to do a video series on DIY marriage counseling. Heaven forbid we go in for some real help."

"So what are you going to do?" The question is heavy. It's loaded. And this really isn't the place for it.

"Go to work, do my best, and try to stay out of frame. It's all I can do." It's a nonanswer, but all I'm entitled to, especially at the moment. "You'd understand if you were married. With someone else it would just be a different set of frustrations."

I think back on my little adventures with Rosaline six months ago. There's rarely a day when the memories don't make at least a cameo in my consciousness. Days like today? They're more like a significant secondary character. He's right in a sense. Every person I dated had their own set of foibles that drove me mad. Even Nikolai has a few minor quirks that get under my skin. But there's a difference between annoying behaviors and deal-breakers. And I get the sense that Annabelle's Instagram addiction is encroaching on the latter territory. But Brian will never leave. He'd implode first.

In true Brian fashion, he shifts the conversation back to me. "So what is it you need?"

"Who said I came over for a favor?" My voice feigns innocence.

He gives me a deadpan glare. "I've known you your whole life and I can identify the Sabrina-on-a-mission walk from a mile away."

"I was actually going to ask you to walk me down the aisle when

I get married next year. Whaddya say?" I playfully punch his arm like I used to do when we were kids.

He takes a long pull of his beer and stares off into space. "Nope."

I gasp. "What do you mean, 'nope'? I'm not asking to borrow your car when you need it for something else. This is a big deal. I was going to hook you up with the plane tickets and everything."

"It is a big deal. And I'll be there in the front row. But walking you down the aisle would have been Dad's job, and I don't want to pretend I can fill his shoes, because I can't. And besides, of all the women I've ever known, you can stand on your own two feet better than any of them."

"Thanks for the compliment, but most of my sex are perfectly capable of that, thanks." I wonder how much of this soft misogyny is because of Annabelle and how much of it is innate, but I try to keep my temper in check. The simple callout was good enough—for now. "But I really would love it if you did this for me."

"Sabrina Fair, you need to read that poem over again. Mom might have painted her as the delicate little water nymph, but she's the hero. I'll be there to cheer you on, but you don't need me there to 'give you away,' because you belong to yourself."

He looks over at Annabelle, who is still fixed to her phone screen. "Better yet, walk down the aisle with Nikolai. Start the marriage as you mean to continue it—as partners." It's his turn to punch me in the shoulder.

"That's a brilliant idea, brother. But be careful and save some of those brilliant ideas for work. I don't want you using up your yearly quota on me."

He sticks his tongue out at me, and I return the favor before going to find Nikolai.

I turn serious for a moment. "Just be good to yourself, okay, brother?"

He gives me a mock salute, like a subordinate accepting orders. Unfortunately, I don't think he will be.

I find Nikolai finishing off a conversation with Tim Espersen, of all people. Nikolai knows of my adventures at Burbank Airport, but not the vision Rosaline had shown me of the grim fate that would have awaited me if I'd stayed in Solvang. To his credit he never acted like I was crazy, though he has never fully known what to say about it. He's only happy that despite the crazy odds against it, we've managed to find each other.

I smile and exchange pleasantries with Tim and try not to think of the future we'd have had together if I'd caved to Robin's badgering or he to his own mother's.

Chloe and Chris are dancing to a slow number, and the love on her face is so genuine, my heart strains against my rib cage. Her day is perfect, and I'm glad for my role in it. And glad Robin can be at peace with it too.

I pull Nikolai onto the dance floor, and we sway in time with the music. "Espersen seems nice enough," Nikolai muses as he pulls me closer.

I give a noncommittal verbal shrug. "I suppose. Robin tried to push us together for ages, but I rebelled."

"Not your type?" He leans in and tries to be subtle about smelling my hair and fails. He loves my shampoo.

The vision Rosaline showed me, with us unable to mask our contempt for each other, looms large in my brain. "Not in the least."

He twirls me once on the dance floor before he pulls me back to his chest. "I can't say I'm disappointed. If you'd settled down here with him, I wouldn't be dancing with you now."

I shake my head. "No. If I'd taken that path, the world would be a very different place."

"Any regrets?" He lifts a brow, fishing for a compliment. It's endearing, so I indulge.

I lean in and kiss his cheek, leaving a perfect imprint of my lips in crimson on his cheek. "Of course I have some. But never this. Never you."

He whispers into my ear, "I hope you'll always think that, *min elskede*."

I look deep into his soulful blue eyes and know, with the certainty of the rising sun, that there *will* be moments of regret in the future. Moments of anger when I question why I chose him. There is no such thing as a meaningful marriage without discord, after all.

But I don't think I will ever regret *him*. Because he, unlike so many others, isn't fixated on the way things are "supposed" to be. He loves that I am passionate about my work. He shares my passion for food and travel. He never seeks to make me smaller than I am. Because he has passions of his own, he isn't threatened by who I am or what I want out of life. We can create a marriage on our own terms and be true to ourselves instead of the expectations of others. And in honoring our own expectations and in valuing each other, we will find happiness.

I brush a wayward lock of blond hair from his brow and kiss him, unbothered by who might be looking on. "So do I, darling. So do I."

Author's Note

Dearest Gentle Reader,

I don't think one reaches my age (specifics not needed here, but I wasn't a particularly young first-time mother and I have a kid in high school, so I'll let you extrapolate) without occasionally wishing for a remote control for one's own timeline. I spend (waste?) more time than perhaps is prudent wondering about the things I would do differently if I had access to what Sabrina calls a "cosmic do-over." Given that I have just about everything in life I could possibly ask for (except a set of Mauviel copper pots and pans, maybe), I would be hesitant to meddle with much. All the same, I can't help wondering what things I would change if given the chance. What strikes me when I indulge in these day-dreams is that usually what I would change are the *small* things. I wouldn't undo all my red-letter mistakes, because those brought me to where I am now. For me, it's the little moments when I gave in to self-doubt or insecurities that cause me to look back with a twinge of dissatisfaction.

What if I'd stood up for myself?

What if I'd been brave enough to say no? (Or yes!)

What if I'd believed in myself enough to try something sooner? (Like . . . writing a book?)

This is what my beloved protagonist Sabrina is dealing with throughout *Missed Connections*, though she has the benefit of that timeline remote control in the guise of an Irish fairy godmother (I'm convinced all fairy godmothers have to be Irish) and a very cool retro lounge and time-traveling airplane at Burbank Airport. Despite her being so hyper-competent and (usually) confident in her professional abilities, she pulls her punches in life. Specifically, she doesn't apply for her dream job because she's convinced the timing needs to be perfect. Spoiler alert: The timing will never be perfect, so you have to hold your breath and take the leap, or nothing truly great will happen in life. It takes a lot for Sabrina to learn this, but I am glad she finally gets there.

Sabrina's timing dilemma is not quite as intense as that of our heroine Veronica in *The Wandering Season* who, as a trauma response, completely gives up on her dreams for many years. But like Veronica, Sabrina has a great talent for getting in her own way when it matters most. I think self-doubt is one of the most pernicious and destructive of impulses, and exploring this theme with Sabrina was poignant for me, as well as a lot of frustrating fun.

Frustrating because, honestly, it took three near-total rewrites for Sabrina (okay, me) to figure out the right approach to each jump backward in time. I think if most of us were let loose with that pesky old timeline remote, many of us would end up in a *Groundhog Day* situation where we live the same key moments over and over again until we get them *just* right. And since that concept has been done, I decided to spare you all having to experience each jump three or four times. The only one where I take you back a second time—New Orleans—was not even planned that way originally.

For those of you who have read my historical fiction (please do!), this process of writing and rewriting until everything comes together is not my usual custom in that genre. For my historical novels, even my outlines have outlines, and so much is mapped out in advance that usually the second draft is just a read for polish. That's not to say I don't take things off course or I don't have the fun of organic discovery. At the end of the day, I just try not to get in my characters' way. But the difference is that my historical characters pack carefully for their adventures and bring a map. My contemporary characters throw some random stuff in a duffel bag, hit the road, and hope for the best. It's up to me to figure out where they're going as I try to keep pace. Neither approach is *better* per se, but it does feel like two completely separate careers sometimes.

One thing that doesn't change between the two genres, however, is research. I scoured the earth (read: the internet) to find a copy of the out-of-print *L'Inspecteur Se Met à Table* by Pascal Remy. As far as I can tell, it's the only tell-all book in existence written by an actual Michelin inspector. As you might well imagine, the book cost Remy his job, but it was definitely a useful behind-the-scenes look for writing Sabrina's story. A handful of anonymous interviews with Michelin inspectors are in existence as well, all of which proved invaluable. Unfortunately, my budget didn't stretch to sampling all the Michelin-starred restaurants in the great state of Colorado, so I had to rely on the Michelin app and some top-notch YouTube content to fill in my gaps. Of course I watched said content about food I will likely never be able to afford while eating Twizzlers on Mother's Day, because life is all about balance. (Fun fact: Sturgeon being raised for caviar get better prenatal care than most American women in the twenty-first century.)

It must also be said that I became incredibly ill in the middle of writing this story. I spent a week in the hospital with pneumonia and was laid up at home for weeks afterward, tethered to an oxygen machine. It was a sobering experience for someone who (despite my opening quip) really isn't all that old. I spent weeks unable to work, and it gave me a lot of time to reflect on what I want to do differently in my life. Not in my past, as I've yet to have a visit from my fairy godmother, but rather moving forward.

Without a doubt, the true magic of the human experience is that, while we don't have the ability to change the past, we do have the power to influence our future by acting in the present with those desired outcomes in mind.

They call it the present for a reason—it really is a gift.

So, dearest reader, as you look back on Sabrina's journey through her regrets, I hope you don't long too much for a visit from Rosaline, as charming as she is. I hope you see that you already have the power in your own hands to create the future you want.

With love,
XOXO
Aimie

Acknowledgments

As always, I am humbled by the people who have stood with me on this crazy writing endeavor of mine, and I will do my best to thank them all here. My heartfelt thanks to:

My amazing editor Kimberly Carlton. Thank you so much for your understanding and support with this book, especially as we both dealt with health woes. I appreciate your grace more than I can express. That Sabrina's story came out as well as it did (and on time) is nothing short of a modern miracle in my eyes.

Kevan Lyon, my brilliant agent, for her loyal support and encouragement. I am beyond lucky to have you in my corner.

My various writer "families," the Lyonesses, the Tall Poppies, and the Business Hat ladies. You all help keep me sane in a business that seems determined to drive me otherwise. And especially my dear writer friends Kate Quinn, Heather Webb, Andrea Catalano, Sara Goodman Confino, Kimberly Brock, Rachel McMillan, and J'nell Ciesielski—warmest thanks for all your support over the years.

Kerry Schafer, aka Kerry Anne King, my friend and author genie. Thank you so much for your support of this project when I was ready to give up, and for all the nurse-ly advice when I was feeling poorly. Thank you for being my friend when I needed you most . . . I don't think I'd have finished this book without you.

Caroline Hewitt, audiobook narrator extraordinaire, who works so tirelessly to give my work its voice for the listening public. I admire your commitment to the craft and value our friendship so much! (Don't forget to buy your audiobooks from Libro.FM to support your local independent bookstores, and always support #HumanVoices!)

My incredible line editor, Julee Schwarzburg. It is such a privilege to work with you over multiple books. You've made me a better writer.

Taylor Ward, Kerri Potts, Margaret Kercher, Amanda Bostic, and the whole crew at Harper Muse, thank you so much for helping me bring Sabrina's story to the world.

My dear friends at Macdonald Book Shop for their unwavering support since I moved into Estes Park, and to my beloved indie bookshops everywhere. You are the backbone of our bookish community.

My book blogger friends and Bookstagram rock stars—I appreciate all you do to shed light on undercelebrated books. Every book-loving post makes a hard business seem a little less impossible.

JijiCat for his loyal support of my career, and his insistence that I put a cat in every manuscript. Pjuske is for you, buddy. And to Zuri for being a very fierce Tiger Princess.

The Vetter and Trumbly families for their unflagging support. You're the best cheering section a writer could ask for.

My beautiful, talented, kindhearted children, Ciaran and Aria, who remind me daily what life is really about. And for making me laugh a lot. Also, thanks for watching YouTube specials about bluefin tuna with me. That was a fun Mother's Day.

As always, all my love to Jeremy. I wouldn't change much about my life, but if given a remote control of my own timeline, I'd go back and find you sooner.

And . . .

To my readers, without whom none of this would be possible. You have my gratitude.

Discussion Questions

1. If given the opportunity, what era of your life would you redo? What do you think the consequences might be?

2. Why do you think Sabrina was so afraid to apply for the job at Michelin?

3. Do you think Sabrina handled things well with Edward? What would you have done differently?

4. Why do you think Orla worked so hard to destroy Sabrina and Rian's relationship? Was she as magnanimous as the note made her seem, or more self-serving?

5. Sabrina goes to Denmark and realizes she was right to think the job at The Mesmerist was a bad fit, but taking a chance on that job would have been the right course for her, mistake though it was. What do you think this says about the value of our mistakes?

6. In Paris Sabrina learns the hard lesson that sometimes

the game of life is rigged. How do you think learning this will affect her?

7. After Sabrina's second trip to New Orleans, do you think the course of Edward's life will change? How so?

8. What do you think was the biggest risk Sabrina took in her time travels?

9. What do you think was at the root of Robin and Sabrina's rocky relationship? How do you think Sabrina's relationship with her mother will change moving forward? And with her siblings?

10. Overall, what do you think Sabrina will take from the experience of time travel? What lessons has she learned, and how will they impact her future?

Recipes

Here are a couple of recipes mentioned in the book. For more, visit www.aimiekrunyan.com/blog.

SABRINA'S CURRY CRÉOLE SAUCE

A versatile sauce that pairs well with various meat- or vegetable-based dishes

INGREDIENTS

- 2 tablespoons olive oil
- 1 medium onion, diced
- 2 stalks celery, diced
- 1 medium green bell pepper, diced
- 3 cloves garlic, minced
- 1 (14-ounce) can diced tomatoes
- 2 cups chicken stock (low sodium is a good choice)
- 1 tablespoon (or more to taste) Louisiana hot sauce
- 2 bay leaves
- 2 tablespoons Maharajah curry powder (I love Penzey's)
- 1/4 teaspoon cayenne pepper

$^1/_2$ teaspoon dried thyme leaves
4 tablespoons butter
Kosher salt and black pepper to taste

DIRECTIONS

1. Heat oil in a cast-iron cocotte (or saucepan) over medium-high heat until shimmering.
2. Add onion, celery, and green pepper and cook, stirring occasionally, 3 to 5 minutes.
3. Stir in garlic and cook until fragrant, about 30 seconds.
4. Stir in tomatoes, chicken stock, hot sauce, bay leaves, curry powder, cayenne pepper, and thyme.
5. Bring to a boil, then reduce heat to low.
6. Simmer until sauce slightly thickens, about 20 minutes.
7. Discard bay leaves.
8. Add butter and stir until completely melted.
9. Remove from heat and season with salt, pepper, and additional hot sauce to taste.
10. Taste and adjust seasonings to your preference.
11. Serve over fish, chicken, pasta, or whatever moves you!

NIKOLAI'S STRAWBERRY TART
(*Jordbærtærte*)

A luscious pie with an almondy marzipan-based filling, dark chocolate, vanilla pastry cream, and (of course) strawberries! Best made in season.

INGREDIENTS

Piecrust

Prepare using your favorite recipe (or premade, no judgment here). For a pastry crust, blind bake for 8 to 10 minutes, but don't bake completely. Feel free to experiment with a graham cracker or cookie-based crust, which won't need to be prebaked.

Mazarin (marzipan-based) filling

1/2 cup superfine sugar
7 ounces marzipan
1 stick (8 tablespoons) butter, room temperature
2 eggs, room temperature
1/4 cup flour (gluten-free is fine)
1 (3.5-ounce) bar dark chocolate, finely chopped (preferably Godiva or Ghirardelli)

Pastry cream

1/2 cup milk (whole is best)
1 egg, room temperature
2 tablespoons superfine sugar
1 tablespoon flour (gluten-free is fine)
2 teaspoons vanilla extract (go for broke—make homemade!)
3/4 cup heavy cream
14 ounces fresh strawberries, quartered or roughly chopped (the fresher the better)

DIRECTIONS

1. Preheat oven to 350 degrees.
2. To prepare mazarin (marzipan-based) filling, combine sugar, marzipan, butter, and eggs in food processor. Blend until smooth.

3. Add flour and blend completely.
4. Pour into prepared crust and bake in preheated oven for 30 minutes or until browned and barely wobbly.
5. Cover crust with silicone pie shield or aluminum foil to keep from scorching if needed.
6. Remove from oven and evenly sprinkle chopped chocolate over filling, carefully spreading with spatula.
7. Set aside to cool and refrigerate for 1 hour to cool completely.

1. To prepare pastry cream, add milk, egg, sugar, flour, and vanilla to medium saucepan.
2. Stir over medium to medium-high heat until thickened and mixture coats the back of a spoon.
3. Pour into bowl and allow to cool completely.
4. Cover mixture once it's not steaming.
5. Place heavy cream in the bowl of a stand mixer and beat on medium until soft peaks form (or use a hand mixer).
6. Add whipped cream to cooled pastry cream and whisk until smooth.
7. Spoon on top of chocolate layer and smooth with spatula.
8. Add a generous layer of sliced strawberries, either in an artistic pattern or willy-nilly.
9. Serve and enjoy!

About the Author

Internationally bestselling author Aimie K. Runyan writes to celebrate unsung heroines. She has written eight historical novels (and counting!) and is loving her foray into the exciting world of contemporary women's fiction. She has been a finalist for the Colorado Book Award, a nominee for the Rocky Mountain Fiction Writers' "Writer of the Year," and a Historical Novel Society's Editors' Choice selection. She is proud to be an adjunct professor in the MFA in Creative Writing program at Drexel University and is active as a speaker and educator in the writing community in Colorado and beyond. She lives in the beautiful Rocky Mountains with her wonderful husband, two (usually) adorable children, and two very sweet cats.

Visit her online at aimiekrunyan.com
Instagram: @bookishaimie
Facebook: @aimiekrunyan
X: @aimiekrunyan
TikTok: @aimiekrunyan
Threads: @bookishaimie